Praise for
The Vampire's Seduction

"Suspenseful . . . and sexy . . . This foray into
fangoria is atmospheric and occasionally funny."
—*Publishers Weekly*

"A real treat . . . an excellent read!"
—Freshfiction

"An exotic, exciting thriller."
—*Futures MYSTERY Anthology Magazine*

"One can almost feel the heat rising from the
pages. . . . A stimulating read."
—Curledup

"Dark, seductive, disturbingly erotic, Raven Hart
drives a stake in this masterful tale."
—L. A. BANKS, author of the Vampire
Huntress Legend series

By Raven Hart

The Vampire's Kiss

RAVEN HART

BALLANTINE BOOKS • NEW YORK

The Vampire's Kiss is a work of fiction. Names, characters, places, and incidents are the products of the author's imagination or are used fictitiously. Any resemblance to actual events, locales, or persons, living or dead, is entirely coincidental.

A Ballantine Books Mass Market Original

Copyright © 2007 by Raven Hart
Excerpt from *The Vampire's Betrayal* by Raven Hart copyright © 2007 by Raven Hart

Published in the United States by Ballantine Books, an imprint of The Random House Publishing Group, a division of Random House, Inc., New York.

BALLANTINE and colophon are registered trademarks of Random House, Inc.

This book contains an excerpt from the forthcoming book *The Vampire's Betrayal* by Raven Hart. This excerpt has been set for this edition only and may not reflect the final content of the forthcoming edition.

ISBN 978-0-345-49856-4

Cover illustration based on a photograph © Studio MPM/Getty Images (top) and © Franz Aberham/Getty Images (bottom)

Printed in the United States of America

www.ballantinebooks.com

OPM 9 8 7 6 5 4 3 2 1

To my readers.
Thanks, everyone!

Acknowledgments

Thanks to Chris Schluep, Claudia Cross, everyone in Georgia Romance Writers, Jennifer LaBrecque, Berta Platas, Rita Herron, Kelley St. John, Rhonda Nelson, Elena Pedri, Donna Sterling, Sandra Chastain, Julie Linker, Caridad Pineiro, L. A. Banks, Michele Moore, and Richard Tuft. Thanks also to my *other* writing buddies—Mike Roberts, Melissa Carver, Joanne Bullington, Clarence Jones, Dorothy Northrip, Mark Jackson, Ginger Carter, Carrie, Frank, Leslie, Tricia, Sonya and bro Mike. Thanks to Madee James for the great website, and to the pink-pencil-wielding copy editor who did such a great job on the manuscript. As always, thanks to Mama and Daddy and the home folks. Sorry if I missed anybody.

Letter from William, a Vampire

I am William Cuyler Thorne, and I have been a vampire for five centuries or so. For most of that time, I've had what you moderns would call a death wish.

You may well ask why I've yearned for death. Why would an immortal creature, forever young and strong, with a vast fortune at his disposal and an endless supply of beautiful women to fulfill his every carnal need, wish to end his existence?

My fascination with my own extinction was born on the night I was made. The night I became a blood drinker I witnessed the slaughter of my wife and child, whom I loved more than life itself. The pain of that memory has seared me like a firebrand for half a millennium. I longed for a final death to snuff out the agony, even though it meant damnation for all eternity, since my soul had been taken when I was turned.

I cannot honestly say how I have managed to stem the desire to bring on my own demise. I suppose the semblance of family that I have managed to cobble together over the centuries has helped me more than I know. A royal line of strong, beautiful women—descended from Lalee, the greatest voodoo priestess ever to grace the shores of the New World—have been my daughters. My immortal offspring is one Jack McShane, whom I made into a vampire as he lay dying on a Civil War battlefield. The rest of my household consists of two loyal retainers in the form of twin half-canine/half-human bodyguards, Reyha and Deylaud.

And now there is Eleanor. My beautiful, raven-haired madam seductress whom I made into a blood drinker so that she could serve as my companion for the rest of my nights on earth. Her devotion, not to mention her ravenous sexual hunger for me, had finally eased the pain of my hellish memories and made me want to live to be with her.

And then the impossible happened. My mortal wife, Diana, my goddess, returned to me as a vampire. She whom I had thought dead and buried for the last five hundred years came to me—along with the son she had borne me.

My joy was tempered with anger, for she arrived in the company of another man, a powerful blood drinker whose life and bed she had shared for these centuries. My son, now a vampire created by this same evil monster who had taken my wife, did not even know of me—and still to this day does not know I am his mortal father. With that, my anger turned to rage.

A pox of the undead, an awful, rotting scourge, overtook my son in Savannah. The only treatment proved to be the voodoo blood that I carry inside myself. A drink from my own veins strengthened him, but the cure could only come from a purer form of voodoo blood. That is, blood taken from the descendants of Maman Lalee. From the daughters of my heart.

Hugo and the others took the smallest and most vulnerable of them, my precious little Renee, for her life's blood. And with her fled the sanity of her mother, Melaphia, my treasure, now left with a broken heart and shattered mind.

I gave Melaphia my most solemn vow that I would move hell and earth to get her daughter back. I left her and my beloved city—Savannah—in the tender care of my trusted offspring, Jack, who, for all his erstwhile humanity, is a very fearsome creature indeed.

But not as fearsome as I, a vampire betrayed in the cruelest way imaginable, left distraught by the two women that he has loved most in his life and in his death. Eleanor led Diana to Renee, and together they kidnapped her.

My rage rises within me, as powerful as the tide. As I pursue these women I can smell the blood of those who stole from me as the wolf can smell the hare. When I find them they will wish they had never drawn breath as humans, much less drawn blood as vampires.

As my dear Jack would say, payback is a bitch.

Beware the vampire betrayed—for his kiss is death.

Letter from Jack, a Vampire

You know those country songs about some down-and-out bastard whose woman just ran off with his best friend and his double-wide? Somebody who just lost his job and his dog done up and died, he's out of money and liquor, and his TV flamed out right before the Daytona 500 came on?

I feel like that guy. Only worse.

Things were perking along real fine for me until a few months back. Yes, I had about everything a vampire could want—my own auto repair business, a handful of loyal human and not-quite-human pals, a cozy place to park my coffin, and a budding romance with a hot Latin lady cop. And, last but not least, I had my sire, William Thorne, the baddest vampire on the continent, to watch my back.

Me and William didn't always get along, I admit. He bossed me around for the hundred and fifty years since he made me, and it seemed like we were at each other's throats a lot. But we always needed each other. Mostly we worked together to keep the undead and otherwise unhuman inhabitants in the city in line and under the radar of the police and the public. But the tension between us was always there.

Lately, though, we came to what you might call an understanding, and he started treating me almost like an equal.

That was about the time all hell broke loose.

See, William's own sire—a nasty piece of work named Reedrek—came to town to settle some old scores with his offspring. First he murdered one of William's best friends and then he murdered one of mine.

That *really* pissed me off. Me and William took care of him, locking him away in the cornerstone of a hospital wing under construction. Just when we were starting to relax, even more horse hockey hit the fan. William's long-lost wife and kid showed up with an evil vampire named Hugo.

It was like Peyton Place for bloodsuckers around here, what with the catfights between William's wife and girlfriend, William taking on Hugo, and me mixing it up with Junior, a punk with a foul attitude to go with his fangs.

If that wasn't bad enough, a vampire-rotting plague broke out, I accidentally raised my murdered buddy from the dead as a zombie, and my by-the-book cop girlfriend, Connie, found out I was a bloodsucking fiend.

Talk about a bad week.

And then the most awful thing happened. The new

vamps left town in a hurry—pulled up stakes if you'll pardon the expression—and took our beloved nine-year-old Renee with them. I say "our" Renee because William and I had helped raise her as we'd raised her mother and her mother's mother and so on.

When Renee was taken, a piece of my heart went with her. And the rest of my heart broke when I looked into the eyes of her mother, my beautiful Melaphia, and realized that her daughter's disappearance had driven her to madness. She is like a wild thing made of loss and sorrow.

William has gone off alone to bring Renee back or die trying, leaving me to take care of Melaphia and keep Savannah's denizens of the dark from making the city into some demon's feeding ground.

How long do you think it will take for an upstart bloodsucker or opportunistic shape-shifter or three to try and take me on once word gets out that William is out of town indefinitely? Pretty much any time now, I figure.

But what the hell. William may be the baddest dude on the continent but good old Smilin' Jack ain't too far behind. Besides, maybe a good rumble would take my mind off my troubles.

All I've got to say is . . . bring it on.

One

William

I stared across the frozen landscape and watched the flames lick at the mansion I had just set on fire, consuming it bit by bit, much as I had consumed its inhabitants. I've never been much of a flesh eater, preferring instead to drink a creature's blood, as I am a man of refinement. But I can make an exception now and then.

My offspring Jack has been known to run down a buck from time to time, wrestling it by its antlers and delivering a killing bite to the jugular before feasting on its flesh. Only in season, of course. I believe it has as much to do with his ideas of southern machismo as it does with a sincere craving for the flesh of a living creature. Still, for decades it has kept at bay his lust for the human kill to which we vampires are born.

Ultimately, my Jack is a civilized blood drinker who knows how to keep his baser needs in check. As do I, for the most part. But tonight was different. Tonight was special. I indulged in a kind of savagery I had not allowed myself in centuries. One by one I ripped out the throats of the vampires inside the now-burning manse, sampling the blood and flesh of each one in turn. And I enjoyed it.

My fangs to their throats, I bade each of them tell me the whereabouts of their leader. I heard the names of several cities, but I could smell the lies on their lips, so I ripped out their throats. I severed the heads of some, and I even staked one with a spindle ripped from a wooden chair. I knew I would discover the truth before the night was done.

It was pleasing to vent my wrath on the small band of blood drinkers, especially since I'd been forced to come all the way to this wild and most frigid part of Russia to find Renee. The ones who fled with her had not returned to their home, however. Hugo and his clan would not have wished to lead me to the rest of their "family," or to expose them to the rotting disease the traitors could all now be carrying.

Ironic that the pox had been developed on this very site as a form of biological warfare against us, the peaceful vampires of the New World. But the plague had escaped Hugo's control, and one of their own— my son, Will—was stricken half a world away.

As I reflected on these matters, one of the mansion's magnificent domes collapsed upon itself in a shower of sparks, making a sound like the hinges on the gates of hell creaking open to collect its due. A figure scrambled out of the burning shell of what an hour ago had been an impressive example of Russian baroque architecture.

I smelled a lone survivor of the carnage before I left the mansion, but it would have been too tiresome to ferret him out of the massive building with its surely inexhaustible variety of hiding places. I simply torched the place and waited for the rat to desert the burning ship.

I stood in the shadow of a giant fir tree and watched him run, half-staggering, from the structure, beating at his burning hair with his bare hands. He looked so comical that I briefly thought of letting him live; there are certain advantages in leaving an individual to tell the cautionary tale to others.

But I wasn't feeling particularly charitable.

I was on him in an instant, dragging him down to the snow-covered ground. I forced his head around to face me, nearly breaking his neck in the process, and let him see my fangs, which still held shredded bits of his comrades' flesh.

"What is your name?" I asked.

"Vanya."

"Where is your master, Vanya?" I asked him. "Where has he gone?"

"I don't know," he whimpered. "I swear it."

"What good is the oath of the damned to me? Besides, you *do* know where Hugo and his mate are. I can smell it on you like I can smell your terror."

"You'll just kill me anyway."

"Perhaps. Perhaps not. Know one thing for certain: If you don't tell me you'll be dead sooner than if you start speaking the truth."

I saw the decision in his eyes. "London," he said.

A less powerful vampire than I would not have known if he was lying. But I knew in my blood and in my bones that he was telling the truth. Tightening my grip on him, I pressed his throat to my mouth, almost like a lover, and delivered a killing bite that half severed his neck. I left him staring sightlessly at the stars.

"London," I breathed, feeling myself smile for the first time since my beloved Renee had been kidnapped.

It would almost be like going home again.

Jack

"Ta-da!" Werm stretched out his skinny arms and twirled around the abandoned shell of a room like he was showing off the Taj Ma-freakin'-hal. The one bare lightbulb overhead illuminated a dingy, dirty hovel with peeling wallpaper and rats' nests in the corners. I didn't need my super-duper vampire sense of smell to tell me that some of the homeless people of the city had been making it their home. Or at least their toilet.

I looked at my little fledgling vampire friend in his usual getup of black leather and silver bling. His hair was an inky black, thanks to the modern miracle of Miss Clairol. "*This* is where you want to start your own goth bar?" I asked. "With *my* money?"

"It's perfect!" He gestured to one side of the room. "We'll have the bar over here, and back behind me we can have the stage."

"Stage?" I wondered just what kind of shows Werm's weird friends could come up with. Probably something like those crazy performance art pieces you hear about coming out of New York. I could see in my mind's eye one of Werm's little pals stuffing dimes up his nose while he recited the Gettysburg Address.

"Yeah, we can get some bands, some spoken word artists—"

"Whattaya mean 'we,' white boy?" I was planning to be a silent partner only. Silent as in never setting foot in the joint if I could help it. I had only agreed to the loan to help Werm get on his feet financially and keep him out of trouble. In the movies, vampires never seem to have to make a living. Welcome to the real world. Besides, idle hands are the devil's workshop, as my poor sainted mother used to say. And when the idle hands belong to a bloodsucking demon to begin with, well . . .

"C'mon, Jack," Werm wheedled. "You're gonna love this place once we get it fixed up."

"There's that 'we' thing again."

Werm continued to ignore my skeptical tone and splayed out his hands in front of him. "This is going to be the most happening place in town. Everybody who's anybody is going to want to hang out here. I've hired a decorator who knows just what I want."

Being a country music fan, I thought about that song "I'm Going to Hire a Wino to Decorate Our Home." I wondered what a bar would look like after Werm's goth friends got finished with it. A funeral parlor, most likely. Not altogether inappropriate for a vampire, I reckoned. After all, Werm would be settling his coffin in the cellar of this place if this was where he wound up. His society parents were on the verge of kicking him out of the house.

"Aren't you putting the cart before the hearse?" I asked him. "You've got to get the thing built out before you decorate. Did you get bids from that list of contractors I gave you?"

"I did better than that." Werm beamed. "I have a great idea about how to get the work done around here and save money at the same time."

Werm and "great idea" were not exactly two things that went together hand-in-hand. "Lay it on me," I said. "I'm keen to hear this."

"I'm going to hire Eleanor's whores to do the work. Think about it. They've been unemployed for weeks and this will let them make some money and keep them off the streets."

"That's the craziest damn fool idea I ever heard! They're *used* to being on the streets. They're *whores*. If they could do carpentry and drywall, they wouldn't have to be *whores*." I wasn't expecting an awesome display of brainpower from Werm, but by *dang*.

"Just because they're whores doesn't mean they can't learn. If they ever decide to go legit, they'll need to know a trade. If they applied themselves they might even learn to do something high-class."

"You're forgetting that old saying," I told him. " 'You can lead a whore to culture, but you can't make her think.' "

"I know what your problem is. You're thinking of stealing them away from Eleanor. Maybe I should call you 'Jack, the killer pimp.' " Werm busted out laughing. "I can just see you in a purple suit and a hat with a big feather in it."

"Laugh it up, fang boy," I said. "Babysitting a bunch of homeless hos is not as much fun as it sounds." I'd had to find temporary accommodations for five working girls while Eleanor's house was being rebuilt at William's expense.

Reedrek had torched the classy brothel just for the

sake of meanness. I'd financed the prostitutes' new housewares and wardrobes, held their hands and listened to their troubles. Hell, I'd even painted their toenails and braided their hair.

"It sure *looks* fun," Werm said. "I'll bet the girls are offering you all kinds of perks for being nice enough to help them out, you lucky dog, you." He punched me weakly on the shoulder.

It was true—they'd all offered to show me their appreciation in various ways, but I'd decided to keep things on a professional level. "I've got enough stress right now without having jealous catfights break out."

"I think they're all in love with you. Cheryl says you're the best-built and best-looking man in town. She says she wants to run her toes through your wavy black hair."

"Stop it," I said.

"And Souxi says she wants to paint her new room the exact shade of blue as your eyes."

"I'm going to bite you if you don't hush up," I said.

"They follow you around like little ducklings. It's really funny."

I gritted my fangs. Herding whores. This is what I had come to. Oh yes, I was going to look really tough to the other badasses in this city when they started challenging me for dominance over the territory hereabouts now that William wasn't around to back me up.

"Seriously, Jack. I think the bar would be the perfect place for them to work until Eleanor gets back."

If Eleanor got back, that was. I'm not sure the seriousness of her situation had fully dawned on Werm. Her decision to leave her sire so soon after she was made was a dangerous one.

Unless William released Eleanor formally and in person from the mystical two-hundred-year bond of sire and offspring, she would start to physically "deteriorate," as William put it. In other words, she would rot on her feet, return to being the dead thing she was. I only hoped William made it to her in time.

Also, as a fledgling without William's protection, she was vulnerable to all kinds of predatory vamps. There was no telling what Hugo had promised her to make her agree to go to Europe with him and the others. But if she chose to trust Hugo instead of William, that might well prove to be a fatal mistake.

"Maybe you're right about them learning a trade," I said. "Once the place is finished, I think they'd be better off as cocktail waitresses than carpenters, though. I just doubt if their skills extend to the finer points of construction. Maybe they might be able to spackle the ceiling if they can do it lying on their backs."

"I can hang wallpaper," a little voice behind me said. "And I do it standing on my own two feet."

I turned to see Ginger, one of Eleanor's girls, standing there in a pair of pink overalls with a sample book under one arm. Oh, man, did I ever feel like a heel.

"I'm sorry, darlin'," I said. "I just meant—"

"I know what you meant, Jack. But just because I'm a whore doesn't mean that's all I know how to do." She thrust out her pouty, painted lip and sniffed. "I took a correspondence course in interior design."

I started to ask her if she had to copy a picture off a matchbook cover to qualify, but I bit my tongue in time to stop myself. Ginger was actually one of the brighter prostitutes in Eleanor's employ. Unfortunately, that wasn't saying much.

"You're the new decorator?" I scratched the back of my head. So the decor would run more toward contemporary whorehouse than gothic dungeon. I guess that might be an improvement. Either way, this was going to be the craziest drinking establishment in town. In fact, I wanted to get good and drunk just thinking about it. "I'm sure you'll do a dandy job, darlin'," I said.

She smiled a little before her girlish face broke out in a sad look. Werm took the sample book from her. "Listen," he said, "Jack didn't mean—"

"It's not that," she said, waving a hand dismissively. "I'm worried about Sally."

"What about her?" I asked. I'd noticed that Sally, the youngest of the prostitutes, had been a bit nervous and standoffish lately, and her skin didn't look like healthy living human skin should. I'd figured she was just stressed out by losing so many of her belongings in the fire as well as her mentor, Eleanor.

"Promise not to get mad?" Ginger said, looking up at me between fanlike false eyelashes.

I started to make the sign of the cross on my chest in a cross-my-heart gesture before I remembered. You'd think that after a hundred and fifty years I'd recollect I was damned. "I promise."

"She's on crystal meth," Ginger said.

"Oh, geez," Werm said. "Are you sure?"

"Yeah. Marlee saw her with a pipe. The kind they make from a lightbulb with the metal end sawed off and the guts taken out. Plus, she's not eating and she's letting herself go. Her skin looks terrible. She's even getting speed bumps."

"That's what formication will do," Werm said, shaking his head.

"It's not from fornication. If it was, all us whores would have it," Ginger said.

"Not *forn*ication," Werm corrected, "*form*ication. That's when a meth addict feels like there's spiders and snakes crawling under his skin."

"So they scratch themselves until they've got sores all over, like Sally's done," Ginger said, understanding.

"How do you know so much about meth addiction?" I asked Werm.

"A guy I worked with at Spencer's at the mall was a tweaker," he said. "He was messed up."

"Ginger, are you absolutely sure that Sally is smoking ice?" I asked. This was serious. One of the things William had told me to do before he left was to take care of Eleanor's girls, and I didn't want to let him down. Much less Eleanor herself.

"I'm pretty sure. But that might not be her only problem."

"What else?" I asked.

"Some guy has been following her," she said. "We think he's a stalker or something."

"Why hasn't somebody told me about this before?"

Ginger shrugged. "She just told us this morning at breakfast. She says it's been going on a few days now."

Werm asked, "Could he be a pusher or something, or maybe a john who's obsessed with her? What does he look like?"

Ginger shook her head. "She swears she's never seen him before. He's tall and skinny and has these parallel scars down one side of his face. Like something with huge claws got hold of him."

"Meth users get paranoid a lot," I said. "Maybe it's

her imagination. But just in case, I'll check out her source. Do you know where she's getting the ice?" I could really get off on draining anybody who would sell that poison to people, especially to an innocent like Sally.

It seemed strange to think of a prostitute as innocent, but there was something naive and vulnerable about her that had made me afraid for her even before I heard this disturbing news. She seemed to need somebody to take care of her. I guess Eleanor as her madam had filled that role.

"She gets it from a gang of cookers that live down by the marsh. There's a whole family of them. Their name's, um, Thrasher."

"Oh, crap," I muttered.

"Do you know them?" Werm asked.

"You could say that."

I first met up with that clan in the twenties when they made illegal whiskey and I ran it—that is, delivered it—for them. They tried to shortchange me a time or two, but I could forgive them for that. What really chafed me was when they poisoned a bunch of my friends with some 'shine that they knew was a bad batch but were too stingy to throw out. Killing your customers is bad for business any day of the week, but I was particularly sore about it that time because I gave that jug of rotgut to those old boys whose lives it took.

I sat down to drink and play cards with them one night in a speakeasy out by the river. We all passed out. I was the only one who woke up. That one was tough to explain to the authorities. They didn't exactly buy my "cast-iron stomach" excuse, but they couldn't prove I brought in the 'shine since all the witnesses had gone toes-up.

It seemed that the Thrashers hadn't learned a thing in eighty-something years. Nowadays the contraband was methamphetamine, hillbilly heroin, the drug of choice in the rural south. And they were still just as willing to ruin somebody's life for the almighty dollar as their granddaddy had been.

Maybe the worst part was, the stuff couldn't hurt *them*. See, they're werewolves. And any kind of shapeshifter is almost as hard to kill as a vampire. So they could take the stuff, no harm done, but their regular steady customers were in for a world of hurt.

I said good night to Werm and Ginger, left them to go over their wallpaper samples, and went out into the frosty night. I'd known this night was coming since the day William left for Europe. I was going to have to take on the monsters who lived in the dark places in and around this city to prove I was large and in charge.

It was time to kick some werewolf ass.

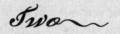

Two

William

Did I say that two women had betrayed me?

Make that three.

I looked up at the lights in the windows of Olivia's town house as the freezing mist swirled around me like a damp velvet cloak. The Georgian terrace-style home on Bedford Row had four stories aboveground, plus a basement. Plenty of room for my hand-selected leader of the European Bonaventures and her merry band of vampires to live in comfort. One big happy family.

We vampires who had chosen to fight the old lords rather than go along with their plans for world domination called ourselves Bonaventures. We'd been convening in Savannah when the plague leading to Renee's kidnapping had disrupted our planning session.

This area of Bloomsbury, north of the City of London, was home between the great wars to scholars, artists, and writers like Virginia Woolf. It now had an air of faded gentility. I took a quick glance over my shoulder, but as it was not a fit night out for man nor beast, as the gothic stories go, nobody was there to see me leap the wrought-iron fence.

Once on the other side, I paused to admire the house. It would be a shame to have to torch it like the one in Russia, but it would give me almost as much pleasure. Olivia had discovered that my Diana was a blood drinker—but she had chosen to keep that fact from me and even worse, coerced Jack to keep her secret. Because of that choice I was blindsided by Diana's arrival in Savannah and unprepared for the disastrous events that followed.

I reached the front door and lifted the large brass knocker. But I stopped, deciding that I should give Olivia the same warning of my arrival that I'd had of Diana's.

I grasped the door knob and twisted. When it came off in my hand, I cast it aside along with the remaining hardware from the hole it had left in the door. Then I wrenched the door open, splintering the wood away from the series of dead bolt and chain locks that had been attached to it a moment before.

Inside the entrance hall a staircase led up to a landing where a number of pale faces appeared from behind separate doorways.

"Come out, come out, wherever you are!" I bellowed.

A dark-haired female vampire in emerald green satin came out onto the landing. From behind her stepped Olivia in a flowing white silk gown. "Everyone, this is William Cuyler Thorne. He and I have a lot to talk about. Go back inside your rooms. I'll introduce you another time."

Olivia started down the staircase slowly. I could smell her fear of me. Two vampires, ignoring her orders, followed along behind her—the dark-haired female and a male of average height and build with reddish brown hair and beard and vivid blue eyes that spoke of Celtic ancestry.

When Olivia reached the entryway, she raised her arms as if to embrace me, but the look in my eyes made her think better of it. "William, I'm so sorry about Renee," she said.

"Jack called you," I stated. Of course he had. Jack would do that—keep everyone informed and on the same page, as he would put it.

No matter. I didn't care if Olivia was prepared for my arrival. If she had been expecting me, she had clearly not thought out what she would say in her defense. Her gunmetal gray eyes betrayed her indecision and dread.

Olivia's platinum hair and alabaster skin against the backdrop of the sheer white gown gave her an ethereal, ghostly appearance. She looked positively delicate now, much different than the first time I met her. Then she was dressed from head to toe in black leather, playing the young tough. I wondered what a vivid slash of red would look like across that lily-white throat.

"William, I can explain—"

In one lightning-fast motion, I ripped a wooden spindle from the staircase and pressed the jagged end to Olivia's chest. A circle of red began to stain the pristine whiteness of the gossamer gown where the sharp point of the wooden shard pierced her flesh.

"No!" screamed the woman standing on the last step

of the staircase. She lurched forward but was caught from behind by the male vampire, who held fast to her.

"Give me one good reason why I shouldn't kill you," I rasped, pressing my face close to Olivia's and extending my fangs to full length.

"I can give you many," Olivia said.

"Come now, mate," the man said in a forced, jolly tone. His accent held a touch of Aussie twang. "Let's talk about this, shall we?"

I ignored him and pressed the stake harder into Olivia's flesh. The force of my anger raised me off the floor so that I hovered above her, my fangs inches from her face. "Do you know what it's like to be confronted with the fact that the love of your five-hundred-year existence, whom you thought dead and buried, is a vampire? Imagine, if you will, my horror as I stood on my own dock and saw my long-lost wife and son—blood drinkers both—in the clutches of one of the most vile creatures I have met in my long life.

"Imagine the shock, the total horror of being unprepared for such a sight, even though the two most trusted of your own bloodline could have warned you in advance. Could have spared you."

"I was afraid, William," Olivia said. "Afraid for you. If I had told you Diana was alive, I knew that you would move hell and earth to go to her. Even if it meant you would be walking into a situation where you would have been vastly outnumbered. I thought if I waited until we knew more about Hugo and how to fight him together, then you would have a better chance of survival."

"That's amusing. I just walked into that very situation in the wilds of Russia and I slew a dozen or more vampires single-handedly. Vampires who had surely been forewarned by their leader, Hugo. And still they could not stop me from spilling their blood and burning them to crisps."

Olivia's eyes widened and I heard the other two vampires gasp. All three of them reeked with fear of me. As well they should.

"I had just lost Alger!" Olivia said with a hitching breath. "In the few short days I spent with you, you had become my new father. I couldn't lose you, too, not so soon after I had lost my sire." One pink-tinged tear escaped the corner of her eye. "I love you, William. I love you like I loved my Alger."

She loved me. I was suddenly overcome with a staggering weariness. The events of the last few days— Renee's kidnapping, Melaphia's hysteria, my betrayal by Diana and Eleanor, my slaughter of the Russian clan—hit me with the force of a cannonball to the gut. My feet touched the ground and I sagged against an antique grandfather clock.

Olivia came to my aide, supporting me. I would allow her to believe that her profession of love brought me back to my senses. I would let her believe that I was such a fool for the love of my fellow blood drinkers. After all the betrayals, among my own kind it was only the affection of my offspring Jack that I valued. For reasons I would never understand, I prized his lingering humanity. But for the present I needed Olivia and her coven to help me rescue Renee, so I couldn't afford to indulge myself by punishing her, even though I longed to. As Jack would say, I needed to get it together.

I let the improvised stake drop to the oriental rug

and Olivia collapsed against me with a sob, throwing her arms around my neck. She clasped herself to me as if I'd just saved her from a horrible fate, instead of almost killing her myself.

"William, I am so sorry. Please, please forgive me. I will never keep secrets from you again. I swear it on my existence as a blood drinker, on the memory of Algernon."

My vision no longer swam with the bloodred haze of my bad intent. Yet I couldn't quite muster the goodwill to tell Olivia that I forgave her. Because I didn't.

But I put my arms around her and hugged her back as if I did.

They seated me in the parlor and Olivia went upstairs to change out of the bloody gown while the other woman went into the kitchen to make tea. When the women were gone, the man introduced himself. "I'm Donovan Baird," he said. "I'm what you'd call Olivia's right-hand man."

I shook his proffered hand and he continued, "Since Jack called, we've been making inquiries."

"Inquiries?"

"Into the whereabouts of Hugo's gang," he explained. "Our spies on the Continent told us they didn't go back to Russia. If you'd contacted us we could have saved you the trip there." He looked away nervously. He was diplomatic enough not to say outright that I had done anything wrong in not informing their coven of my plans. He was a wise man.

"What else do your spies tell you?"

"That they're here in London. But I guess you know that already or you wouldn't be here."

"Do you know where they are?"

Olivia appeared then, wearing jeans and a T-shirt. The other vampires I had glimpsed earlier followed behind their mistress. They entered the parlor quietly, filled the seats on the far side of the room, sat cross-legged on the floor, or stood in the shadows. As far from me as they could get.

Olivia answered my question. "We think so. To-night we were going to have a session to plan strategy for approaching them. But first we need to surveil them. See how many are in their party. Observe their comings and goings."

"You'll leave that to me," I said.

"Of course. Anything you say," Olivia demurred.

The dark-haired one returned from the kitchen with tea and blood on a tray. She left the others to serve me and went to Olivia, putting her arms around her and laying her hand gently on Olivia's chest where the wound from the stake was healing already.

Olivia introduced the others while I drank to rehydrate myself. The dark-haired one's name was Bree. I scanned the room looking from one blood drinker to the next. "How fares the one you sent to spy on Hugo, the one who was so gravely injured by his clan?"

One of the women sitting on the floor broke out in sobs and the man nearest her laid a comforting hand on her shoulder. "She didn't make it," Olivia said. "She used the last of her strength to make her way back to us, but she'd lost too much blood and too much flesh from her throat. She had fang marks all over her body. Judging from the wounds, many different vampires had been at her for who knows how long. No amount of feeding from our veins could save her."

"I'm sorry for your loss," I said. It was rare indeed for anything other than fire, sunlight, a wooden stake through the heart, or decapitation to kill a vampire. Vampires could almost always recover from blood loss in time. While it was true that females were the weaker vessel in the world of the blood drinker, the fact that this one died of exsanguination bespoke of how terrible indeed must have been her wounds.

Donovan changed the subject. "You know, of course, that we are all at your disposal," he said. "Whatever you want us to do. We're all ready to fight."

"I wonder," I said, "if you are. If you really are ready."

Bree looked around at the others. "What do you mean?"

I stood up and walked to the center of the room. I stared into the eyes of first one vampire and then the next, taking their measure. "You have managed to steer clear of the dark lords by keeping your heads down, by keeping yourselves cloistered behind these walls for the most part, and by being discreet in your activities."

I knew these facts because I had kept in close contact with Algernon, who until his recent murder led the little coven of vampires. The city helped shield them while the old lords traditionally preferred the countryside.

"All that will change when we take on Hugo and his clan. Nothing draws out the old sires like conflict. The bloodier the better, as far as they're concerned. When we go in for Renee, it could be a bloodbath. Hugo will call for the darkest forces at his disposal.

There is no predicting what we will face before all is said and done."

"So, you're saying we could face something more evil and powerful than Hugo?" Bree asked.

"Most certainly," I said. "We all know that the dark lords have been preparing something very bad for us. Their opening salvo was to send Hugo to the States to unleash the vampire plague. Since we were able to stop the spread of the contagion, they will hit us with something even more dangerous. If we start a war with Hugo's clan, it may cause the old sires to move up the timetable for their next attack on us. Especially since I'm here now."

"Why will that make a difference?" Donovan asked.

"They will probably interpret my arrival on European soil as an attempt to answer Hugo's attack, and they will expect me to have something up my sleeve as payback. They won't believe I am here simply to rescue a human child, even now that Hugo has undoubtedly told them about the voodoo blood. They just don't think that way."

"Are you sure Hugo would tell them about the voodoo blood?" Olivia said. "Maybe he would want to keep that to himself and his clan in case the dark ones wanted Renee for themselves."

"That's possible," I said. "It depends on how much he wants to ingratiate himself with them. For him to keep Renee for his own little family and not tell the dark ones about her would be the best that we could hope for. In either case, we've got a serious battle on our hands."

The one called Bree spoke up again. "Why should

we endanger ourselves by calling the attention of the dark lords to us?" She ignored the gasps of the other vampires in the room. "But for her magic blood, this human child is nothing to us," she said, looking around for signs of support. No one stepped forward.

Olivia, eyes fiery with rage, slapped Bree across the face with enough force to send her backward across the room into the arms of the vampire directly behind her. "How dare you defy my orders?" Olivia demanded. "Don't you understand the struggle we're in? The dark lords will come for us eventually. Even though he lives on another continent, William is our leader. He has been helping smuggle peace-loving vampires to the Americas for decades. Reedrek told us that the dark lords will attack us, so there's no time to move the rest of us in safety. Now that William is here he can help us plan our strategy, our defenses. Isn't that right, William?"

"Of course," I said, making my face a neutral mask.

Bree was on her feet again, a livid handprint visible on her pallid face. "But only a moment ago he was threatening to kill you! And now you trust him with the well-being of us all?"

"William has been through hell," Olivia said. "He's overcome his emotions. I know he has." She reached for my hand and held it tightly, as if to reassure herself. "We'll be prepared to fight for Renee, and then to do whatever is necessary to insure our survival after that."

She looked around the room at her vampires. She must have seen some skepticism in my face because she drew herself up to her full height and said finally, "Don't worry, William. We're tougher than we look."

"Good," I said, leaving out the natural conclusion to that thought: *They'd have to be.* For now at least, I let it go at that.

Jack

I stood behind a cypress tree and focused on the cabin about seventy-five yards away. I'd parked my truck on the side of the road half a mile back and slogged through the swamp to get this far. The marsh water chilled me to the bone. I am, for all intents and purposes, a cold-blooded creature, like the frogs and toads hibernating in the muck all around me. Savannah never gets that cold in the wintertime—not to humans. But vampires can feel the cold, I can tell you. It feels like death putting its hand against the middle of your back and trying to steer you toward the grave. Reminding you that the warmth of the sun will never shine on you again.

As if the cold wasn't bad enough, the feeling came over me that I was being watched. The last time I felt like that was when dear old Granddad Reedrek was shadowing me around the city. I looked behind me and everything was stillness. There wasn't even a breeze to move the swamp grasses.

I heard things, though. There were unquiet souls around me. In the distance I could hear the chains rattling and that sent still more shivers up my spine. I wasn't far from one of the places where the slave ships landed with their human cargo from western Africa. The cries of the men and women as they were herded on shore, some of them sick or dying from their hard journey across the Atlantic, came to me out of the stillness. The abject sorrow, grief, and fear in those desperate cries made me want to cover my ears.

It was times like this when I wished I could give back my powers of communication with the dead. William always said it was a gift and that I was lucky to have it. He seemed to think it would stand me in good stead one day. Problem was, this little gift that kept on giving reminded me over and over of my former fellow humans' inhumanity to one another. Where presents are concerned, I'd rather have a tacky necktie.

To get the voices out of my head I turned my attention back to the business at hand. There was no activity around the cabin, but there was a light on, and I could see shapes moving around behind the thin curtains. I was tempted to sneak up on the place and just burn it to the ground, scattering werewolves to the four winds. And if a few were killed, let God sort them out.

The authorities would just figure the house went up like so many places where meth was being cooked. The chemicals used were so volatile that fires and even explosions were common. But I couldn't take the chance that there were innocents in there with the bad guys. What if there were puppies—er, kids—around? I had to be sure, and the easiest way to find out and not tip my hand by asking questions was to just wait and watch.

There was that feeling again, like a warm breath on my neck. It was downright creepy, made my skin crawl and the hairs at my nape stand at attention. I took a deep breath and smelled something that touched a chord of recognition in my memory. It was a wild, musky animal smell. Then I heard a noise, starting with a faint, vibrating rumble and building to a full-throated growl. Something wily enough to get the drop on a vampire had managed to sneak up behind me.

Something like a werewolf. *Shit*.

I whirled just in time to look into the yellow-green eyes of a wolf as tall as me, reared up on his hind legs and ready to strike. I saw the intelligence in those eyes as well as some supernatural element that only another cursed creature could identify.

He launched himself and hit me full in the chest, knocking me to the ground. With a roar, the beast came at my throat with a massive display of powerful jaws and razor-sharp canines. I put my hand against his throat and shoved as hard as I could, sending the wolf sprawling backward just long enough for me to get back on my feet.

The wolf righted itself and when he saw my fangs extend to full-length he hesitated a moment—but only a moment—before he hurled himself toward me again. In the meantime I realized why the scent of this wolf was familiar. As I did, I saw something in his own eyes change.

He leapt at me, knocking me on my back again. I could feel his incredible power as he came at my face. His head seemed as big as a tree stump, and his massive maw opened an inch from my face, bringing us eye to eye and fang to fang.

His body began to sway with the force of his wagging tail, and his tongue lolled out and licked my cheek wetly.

"Get off me, you mangy, flea-bitten bastard. If I wanted a kiss from the likes of you, I'd ask for it." I shoved the wolf away from me again, and this time when he landed on his back he stayed put, grinning a goofy doggie grin at me, his still-wagging tail thumping happily against the soggy ground.

Before my eyes, the wolf began to do his morphing routine. I'd seen Reyha and Deylaud do it once before, only in the opposite direction—that is, turning from humans into canines. I'd never seen the reverse, but it was just as awe-inspiring and horrifying. The sound of the bones crunching was the worst, but the creature didn't seem to mind. I gritted my teeth at the sight and sound of his long bones re-forming.

When it was finished, Seth Walker lay naked in the grass and stretched like a guy just waking up after a long nap in the sun. Finally he propped himself on his elbows and said, "I thought you'd never recognize me, you toothy sonofabitch. I always said that vampire sense of smell ain't all it's cracked up to be."

"Bullshit. It's better than yours. Hell, I'd know your sorry hide in a tan yard," I said. I wiped at the place where he'd licked me.

"Sorry about the slobber. Sometimes my wolf acts like a pup around old friends."

"Just don't let it happen again. People might get the wrong idea, what with you nekkid and all."

"Hey, it's not like when you shape-shift the Fruit-of-the-Looms can come with you."

"Whatever, just keep your fruits to yourself."

He laughed. "My clothes are stashed behind some rocks about a mile from here. I'll tell you what, meet me at that juke joint down by the highway and I'll buy

you a beer, you old bloodsucker, and we'll tell each
other what we're doing here."

Seth Walker, also known as Skinwalker, squeezed the
juice from a lime quarter into a Corona and then
stuffed it into the long-neck bottle. "So what *are* you
doing here?"

"I live here," I said, taking a pull on my own brew.
"Which is more than I can say for you." Seth was police chief of a small town in north Georgia. The citi-
zens he served just thought he was a damned fine
lawman, not something out of a Lon Chaney Jr. movie.

He was also a self-styled naturalist and folklore ex-
pert. He could entertain you for hours with stories of
native American skinwalker lore and shape-shifter
myths from around the world.

He told me once that every culture on earth had a
shape-shifter myth. What does that tell you? Where
there's smoke, there's fire, as the saying goes. Just because a story is called a myth doesn't mean it's not
true.

"I know you live in Savannah," he said. "I mean,
what are you doing here in the marsh? Do you have
some unfinished business with the Thrashers that I
don't know about?"

"Ain't it just like a lawman to ask so many questions that aren't any of his business," I observed.

He grinned at me. "I just know that you wouldn't
be caught dead—if you'll pardon the expression—
within spitting distance of these poor, furry trash unless something was up, that's all."

"You got that right." I took another gulp of my beer
and paused long enough to watch a shapely barmaid's

rear wiggle as she sashayed by us. "Here's the story: I have reason to believe the Thrashers are cooking meth and selling it to someone I'm supposed to be taking care of. That's it in a nutshell."

Seth grew serious and took a bite of a steak so rare I'd half-expected it to moo when he'd first cut into it. "That's pretty much why I'm here, too. One of the Thrasher cousins tried to set up an operation in the north Georgia mountains."

"What happened to him?" As if I didn't know.

"Ate him."

"Good for you."

Seth burped and held up his empty bottle to signal the barmaid that he wanted another. "But not before I made him tell me about the rest of the family operation. There's nothing like baring a good set of fangs to loosen somebody's lips, not to mention his bowels. Am I right?"

"I've scared the shit out of a few old boys myself," I agreed. The barmaid handed him another Corona over the bar, and we clinked bottles.

"So I came on down here to check things out," he said.

"And just when were you going to tell me you were in town?" I asked.

He turned serious again. "There were a couple of things I had to figure out first."

"Such as?"

"Such as why one of the Thrashers hangs out at your garage most nights."

"Who are you talking about?"

Seth sawed at the bloody steak with a dull steak

knife. "The one named Jerry. He's a Thrasher on his mother's side."

"You're shitting me." I had always known that a couple of the old boys who liked to hang out at my auto repair business were not 100 percent human, but I never made it my business to find out what they were exactly. Not to mention who their people were. If *people* was the right word.

Jerry and Rufus smelled like shape-shifters, and I was always pretty sure Jerry was a werewolf. Us boys who have what you'd call inhuman tendencies can usually recognize one another, vampires and shifters (especially the canines and felines) by smell. Other kinds of creatures had other means.

Anyway, the boys who hung out at the garage had the good manners not to ask me what *I* was and, being a good southern host, I returned the favor. I guess you could call it a don't-ask-don't-tell policy, although I'm pretty sure they always knew I was a vampire. If they'd had any doubt, it had been shot all to hell when Reedrek came to town and murdered Huey, one of my employees and a good friend of my irregulars, as I called them.

"So I take it you didn't know Jerry was part of the Thrasher pack?"

"Hell, no, and how do you know what goes on at my garage anyway?"

"Because I've been casing the place when you haven't been there." He grinned at me, flashing a row of perfect, white, human-looking teeth. "And sometimes when you have been."

I opened my mouth to express my doubt that a

werewolf could catch a vampire unawares but remembered he had done just that in his animal form an hour ago. I didn't feel too bad about it, though. Seth was no ordinary werewolf.

He was the baddest shape-shifter in the south.

I first met him years ago when William had sent word through the unhuman grapevine for him to come down to Savannah and help us with a little problem. A local werewolf was chowing down on the citizenry and leaving half-eaten bodies out in the open in front of God and everybody. It wouldn't do. An in-depth police investigation could lead to all kinds of discoveries that would cause a general panic among the human population.

William, through his network of informants in the undead and otherwise unhuman world, knew that Seth had a reputation much like William's own in the vampire world. Seth was a lawman and didn't put up with any mess, and he liked to help maintain the secrecy of the existence of shape-shifters, as well as vampires and other things that go bump or growl or purr in the night. His philosophy and approach were also like William's: If you were a shape-shifter and didn't behave yourself and help maintain the status quo, he would eat you. Simple as that.

Since werewolves like to take care of werewolf business, just as vampires like to keep their own troubles within the bloodsucking ranks, William called Seth as a courtesy before he took it upon himself to go out and bag himself a big, bad wolf.

Seth came down to Savannah and dispatched the bad guy with nary a trace of blood or fur before you could say Jack Robinson. No muss, no fuss. All nice and tidy, just the way William liked things to be done. William liked him immediately. Even the Rin Tin Twins took to him, and things could get dicey whenever you introduced them to other folks with, let's say, canine tendencies. The twins' judgment of character was almost never wrong, and that was good enough for me.

Seth stayed on a couple of days and nights to see the sights and that's how we got to be buddies. Since then he came down to Savannah every year to go hunting and drinking with me and just hang out. He would raise hell with me by night and play golf with the polo-shirted, former frat boy crowd by day. To look at him in a pair of khakis, you'd think he stepped right out of the Kappa Alpha house. But he was just as comfortable roaming through the woods hunting deer with me, his fangs and claws his only weapons.

I think he also liked to use his time in Savannah to maintain his stable of contacts among other shifters, particularly werewolves, in south Georgia. I wondered sometimes if one or two of those country club boys he hung out with in the daytime might be werewolves who could come and fight with us, but outing a nonhuman was serious business and I knew Seth wouldn't have asked.

I had no idea what Seth's real age was. Shapeshifters aren't immortal like vampires, but they live longer than humans, don't show their age much, and are a bitch to kill. The only things that would do the job was a silver (you guessed it) bullet or silver stake to the heart, fire, or decapitation. Seth, who looked like a thirty-year-old human, could be fifty or a hundred. I couldn't tell; I don't even think other werewolves could necessarily tell.

I also had no idea how he had established himself as the foremost furbearing badass in the south. I tried to ask him about it a time or two, but he always deflected my questions. So I decided I'd better extend him the same "don't ask" courtesy as I did everybody else. What he *did* like to talk about was his work as an amateur naturalist and ecologist. He'd raised a lot of green in and around Atlanta for green causes and had a lot of interesting stories to tell about how he went after the more notorious polluters of the Chattahoochee and public lands. He was not above putting someone in their place with teeth and claws if he could do it discreetly.

There was one particularly unlucky politician locked up in the state mental hospital in Milledgeville who as far as I know is still babbling to anyone who will listen about seeing a man change into a wolf and come at his throat. I don't imagine he's ever made the connection between that incident and the bribe he took from a chemical plant to excuse them from dumping enough poison into the Hooch for a gigantic fish kill. No matter. He'll never murder another trout again.

Seth was roughly my height, more than six feet, and your typical—for this part of the world, at least—mixture of Native American and Scots-Irish blood. His brown hair was cut preppy short and those green-yellow eyes looked almost exactly like they did in his wolf form, except for the shape, of course.

Women must have found him handsome because

between the two of us—I don't mean to brag, but I'm not exactly chopped liver myself—we commanded the attention of pretty much every female in the room. Their reactions ranged from sly sidelong glances to out-and-out ogling. They were checking us out in a big way.

"I must be getting sloppy in my old age," I said. "I couldn't tell you were even around the garage."

Seth grinned. "In vampire years, you're just a tyke."

"So what was the other reason you didn't let me know you were in town?" I asked him.

"You know how I like to keep things on the down-low, especially when I'm dealing with other supernaturals," he said. "I was going to come and say howdy eventually. I just wanted to get this business with the Thrashers finished and keep you from getting involved. Whenever you get mixed up with them, nothing good ever comes from it."

"I can't argue with that," I said. "But now that I am involved, how do you suggest we go after them?"

Seth sighed. "I don't suppose I can convince you to just stay out of this and leave it to me?"

"Nope."

"Didn't think so. Okay, then, why don't you shake down that Jerry guy and make him tell you anything and everything he knows about the meth operation over at the cabin. Then we'll compare notes and decide what to do from there."

"Sounds like a plan," I said, throwing a wad of cash on the bar. "Come on, fur-for-brains, you can bunk at my place for the rest of the time you're here. I'm staying over at William's for a while anyway."

"That's mighty neighborly of you. You still sleep in

that coffin painted up like Dale Earnhardt's number three?"

"Sure do."

"You're a true son of the south, my friend," Seth said as we made our way to the door.

"And don't you forget it," I said. One of these days I'd get Seth to tell me about *his* origins. His real ones. That should be quite a tale.

Three

William

As still as standing stones, Donovan and I watched the town house where Hugo and his gang were hidden. Dressed in black, we stood in the shadows afforded by a grove of elms in the park across the street. He had insisted on accompanying me, announcing his intention to be my lieutenant while I was in London.

Olivia's spies had indeed identified the house where Hugo, Diana, and Will were staying. I could smell them from here. But I also knew that Renee was not in or around the house. I knew this only through the instinctual connection I had with the head of her bloodline, Maman Lalee. The mystical seeing shells Lalee had bequeathed me had failed. I'd brought them with me in the hope that they would show me Renee, or at least the way to her. But they evoked no telling visions. I sensed that they needed to be used on the soil that Lalee had trod, needed that ancient and mystical connection through the earth to her. On this continent, they were as silent as the dead things they were, and my psychic connection to Renee through her fore-mother would take me only so far. I would have to rely on more or less conventional means to track her down.

I closed my eyes and pictured Renee as I'd last seen her. She was wearing her school uniform of a navy plaid skirt and vest with a crisp white shirt. One of her knees had a scrape covered with a cartoon adhesive bandage. Her hair was carefully plaited, each of the little braids topped with a different colored barrette. She'd kissed my cheek before she headed to the kitchen table to do her homework. My chest ached with missing her, and I rubbed at it absently.

Out of the corner of my eye, I observed this Donovan, if that was his real name. He was an obliging fellow, popular and gregarious judging by his interactions last night with the others in Olivia's coven. It was clear that she leaned on him quite heavily. She obviously assumed him to be trustworthy and dependable. But I wasn't in a position to assume anything.

"It's been a long time since I've been on a *stake-out*," he said with a grin, then cleared his throat awkwardly.

"A vampire joke," I said, hardly in the mood for jest. "You would enjoy meeting my offspring Jack. He has a much better sense of humor than I."

"If you say so," he said.

"What's your background?" I asked him.

"What do you mean, mate?" he asked, not taking his eyes off the house.

"How did you come to be in Alger's coven? I never heard him mention you."

"I only just arrived right after Alger was killed," he said. "I'm a bit of a wanderer, you see? I've spent most of my life in Oz—that's Australia to you Yanks—but I've got to go on walkabout from time to time. I travel here and there—stowing away on ships is my specialty—and try to keep one step ahead of the dark lords. I'm of a mind to settle down for a spell now, though."

"Oh? Why now?"

He glanced at me just as the clouds overhead broke and the moonlight spilled down, illuminating his face more clearly. His skin was very white, whiter than even the natural pallor of a vampire, as if mention of the dark ones had caused the blood to drain from his face.

"I long for what strength there is to be had in numbers," he said finally.

"Again I ask you, why now?"

"I can feel them coming," he said in a suddenly raspy voice. "Can't you?"

"Yes," I said. "I can." From the moment I touched down on European soil from my chartered aircraft, I felt the difference. There was a roiling underneath my feet, below the surface of the earth. It felt as if hell itself was mobilizing.

"I'm glad you're here," he said.

I didn't respond. I wondered if Olivia had passed on to her coven members the mythology that had built itself up around me. Algernon had regaled her with so many tales of my exploits through the ages that when she first met me in Savannah, she knelt to me as if before a god. I hoped those in her coven were not looking to me as their sole salvation.

I'd had much time to think on the journey to and through Europe, and much time to stew in my own resentments. I once had great ambitions to help the more peaceful of my race triumph over the dark lords who would enslave them. After having been betrayed by some of those I loved best, I realized that I was beginning to care little whether any of us lived or died. Now my only concern was for Renee. Let Olivia's clan believe that I was also here to help save them. When they had served their purpose by helping me get Renee back, I would leave them to their fate.

It was a sea change in my attitude. Olivia was right in saying that I had devoted decades to saving my fellow vampires from the dark lords. But I realized that after all that had happened in the past few weeks, I had stopped caring. Let them save themselves.

"Oy!" Donovan jerked his chin in the direction of the house we were watching as Hugo and Diana stepped out of the front door. From behind them stepped Will. He looked thin but well. He had seemed cured by the newly engineered vaccine right before he'd left Savannah. But had he drunk little Renee's blood to finish repairing himself to this extent? There was no sign of the rotted flesh that had been sloughing off his face that last time I saw him. He still looked like a lean, hard, twenty-something punk rocker, with his close-cropped red-gold hair and pierced ears. He walked with the same swagger and wore the same insolent expression.

Eleanor was nowhere to be seen, much less Renee.

"I'll follow them," Donovan offered, and he was off.

I watched the evil little family walk casually down

the street, going to feed on some unsuspecting humans, no doubt, while Donovan followed at a discreet distance, too far away for his scent to be noticed by the other vampires, but close enough so that he wouldn't lose them. He looked as if he had done that sort of thing before.

When the others were out of sight, I crossed the street and entered the side yard of the house. The house was not as secluded as Olivia's, and I didn't care to be seen breaking down the front door. Once in the darkened back garden I found a cellar window unlocked, raised it, and lowered myself inside. If there was anyone home, I didn't wish to alert them. I listened and breathed deeply. The scent of Eleanor's fear came to me. I followed the odor.

Jack

I strolled into the garage and got myself a cup of coffee. Rennie and the irregulars were playing cards as usual. Rennie was my business partner and the best master mechanic in the great state of Georgia, and he was human. The irregulars consisted of a motley collection of guys who liked to hang out at my all-night auto repair business, Midnight Mechanics. Just why they were almost always here and not in their homes—wherever that was—was anybody's guess. Like I said before, my policy was not to ask anybody too many questions.

The irregular who had been hanging out the longest was Otis. Otis smells like a human—a human with severe hygiene issues maybe, but a human nonetheless.

Still there was something about him that was just, well, different. Different as in supernatural different. He doesn't have pointy ears or too many teeth, so I haven't quite figured out just what he is. But one day I will.

Rufus I'm pretty sure is a shape-shifter—not a werewolf, but some other variety I can't quite identify. Jerry is definitely werewolf all the way. I knew that even before Seth confirmed it. There was something really primal and elemental about werewolves that was fairly easy to spot—or to smell. Plus there's that full moon thing. Jerry never came around during a full moon. Neither did Rufus for that matter. Whatever that meant.

Then, in a class by himself, was Huey. Huey is the guy who Reedrek murdered, although he's here every night with the irregulars, playing cards when he doesn't have any car detailing to do. You might well ask why Huey is still hanging out when he's been dead for, oh, several months now.

It's because I accidentally raised him from the dead. Huey is a bona fide flesh-eating zombie. That communication-with-the-dead thing I mentioned earlier can get away from you. It went haywire one night during a voodoo ritual I performed while knee-walking drunk. You know how they say that drinking and driving don't mix? Well, neither does drinking and beseeching a voodoo *loa* for extra vampire powers.

Long story short, Melaphia created a spell so that Huey wouldn't rot any more than he already had. Even though he was past his expiration date when he clawed his way out of the ground, he hadn't completely turned sour. He could pass for human. A human with a body odor problem and a complexion so bad he looked like he'd at some point come in third in a hatchet fight. In fact, you didn't particularly want to get downwind of either Huey or Otis, but at least Huey had an excuse. He was dead. Otis was just a slob.

I waited for the hand to be over and then called Jerry to the kitchen area by waving the new issue of *Field & Stream* and telling him I wanted his opinion on a new shotgun. As soon as he was out of earshot of the others I said, "I need you to tell me everything you know about the Thrashers' meth operation, and don't even think of telling me you don't know anything."

I like to keep a low profile, but sometimes there's an advantage to having people know you're something big and bad. I could tell I wasn't going to have to shake Jerry down hard. He knew how dangerous I was, and that I didn't mess around. He blanched and swallowed hard.

"How did you know?"

"Never mind that. Just tell me everything. And while you're at it, tell me why one of the Thrasher clan hangs around my garage every night."

"I ain't a Thrasher," he said with conviction. "My ma was one, is all. I grew up in their pack when my daddy got run off. I didn't have no say in it."

"Who ran him off?"

"The law. Something about a killin'."

"Uh-huh. He chow down on somebody?"

"He got crazy drunk on Thrasher rotgut whiskey and got sloppy. I never saw him since I was a kid. The

Thrashers might have killed him themselves, for all I know."

It wouldn't be the first time a pack killed one of its own members for bringing them unwanted attention from the authorities. That was one of the only rules they were damned serious about.

"How did you break away from them?" I asked. Werewolf packs are funny. They treat their weakest members like dirt. They have that in common with regular wolves. Only werewolves then get pissed off when the pack member they treated so bad tries to escape. They can be downright possessive and get all snappish when somebody tries to leave them.

"When my mama died I just went. I wandered around for a while, but I never fit in with any other packs, and being a lone wolf is hard. Besides, I was homesick. So I moved back to Savannah and just tried to stay out of their way."

I expect life as a lone wolf is hard, at that. You need the support of a pack to help you cover your tracks, as it were. I mean, think about it. You have to stay a step ahead of the law because if you get in criminal trouble, you can't risk winding up in jail when there's a full moon. Werewolves can take their wolf form at will, but during a full moon, they *have* to change—no *if*s, *and*s, or *but*s. No choice. So they can't afford to get themselves incarcerated, drafted into military service, or into any other situation where they can't disappear from prying eyes when the moon is bright. They need their pack members to help them cover their fuzzy asses in all kinds of predicaments.

"How do you manage to steer clear of 'em?"

Jerry blushed. "I hang out here at night." He shrugged and looked away.

I'll be damned. Jerry came here every night because he wanted my protection. He was as tall as me, more muscular and broader through the shoulders. It might seem strange to think that a fellow like that felt he couldn't take care of himself, but nobody knew better than me how vicious the Thrasher clan could be.

Besides, I guess a vampire's hangout is a pretty safe place to be as long as you can stay on that vamp's good side. So far, so good.

"So when's the last time you saw any of them?"

"About two weeks ago one of my cousins came looking for me. He wanted me to help in the business. He said he wanted me to bring that meth shit to town and peddle it. Me and him went a round or two and he went on back to the swamp with his tail between his legs."

I figured Jerry meant that literally. Werewolves can change real fast when they get riled up. They usually revert to wolf form when they fight, especially if it's a real knock-down, drag-out. "Do you think you've seen the last of them?"

"Oh no. As my cousin limped off he said they'll be coming back to talk to me again, more than one of them next time. He said it was time for them to start doing business in the city proper." Jerry shivered, and he looked away from me again.

The Thrashers had always been content to stay in the swamp and hire outside contractors to do their retailing, no matter what kind of contraband they were dealing in. I know, since I was their moonshine runner so many years ago, that is, until the stuff killed my buddies. Having family members get into selling the stuff on the streets was a major shift in their business plan.

"What are you not telling me?" I asked. Jerry took a deep breath and stared at the ceiling. "Don't worry. I won't eat the messenger." I had to chuckle, and that made Jerry relax a little.

"My cousin Leroy said they figured since William was gone, it was safe to start expanding the operation."

I felt a bloodred rage sweep over me like a sudden fever. "He said that, huh?" I would make this Leroy eat those words, that plus a bellyful of Georgia red clay, and chase it with swamp water. I had been right when I'd guessed that the beasties were going to come at me once they heard William was away. With our history, I should have known it would be the Thrashers.

"That's all I know, Jack. I swear it."

I believed him. Jerry was a shape-shifter and he knew the lay of the supernatural land. He especially knew better than to lie to a master-level vampire. "Who's the alpha down there now?" I asked. I was hoping against hope that their old alpha had been replaced since I'd had dealings with them.

"It's still my uncle Samson. He's a mean sumbitch."

Didn't I just know it. I once saw Samson Thrasher tear one of his own wolves apart in an argument over the keys to a stolen pickup truck. I had even tangled with him myself when his negligence poisoned those friends of mine. The only reason I didn't kill him outright was that William wouldn't let me. He did, however, let me kick the shit out of Samson and tell him that if he killed anybody else with that rotgut, the two of us would tan his hide and nail it to a tree.

See, you don't kill an alpha wolf lightly. Because when the alpha dies, you leave his pack without protection, and there's no telling what might have come along to challenge his betas for dominance. It might even be worse than Samson. Personally, I wouldn't give you a plug nickel for the whole pack of swamp dogs. They could chew one another to bits for all I care. But William was the chief monster in the region, and he didn't want to let it be known that he was willing to throw the wolves to the wolves.

There was no point in starting a pissing match between the vampires and the werewolves. The other varieties of shape-shifters might get involved on the werewolf side and then all hell would break loose. We already had our hands full fighting off our own dark lords. William was smart about that political stuff. I just wanted to kick some ass. Now that I was the big kahuna monster-wise, I was going to have to try to be as clever as William about these things. Lord help us.

But kick ass was what I'd done that time I'd mixed it up with Samson. I'd had some bites to show for my trouble, mind you. My wounds had taken weeks to heal. His bite was as poisonous as his mangy soul. But he was a damn sight worse off, especially after I drained about half his blood. I expect my fang marks are still in his hide.

"Why are you asking about all this?" Jerry asked.

I told him what Ginger had said about Sally's addiction, but I left out any mention of Seth. There was no point in blowing his cover. Just because I trusted Jerry didn't mean the truth couldn't be beaten out of him—or bitten out. "Say, what does this cousin Leroy of yours look like?"

"He's tall and skinny and he has claw scars down his face on the right side. Is that who you think was following Sally?" Jerry said.

"Yeah, that's the description. Besides, it all fits. The Thrashers are deliberately targeting somebody who's under my protection, selling her their drugs and stalking her. They're taunting me."

"That sounds like them, the cowards. Using girls to bait you instead of calling you out like men. Or wolves. What are you gonna do, Jack?"

I clapped him on the back. "Don't you worry about it, Jerry. The less you know, the better. Let me know if any of the Thrashers tries to hassle you."

"Thanks, Jack. Be careful. I don't have to tell you how nasty those dudes can be." He made his way back to the card table and Rennie handed him the deck.

I drained my lukewarm coffee and turned around to pour another cup. Seth was standing behind me. "Hey man," he said. "Don't you know that caffeine will keep you up at night?"

"Stop sneaking up on me like that," I said. "You're going to give me a heart attack."

"That would be quite a trick since that heart of yours hasn't been functional since before I was born." He sat down at the Formica table and inclined his head toward the irregulars at the card table on the other side of the garage. "You get any useful information out of our boy there?"

"He says he doesn't want any part of the Thrashers

and that he's been steering clear of them. He knows they cook meth, and they've tried to get him to sell it for them here in the city, but he said no."

"It's dangerous to say no to them," Seth observed. "Do you trust him?"

"Yeah."

"In that case, so do I. Any buddy of yours is a buddy of mine."

"So what's the plan?" I got down a clean (more or less) cup from the cupboard and poured him some coffee.

"I'll take it from here."

"We talked about this at the bar," I said, hardly believing my ears. "You're not making a move without me."

"This is police business and werewolf business, Jack. I can't let you get involved."

"Any nonhuman funny business in and around Savannah is *my* business. Besides, it's me they're after. I'm going to have to face them pretty soon anyway." I told Seth about Sally's stalker and about my theory that the Thrashers were trying to draw me out.

"Besides," I said, "how can you go in by yourself against a whole pack?"

"I don't have to." Seth took a sip of coffee. "Damn, Jack, what do you put in this coffee, transmission fluid?"

I started to tell him that it was made by a zombie, so he was lucky it tasted as good as transmission fluid, but I didn't want to have to explain why I had a zombie for a kitchen maid. "What do you mean, you don't have to?"

"I only have to take on old man Samson. Any male

can challenge him for the leadership position in a dominance fight. He doesn't have to be pack."

"A dominance fight? Call it what it is: a fight to the death. Are you smoking some kind of loco wolfnip weed? If you lose, you're dead, and if you win you're in charge of shaping up a bunch of lycanthropic lowlifes who don't know anything but a life of grand larceny. Are you prepared to move into the swamp and ride herd on those flea-infested sons-of-bitches?"

"It's not going to come to that. I think what I can do is bring in somebody to rule by proxy."

"Can werewolves do that?"

Seth hesitated. "In theory."

"Oh, geez." I covered my face with my hand. "Are you sure you know what you're doing?"

"It is a bit of a social experiment, anthropologically speaking," he said.

"What the hell . . . ?"

"If it works in business, why can't it work for werewolves?"

"How long have you *been* a werewolf anyway? Do you know any besides yourself? If they played by the rules, they wouldn't be *werewolves*."

Seth ran his hand through his hair. "There are all kinds of ways to finesse these things, Jack. Just leave everything to me. Once I get rid of Samson I'll have that pack eating out of my hand in no time flat."

"*Eating your hand* is more like it. That plus the rest of you."

"If all else fails I'll threaten to put them in jail. That will get them on the straight and narrow."

"Who's going to put who in jail?" Connie stepped from around behind me. This was just my night to be snuck up on. But if I had to be snuck up on by some-body, I could do a whole lot worse. Every time she came along when I wasn't expecting her—and some-times when I was—the sight of her shocked my heart almost back to life. She was like a sexy, luscious hu-man defibrillator.

She was wearing tight jeans and a fitted white shirt under a leather bomber jacket. Her long black hair flowed over one shoulder and silver jewelry glittered at her ears and throat. I took a deep breath. Even from several feet away I felt like I could breathe in her light and warmth and humanity.

From the direction she had come, she didn't see Seth—and he didn't see her—until she was standing right in front of him. When their eyes locked, both of them went still.

"Seth," Connie said. "I thought I recognized your voice. But I didn't figure it could possibly be you."

"Connie. Well, I'll be a—" He stood up and made a little move like he might hug her, but he stopped him-self. He'd seen the silver pendant and earrings. I'd heard that just touching silver could give a werewolf a nasty burn, not to mention a case of the heebie-jeebies. I found myself feeling really glad that Connie was wearing silver tonight.

Instead of hugging her he just stood there speech-less, his arms hanging awkwardly at his sides. I had seen Seth Walker be a lot of things, but *speechless* was not one of them. He had what you might call the gift of gab, but not now. He looked at her like she was a long, tall drink of water and he was dying of thirst.

"It's been a long time," she said.

It was hard to tell if she was glad to see him or not. She was being very reserved, which wasn't like her at all. I narrowed my eyes, studying her reaction to my old friend.

"I haven't seen you since, well, it seems like ages." Seth seemed to have recovered somewhat.

"Old friends, are you?" I asked, trying to sound casual. "Where do you guys know each other from?"

"The academy," Connie answered quickly.

Well, wasn't this just old home week? "You two couldn't have gone to the academy together," I said. Seth had been a lawman for years longer than Connie had been in uniform.

"No," Connie said. "Seth was one of my firearms teachers there."

"You mean of all the times Seth here has come down to spend his vacations hunting and fishing with me, you've never run into him here at the garage?"

She shook her head, never taking her eyes off my buddy. My good, good buddy.

"I can't believe I'm meeting up with you again here in Jack's garage," Seth said. "I heard you'd moved out of the Atlanta area, but I never heard where."

Connie shrugged. "Here I am."

"Here we all are," I pointed out. I wanted to ask just what the hell was going on between them, but I was afraid of the answer. In my heart I considered Connie to be my girl, but our relationship had become strained lately. For one thing, I'd had to fess up to being a bloodsucking vampire. That would put a damper on any budding romance, let me tell you. I mean, hot chicks never listed "evil dead" amongst their turn-ons in the personal ads.

And if that wasn't bad enough, turns out she wasn't 100 percent human either, and what she was and what I was didn't mix. The only time we'd tried to get it on, when I touched her it was like I'd picked up a live wire. And not in a good way. I ended up with the burn marks to prove it. The best my friend Melaphia could figure, Connie was part Mayan goddess of some sort. The two of them had been trying to discover more about what Connie was—until Renee was kidnapped.

"So, how have you been?" Seth asked her.

"Fine. Actually, I just came to tell Jack my good news," she said.

"What's that?" I asked.

"I made detective. I'm on duty now, in my plain clothes."

Her clothes were anything but plain. Not with that bodacious bod filling them out. I could see that Seth was taking in the sight as well as me. And she was taking in the fact that he was taking her in. I thought about how the waitresses at the honky-tonk had flirted with Seth and realized that Connie probably thought he was something special, too. Why did he have to look like that? Cripes, he was a werewolf for Pete's sake. If there was any justice he'd look like Jo-Jo the Dog-Faced Boy.

I knew what a disadvantage I was at when it came to competing with other guys for Connie's affections. Regular guys, that is. They had the advantage of not being blood-drinking fiends, damned for all eternity. That is what you call baggage.

But Seth here was not a regular guy—far from it. If Connie knew Seth was a part-time carnivorous, man-eating beast, that might even up the playing field a tad. I could just let that little bit of info slip out accidentally, you might say. As in, Say, Connie, did you know that Seth here sprouts a pelt and a vicious set of choppers at least once a month? And if you don't mind your dates baying at the moon now and then, why, Seth's the guy for you.

But there was one problem. The denizens of the dark have a sort of gentlemen's agreement not to rat one another out to humans. It's something that all the nonhumans take very seriously, an honor-among-thieves kind of thing. I couldn't tell Connie that Seth was a werewolf. Only he could do that.

I wondered what their relationship had been. She couldn't possibly know already that Seth was a werewolf. I mean, she 'bout flipped when I told her about vampires. Like most humans, she clearly had no idea that the shadow world of monsters and their mayhem existed just beyond humans' reach and understanding. That's the way God had evidently intended things to be. Those born beasties, shape-shifters like Seth, seemed to understand this instinctively. Those of us who were made instead of born—that is, vampires—had to learn it. Sometimes one of us forgot, went rogue, and had to be reminded the hard way.

"Congratulations, Detective. That's wonderful news," Seth said. "The bad guys in these parts need to watch out. You'd better keep on the straight and narrow, Jack." He elbowed me in the ribs a little harder than I thought necessary for ordinary joshing purposes.

"Yeah," I said. "You've got to watch those bad guys. You never know when somebody's going to turn out to be a *wolf* in sheep's clothing."

Seth narrowed those yellow-green eyes at me, but Connie seemed not to notice. "I guess I should get going. Your tax dollars at work, yada, yada," Connie said.

"Let me walk you out." I put my arm around Connie's shoulders and steered her gently away from Seth, and she let me. I had the impression that she wanted to put some distance between herself and him. I wondered about that, particularly since otherwise they seemed so cordial. I'd try to get to the bottom of that soon.

"Jack," she said when we were out of Seth's earshot, "I really came here to talk to you about something else."

"What's that?" We stopped at her car and she leaned against the hood.

"I've been thinking about that . . . talent you said you had. The one I saw you use at Sullivan's funeral when you communicated with him after he was dead. You kind of acted as an interpreter so that Iban could talk to his old friend one last time."

"Yeah?"

"I need you to do that for me. Sort of."

"You mean—"

"There's somebody in the . . . afterlife I need to reach. It's very, very important to me."

I wasn't expecting that. It had been so long since I was mortal and without the power to speak to the dead, I never really thought about how it must feel to lose someone *forever*. I guess it was only natural to try to get in contact. I looked down into Connie's eyes and saw need bordering on desperation. Maybe William was right after all. Maybe something good could come of my gift if I could use it to help Connie.

"Well, sure," I said. "I'll do my best. You know I'd do anything for you."

"Anything?"

"Yes." I gently reached out to move a lock of hair back from her face. I just had to touch her. "Anything that is within my power to give you, I will give. If I can act as interpreter, a sort of medium for you to speak to somebody important to you who's passed on, then consider it done."

"Thank you, Jack. But you should know, I don't want to just talk to him."

Him? "I don't understand," I said.

"Ever since you told me you were a . . . what you are—"

"Vampire. I'm a vampire." I won't lie to you. It hurt a little to think that she couldn't even bring herself to say what I was.

"A vampire," she said. "Ever since then I've been trying to get my head around the idea of someone being dead but . . . not. I mean, the idea that you are an undead and the fact that Sullivan can speak to us even though he's dead and buried, well, you can see why it's blown my mind."

It wasn't exactly how I wanted to blow Connie's mind, but it would do for a start. "Sure, I can understand that," I said. "It's a lot to absorb, I guess. But what did you mean when you said you wanted to do more than just talk?"

Connie smiled and her eyes lit with a manic gleam that gave me a bad feeling.

"I want to go there, Jack. Wherever he is, I want you to take me to him."

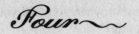

Four

William

It is said that of all the senses, smell has the greatest association with memories, assigning certain scents to specific persons, places, and events. As I glided down the stairs, the scents of Eleanor brought back vivid images. The first time I kissed her long, fragrant neck, the musky odor between her legs the last time I touched her sex. The reek of fear and excitement when she'd first tried to stake me in one of our little games.

The odors of sex, fear, and something I couldn't recognize guided me toward her as my vampire eyes grew used to the darkness. She was here and someone had been at her. Finally I saw Eleanor, my dark angel turned betrayer, chained naked to the ceiling by her manacled wrists. I flipped on a light switch and a bare bulb illuminated the dingy space. She began to stir, as if coming out of a long sleep in the earth. My elegant Eleanor, whose hair was always beautifully coiffed, whose skin was always soft and supple thanks to the most expensive lotions and oils, looked like a rough street urchin. Her hair was grimy and disheveled. Her skin looked lifeless and dirty. The snake tattoo on her torso, which she could make seem almost alive by her undulations when she rode me, looked cheap.

As I came closer I noticed that some of the spots on her body were not dirt but were bruises. When I came closer still, I saw the bites and more. Worst of all, I now recognized the odor I'd been unable to identify. Eleanor's body had begun to decompose.

"William," Eleanor rasped. "My beautiful green-eyed angel. You've come for me. Thank God."

"For you?" I laughed harshly. "Don't flatter yourself. And don't bring God into this or you'll be more damned than you already are. I'm here for Renee. Where is she?"

Eleanor looked as if I'd struck her with one of the implements of torture that were hanging on the wall on either side of her. When she recovered her composure, she said, "I don't know. She's not here. They took her someplace else. And they go to . . . visit her."

"And feed off her," I said.

"William, I never meant for Renee to be harmed."

"Yet you helped them take her. You betrayed me in the cruelest way imaginable."

"You betrayed me first!" She choked back a sob. "When *they* came to town, you rejected me entirely. I'm a fledgling. I needed my sire to survive. You were slipping away from me."

"And when you found out that they were leaving town, you knew Diana would be out of my life. Why didn't you just stay in Savannah? You would have been rid of her."

"I thought you would go after them, just like you have." Her voice held a note of accusation.

"Only to get Renee back."

"You would have come to fight Hugo for Diana even if they hadn't stolen Renee."

I thought about that a moment. Would I have? Would I have followed Diana knowing she had chosen another man? "No. I think not," I said. "I would have let her go."

Eleanor's stricken look said she believed me. She strangled a sob and hung her head, realizing the error of her choice. "He beats me," she said.

"I can see that." While Eleanor was often a facilitator for those with more violent fetishes and could play the dominatrix as well as anyone, she derived no pleasure from being victimized. She had entered into a game over which she had no control. I felt sorry for her for the first time. It was true I could have been more responsive to her needs when Diana had first arrived and proved to be a threat. I should have reassured Eleanor. I thought that she would trust me. But she didn't and the result had shaken my world. I created her to be a helpmate to me, not an encumbrance, and certainly not a traitor.

"He tricked me," she said. "Why didn't you tell me that I couldn't leave you for two hundred years without starting to . . . die?"

"Because I had no idea that you would be so foolish as to leave me," I said.

"You wanted to keep me in the dark like you always did with Jack. It's your way of controlling us."

"Nonsense. I thought I had an eternity to teach you the ways of the blood drinker. How did I know you would abandon me so soon after we started our life together?"

She screamed in frustration. "Because *she* came. And when she did, everything between you and me was different."

I could not deny the truth of that. "That still does not excuse your part in Renee's kidnapping."

"They figured out Renee's connection to the blood on their own. They knew that Gerard had used her blood to experiment with and they put two and two together. I couldn't have stopped them."

My mind reached out to hers for any sign that she was lying, but she blocked my psychic intrusion. An impressive trick for a fledgeling. Jack had taught her well.

She broke down in sobs and sagged against her restraints, and I felt nothing. It was as if what little compassion I had as a vampire was bleeding away as Renee's blood was being let in whatever hovel they had her hidden.

"You saw me in the shells, didn't you? You saw me the first time he—he raped me." For the first time in our acquaintance, I saw shame on the face of my madam mistress.

"Yes, I saw. I was treated to the sight of another man ravishing you and boasting that he now owned everything I called dear. I also saw the moment when you realized you had made a grave mistake by trusting Hugo instead of me. I saw the horror of that knowledge in your face."

Eleanor sobbed again. "Diana couldn't wait to tell me, you know. We were still on the plane when she told me why I was beginning to feel sick. I thought they were giving me tainted blood at first. Then she came to me and said that I had signed my own death warrant by leaving you without being released from our bond. She laughed at me. Even as I first began to die, she laughed."

Eleanor's narrative chilled my blood even further. It was more confirmation that the Diana of my heart and of my memory—the human Diana—was well and truly gone. In her place masqueraded a beautiful demon capable of the most vile of betrayals and the most monstrous acts of cruelty. I realized that my inability to reconcile the sweet and loving Diana of my past to the fiend occupying her body was at the root of my disorientation and disillusion.

"Are they feeding you now?" I asked, noticing under the naked lightbulb her thinness along with the mottled grayness of her decomposing skin.

She shook her head. "I need blood. Please."

I rolled up my left shirtsleeve and offered her my wrist. She bit daintily but hard enough to open a vein. I thought once again what an elegant vampire she made. It was a shame her survival instincts were so poor—when given a choice of whom she should trust, she'd chosen badly. The next few days would tell if that error would prove fatal.

She put her cupid's bow lips to the wound. Her sucking was greedy, and I saw her cheeks grow rosier in moments. She broke the seal between her lips and my flesh well before I could feel the effects of blood loss.

"Take me with you," she said. "Help me out of these chains. Release me from my offspring bond."

"I cannot. Not yet. If they come back and find you gone, or if you begin to miraculously come back into your undeath, they will be alerted to my presence. That might put Renee at even greater risk. You must stay here a little longer."

"Stay here and rot, you mean," she said wildly.

"When I find Renee, I will come back and release you from your bonds, both mystical and physical. In the meantime you must not tell them that you saw me tonight."

She started to protest, but held herself in check with visible effort, knowing she needed what was left of my goodwill to survive. She straightened and tossed her head to clear the unkempt hair from her eyes. "Come closer," she said.

I did as she asked, coming to stand near her. She pressed herself as close to me as the chains would allow and bent one knee, rubbing her leg along the outside of mine. "Is there anything I can say or do to make you want to take me with you now?" she said.

Though her state of decomposition repulsed me, my body began to respond to her as it always had, becoming hard and hot. She reached up, grabbed the chains above her and pulled her body off the floor. She wrapped her legs around my waist and rubbed her sex against me. "I can't believe you're going to leave me here with *them*," she mewled. "I need all the power I can get, William. You know what you have to do."

What she was referring to was plain. In addition to letting her drink my blood, I could in fact give her a measure of my strength without freeing her. In the world of the undead, a female can draw power from a male through sex.

I unfastened my belt and freed my swollen cock. I grasped her thighs and jammed her against me, entering her with such force she screamed loud and long, whether from pleasure or pain I didn't know. She'd been ill-used by her captor in ways I didn't want to think about. But her legs clung to me as I worked in and out of her. I bent her torso backward so I could suck her breasts, laving her nipples with my tongue, tugging hard until they were plump and stiff.

As I tasted her I recognized the stench of Hugo on her skin and I remembered the vision of her and Hugo on the plane. He'd taken her roughly from behind, pinned her to the bed with his massive frame, and rammed himself into her again and again as she whimpered in pain and begged him to stop. When he was finally finished, he'd collapsed onto his back and draped his leg across her body to hold her there until he was ready to use her again.

Revulsion made me decide to end things more quickly than was my habit.

I grasped Eleanor's waist and pressed her to me, entering her fully, and quickened my pace. Soon I came and felt her response as her muscles gripped my shaft in rhythmic waves that made her buck and writhe.

As my demon seed filled her, her body hitched and she arched her back as far as she could against her restraints, her eyes rolling back like those of a doll dropped on its head.

When her body stilled, I slipped out of her and re-clothed myself. Spent, she sagged limply against her chains, but I could feel the power transference. She would be stronger for a while. Still, the fix was only temporary. She would begin to rot again, and soon.

"I'm begging you, William. Take me with you now. I can help you find Renee."

"How can you do that?"

"I'll help you search. I'll do anything you say."

"I can think of only one way you might be able to help. Stay here and try to seduce Hugo into disclosing where they're keeping her."

"Seduce?" Eleanor said with a bitter, near-hysterical laugh. "He's done whatever he wanted with me since the moment we took off from Savannah, no matter what I said or did."

"Isn't that what you volunteered for? I'm surprised that your talents haven't allowed you to wrap Hugo around your finger—much like I once was. I imagine you're quite surprised as well."

Tears coursed down her cheeks, but I found I could not pity her. "It's that damned Diana," she said. "She bewitched both of you. I can't believe that you don't still love me, at least a little."

"Believe what you wish."

Faced with my stern facade, she changed tactics. "I can still bring you to your knees," she said. "Now that I know you're in London, I can call out to you as my sire. I'll remind you day and night what we once were to each other. What we still can be."

"You can't invade my mind unless I let you," I said.

"You'll let me."

My recent gifts of blood and power had allowed her to look like the old Eleanor, elegant and seductive. She lowered her head and locked gazes with me. My head swam with erotic images from the first time we'd made love. She had discovered how I thrilled at the sight of expensive, white Egyptian cotton sheets, pristine except for a few drops of my own blood. I blocked her thoughts before she could persuade me to change my mind and free her.

It occurred to me that—because a female vampire draws power from a male—she can eventually grow stronger than her mate.

Thus it is common for male vampires to kill the females before this happens. That is why so few females survive more than a human lifetime. Those who do survive have learned to make themselves indispensable in some way to the male on whom they depend for protection. That usually means an exquisite sexual relationship. But the male protector, having been weakened through the years by the woman, often becomes the weaker vessel. That is the point at which it is common for the female to kill *him*.

I had planned to stay with Eleanor for the rest of my existence. If she eventually destroyed me, so be it. My death wish would be satisfied and at least the intervening years would be anything but boring. But I didn't think she would kill me . . . because I had actually trusted her.

In five hundred years I had met only two women who could tempt me so sorely that I might let my guard down enough to suffer my own demise. Those two were Diana and Eleanor. Perhaps one day I would see my death wish to fruition by allowing myself to be drawn off my guard by the siren song of some other particularly seductive female. Even let her kill me during sex if she were clever enough. But it wouldn't be either of the two who so recently betrayed me.

"If I can't find Renee on my own, I'll come back to learn what you've been able to discover. Do not disappoint me." I started to walk away but paused at her voice.

"When will you be back?" she demanded. "Will it

be before I start to rot again? Before I die and go to hell for all eternity?"

"That remains to be seen. In the meantime, you will not reveal that I was here. If you do, I'll kill you myself." I turned again to leave but thought of one more thing I wished her to know. "I couldn't help but notice that you didn't think to inquire after Deylaud's health. When I left Savannah he was clinging to life— no thanks to you, who left him for dead. He loved you more than life."

She gave a cry of anguish. "They wouldn't let me see to him. I couldn't help it. I swear!"

"Save it," I said.

I left and made my way upstairs. I quickly searched the sparsely furnished rooms, finding no signs of Renee and no clues as to where she might be. The refrigerator held no stores of blood. That meant they were most likely hunting for live prey.

Once back out on the street, I walked in the direction Hugo and his little family had gone. I lost their scent on the next block so I walked the shadowy streets, lost in my own dark thoughts, until I found myself near King's Cross.

The area had become somewhat gentrified since my last visit to London, what with properties being snapped up for redevelopment near the international Eurostar train station. Still, the odd prostitute and drug dealer were about. A young woman stepped out of the shadows in front of me, blocking my way. "Fancy a bit of a party?" she offered, looking for all the world as if she wouldn't take no for an answer.

"My, but you're a bold one," I observed. Her hair was dyed jet black and her makeup looked as if it had been applied with a spade. On her chin was painted what I believe used to be called a beauty spot. A tattoo on her bare right shoulder said SID V. FOREVER.

"Are you buying or what?" she asked.

"Romantic too," I said.

She made a face. "What you want, then?"

"Like I told you. Romance. Starting w' a bit of a snog," I said, mimicking her accent. I wrapped an arm around her waist and the other around her shoulders and kissed her on the neck while dragging her back into the shadows. Before she could protest, I bit down, covering her mouth with my gloved hand to silence her scream.

I felt her blood flow past my fangs and fill my throat, the sensory delights of feeding on a living, breathing human. Her heartbeat sounded in my ears as if it were my own. I sucked and swallowed, quenching my thirst. As her heart's rhythm began to slow, I sealed the wound in her throat with my lips. She would regain consciousness in a matter of hours with no memory of me.

I picked her up and carried her to a phone booth a few feet away—the picturesque red kind one can see depicted on London postcards alongside double-decker buses. They were largely decorative now that everyone had their own cell phone. I pushed open the door, set her down on the floor of the booth, and closed the door again. If a bobby happened by, he'd assume she was sleeping off a high.

"Don't talk to strangers, little girl," I offered in parting.

When I arrived back at Olivia's house, I found her in the sitting room with a number of her vampires. "What did Donovan find out?" I asked.

Olivia stood. "He's not with you?"

"We split up. Hugo and the others came out of the house and walked down the street. Donovan followed and I searched the house."

Bree appeared at Olivia's side. "You mean he went after those vampires by himself? How could you allow—"

Olivia put a warning hand on Bree's shoulder, went past me to the door, and looked out. He's not back yet."

Jack

Right after sundown the next night I woke up in my coffin with Reyha snuggled against my side. She was accustomed to sleeping in William's coffin, but since he'd been gone, she had insisted on sleeping with me.

I'd taken up residence at William's place to protect Melaphia and the Rin Tin Twins. The twins were Egyptian sighthounds by day and humans by night. They were a gift to William from the King of Prussia. Anyway, they're ancient, immortal, and used to guard the tombs of the pharaohs. Now they nibble their kibble at William's house and guard him while he sleeps.

When he broke his mystical oath to serve William, Deylaud had come within a hair's breadth of giving up his immortality and his ability to assume animal form.

In the last few weeks, after Eleanor moved in with William, Deylaud had developed a strong bond with her. When Eleanor thought William was turning his back on her, she left and moved to her new house, still under construction. Deylaud went with her, and when we found him there after Eleanor left, he was nearly dead. Melaphia did some incantations to restore Deylaud's oath and repair the mystical bonds that he broke, and he'd been recovering slowly.

"Good morning, Jack," Reyha said as she waited for me to crawl from my black coffin. I could tell that she woke up a little disoriented when she realized that I was there with her instead of William. She and Deylaud missed him something fierce.

"Morning, sunshine," I said. When I had my feet on solid ground, I scooped the lanky, leggy blonde up into my arms and out of the coffin. I carefully set her down on the ottoman in front of William's easy chair and handed her the crutches she'd been using since Hugo had broken both her legs.

Thankfully, her healing powers were about as miraculous as a vampire's. She would probably be as good as new in a week or so, but I didn't think I would ever get over the shock of first seeing her or Melaphia after Hugo had beaten them so badly. It had made me sick nearly unto death.

Each and every time I saw Reyha hobbling around, or every time I looked at poor Mel or Deylaud, I vowed that I would kill that sonofabitch Hugo if it was the last thing I did on this earth—that is, if William didn't kill him first.

"Why don't you check on Deylaud?" I said.

Reyha brightened at the thought of her brother and hobbled off while I jumped in the shower. I let water as hot as I could stand beat down on me. I loved the fancy showerhead in William's vault. The pulsating made me feel like I had a pulse and the hot water made me feel warm-blooded. I did some of my best thinking in the shower.

Right now I was thinking about how to handle the situation with Connie. She could tell I was spooked about what she'd asked me the night before, so she had suggested that I sleep on it. Now I knew I had to discourage her from the notion of going into the underworld. William had managed to go there and come back safely, but it wasn't something I was keen to try. Something could go wrong and you could get stuck, like poor Shari had when I tried—and failed—to vampirize her. If Connie wound up there for eternity because I screwed up, I don't know what I'd do.

Maybe Melaphia would come out of the funk she was in long enough to give me some sound advice. Could I possibly get that lucky? I turned off the shower, dried myself, and pulled on jeans, boots, and a black pullover.

I stopped in the doorway to the kitchen, saddened by the scene inside. Reyha knelt beside her brother as best as she could on her hurt legs. Deylaud was still in dog form. He had been so desperately sick when we'd gotten him back to the house that night, he'd morphed into mutthood and stayed that way. William had said it was a good sign, that being a canine would help him heal faster. But it creeped me out to see Reyha in one state and Deylaud in the other. If it was disorienting for me, I couldn't even imagine what it was like for them. They'd been in lockstep for two thousand years.

I bent down beside Reyha to stroke her brother's sleek, pale head as he lay on a pallet by the hearth. When he weakly licked my hand it made me want to cry. He laid his head back down on his paws and sighed as if the effort of holding it up had cost him.

As sad as the twins were, Melaphia was in even worse shape. Her physical injuries were healing nicely; it was her mental state I was worried about.

She sat at the kitchen table hunkered over several small piles of multicolored beads. She worked her needle in and out of a tiny beaded figure, picking up a bead from one pile and then a bead from another. The thing she was weaving had taken shape since the night before, which was the last time I'd seen it. It had limbs and a torso and a head and shimmered with hundreds of tiny orbs of all shapes, sizes, and colors. Glass, crystal, stone, all came together in a frenzy of color and sheen.

"It's called peyote," Reyha said. "The stitch, that is." She joined me at Melaphia's side.

That seemed appropriate. It was crazy-looking, like it had been made by somebody during a long hallucination. And yet it was somehow perfect. There was no logical pattern to the thing, but there was something magic and a little frightening about it. I was afraid to ask what it was going to be used for.

I squeezed Melaphia's shoulder gently. "Has William called?" She only shook her head. That wasn't an entirely good sign. At least she was responsive.

I turned back to Reyha. "Why don't you make Deylaud something warm to eat? Bacon and eggs maybe. He likes that. And make some for Mel while you're at it."

"Yes," Reyha said brightly, and turned toward the refrigerator.

"Mel, I've got to talk to you." I sat in the chair

opposite her and told her about my conversation with Connie. It was hard to determine at first if she was focusing on my words since her eyes never left her needlework. Ever since Renee's disappearance, Melaphia had managed only a few coherent days among mostly incoherent ones. I badly needed this to be a good day for her.

When I got to the part about Connie wanting to go to the underworld, Melaphia's busy fingers froze midstitch, and she blinked as if she was waking from a long sleep.

"What should I do?" I asked. "I mean, we can't let her try it, and she can't do it without one of us. I think I should tell her about William and how he almost got trapped in that dimension and about all the hellish things he saw, the danger he was in—"

"No!" Melaphia said, and, for the first time that morning, she met my eyes. There was a ferocity in her look that startled me, but at least there was some understanding, some sanity. When she saw my reaction, she squared her shoulders and took a deep breath. "No," she repeated more calmly. "Let me think on it awhile. Put her off for now. Tell her that I'll . . . work on the problem and get back to her."

"Wait," I said. "We're on the same page here, right? We're not going to actually try to help her do this." Connie hadn't mentioned getting Melaphia to help with her scheme, but she knew what a powerful *mambo* Mel was.

"Of course we aren't," Melaphia agreed. "I'm just advising you to put her off. If she presses you, blame me. Tell her that I forbid it. It's too dangerous."

"Thanks," I said.

Reyha put a plate of food in front of Melaphia, who picked up a piece of toast and nibbled on it. She had barely eaten since we lost Renee. I started to hope that she was beginning to make her way back to us.

Reyha dangled a piece of raw bacon in front of my face and I grabbed it with my teeth and slurped it up like spaghetti. She giggled and I tugged a lock of her long, straight hair.

"Call me if you need me," I said on my way out. "I've got to see a man about a wolf."

The night before, Seth and I had agreed to meet at the little swamp bar and talk about how to approach Samson. I was still holding out hope that I could talk Seth out of challenging the pack leader outright. I'd rather just have a big brawl, lay down the law, and have done with it. But two against a dozen or more weren't very good odds no matter how strong Seth and I were. I wished we had reinforcements, but the only other vampire in town was Werm. He was a nice enough little guy, but not exactly the man you'd want backing you up in a fight. He was so short and skinny, one huff or puff from any of the big, bad wolves would blow him and his house down.

I thought about how Werm had begged to be made into a vampire so he would be a badass that nobody could push around anymore. If he was really going to be one of us, it was time for him to stand and deliver some badassness. He had to learn to fight for his own good. In the world of the undead, only the strong survive. I decided to stop by his new place on the way to the marsh and have a little chat, vampire to vampire.

When I got to the converted warehouse, I saw that

he was as good as his word about getting the whores involved in the renovation. Cheryl and Souxi were painting one wall red. Marlee was finishing a black paint job on another wall. Ginger and Sally were trying to install a light fixture on the third wall. They all stopped their work to greet me when I came in.

Sally hung back from the others, her gaze darting here and there, not meeting mine. Here was yet another young person I was going to have to have a serious talk with. I was beginning to feel like Ward Cleaver.

"So what do you think, Jack? It's really coming along, isn't it?" Werm asked. He actually had on a pair of coveralls. I think it was the first time I'd seen him wearing anything other than black leather. His spiky hair was poking out from under a bandanna he'd tied around his head.

The first time I'd met him, he'd had his hair dyed black in classic goth style. Then when Reedrek forced William to make him a vampire, Werm's hair had turned snow white. Now he had it dyed dark again.

"Yeah, it's really going to be . . . something." What that something would turn out to be was still anybody's guess. "When's opening night?"

"I figure we can have it ready in a couple of days."

"So soon?"

"Sure. The girls are working practically around the clock."

"What are you going to name this joint, anyway?"

"I want to call it Jack's Place, since you loaned me the money and all. It never would have come together if it weren't for you." Werm slapped me heartily on the back.

"Please. Please, tell me you're kidding." I didn't want

my name associated with any poetry-reading, punk music–playing, rich-kid club. I liked Merle Haggard–playing, throw-your-peanut-hulls-on-the-floor, honky-tonk kind of places.

Werm laughed. "Yeah, Jack, I'm kidding. I know this isn't exactly your style, but I hope you'll want to hang out here some."

"Can't wait," I said, trying to sound sincere. "Listen, that's not what I came to talk to you about. Remember how you wanted to be made into a vampire so that you could whup anybody who ever tried to mess with you?"

"Yeah?" Werm sounded wary, like he was waiting for the other shoe to drop. The kid was sharp. I always had to give him that.

"How's that been working out for you? I mean, do you think you're tough?" I really wanted to know. Maybe my instincts were wrong and Werm was stronger than he looked. I surely hoped so.

"I've kicked some butt," Werm allowed. "None of the guys who used to hassle me can do that anymore since I put them in their place. I think a couple of them are seriously afraid of me."

"I'm glad to hear it," I said. It was good for Werm's confidence that he could beat up his old high school tormenters, but taking on supernatural bad guys was another kettle of fish. "You know how William and I have always had each other's backs all these years?"

Werm nodded solemnly. "Yeah. Ever since he made you during the Civil War."

"That's right. Here's the thing: Now that William is going to be gone for a while, I need you to do that for me. I need you to be my backup when things get rough. You know what I'm saying?"

Werm got a look on his face that was one part rapture, one part stark terror. "Me? Really? Well, sure. I mean, of course I've got your back."

He tried to look casual, but I could tell he didn't know whether he should be really proud or run for his life. He scratched his head under the bandanna. "But please tell me a boat full of dark lords hasn't just sailed into port."

I had to laugh. "No, the dark lords haven't come for us. Not yet anyway."

"Reedrek didn't bust loose?"

"Lord, I hope not."

Werm visibly relaxed. "Okay, good. Then whatever it is can't be that bad. I mean, because I figure something must be up or you wouldn't have even mentioned it, right? But like I said, it can't be all that bad."

"Nah. It's just a little werewolf trouble, that's all."

"A little werewolf trouble?" Werm's voice squeaked at the word *werewolf*.

It had only been in the last couple of weeks that I had introduced him to the concept of werewolves and other kinds of shape-shifters besides Reyha and Deylaud. He'd come into the garage and run smack into Jerry and Rufus, and could tell right away—in that way that all us vampires have of telling—that these guys weren't your average joes. He'd about pissed his leather pants right there when I pointed out to him that us vampires weren't the only things running around with sharp, pointy teeth. I think he was still getting used to the idea.

Werm had figured out that vampires existed all on

his own, through observation and research. You have to give him snaps for that. But he had no idea about the other monsters. Maybe vampires were easier for him because he had romanticized them in his mind and wanted so desperately for them to exist. But the other parts of the nonhuman world had poleaxed him as much as they would have any human who'd had the bad fortune to stumble into their paths.

I often wondered if Werm would still have wanted to become a vampire if he could turn back time and choose, knowing what he knew now. I'd never find out unless I asked, but I didn't plan to raise the question right then.

"Remember the other night when Ginger told us that the Thrasher clan was cooking the crystal meth that Sally's on?"

Werm looked over to where Ginger was trying to get Sally to help her screw in a wall sconce for the light fixture. It was easy to see that Sally couldn't focus on what she was doing. "I remember," he said.

"The Thrashers are *werewolves*. I'm going to take them on because of what they're doing to Sally and other folks in these parts. And you're going to help me."

He looked up at me and blinked. "Uh, Jack . . . who all *else* is going to help us?"

I thought to tell him it would be just him and me so I could enjoy his reaction, but I didn't want to see the little guy faint, so I gave him the truth. "Only the toughest werewolf sumbitch this side of the Mississippi. And maybe we can get Jerry to throw in with us, too."

"How many of the bad wolves are there?"

"Oh, not more than eight or ten."

Werm held up all five fingers of his left hand and started to count them off, but his fingers were shaking so bad, he put his hand down again. "That's *four* against ten. Jack, if ten guys are going to go all Lon Chaney Junior on my ass, I'd like better odds than that."

I squeezed his shoulder in what I hoped was a reassuring gesture. "Don't worry, man. We're vampires, remember? We're badder than any of those mongrels."

"If you say so. Hey, can we shoot them with silver bullets?" he asked hopefully.

"That's not considered sporting. Neither is them coming at us with wooden stakes. It's one of those unwritten rules of etiquette for supernatural dudes. You don't get to use whatever a guy's Kryptonite is on him unless he's one of your own. It pretty much has to be a fair, fang-to-fang fight."

"You mean you or me can put a wooden stake through a vampire's heart, but we can't use silver bullets on a werewolf even though anybody else could?" Werm was incredulous.

"I admit it sounds illogical," I said. "But it's just one of those things. You won't die or anything if you break that rule, not like you would if you killed your sire, for example. It's just that you'd get a bad reputation in the unhuman community."

"What do I care about my rep when a werewolf is chewing off my leg?"

I sighed. "Remember how you felt when all those bullies were beating up on you? It got you a reputation as being a weakling, and you didn't like it, did you?"

Werm shook his head. "No," he muttered.

"It's the same kind of thing. You want to have the reputation as a guy who fights fair and doesn't resort to another supernatural breed's Achilles' heel. But when it comes to fighting amongst us vamps, there's no holds barred, so you can go for it with a stake or fire or whatever."

Werm paused a minute for this to sink in. "It sounds like if you get yourself a reputation as a guy who doesn't fight fair with other species of supernaturals, it can come back to bite you."

"Literally," I said.

Werm moaned. "Maybe when you and this other tough guy show up and tell the Thrashers to quit selling dope, they'll just . . . quit," he suggested hopefully.

"Not likely." I was sorry to have to bring him down when he was so happy about his club opening, but I told myself it was for his own good. Besides, if he survived the big fight, and I planned to make sure he did, it would do wonders for his self-esteem. I've said it before, and I'll say it again: A vampire with self-esteem issues, now that's just sad.

"So when are we going to confront them?" Werm asked.

"I'm meeting with Seth tonight. He's the one I was telling you about. We'll decide and then I'll let you know."

"Is it going to be on the bad guys' turf?"

"Yeah. We can't exactly have a skirmish between the evil dead and their furry friends right here in front of Savannah's humans, can we?"

"I—I guess not," Werm agreed.

"I'll tell you what. Maybe you and me can get in some training time before the big fight."

"Uh-okay."

A crash drew our attention back to Ginger and Sally. The light fixture had fallen to the floor and the glass globe had shattered into a thousand shards. Sally stared at the mess with wild eyes.

"You were supposed to hold that still while I screwed the base in the wall," Ginger scolded the younger woman. "Get the broom over there and help me clean this up."

Instead, Sally bolted from the room and into the darkness as the others stared after her. "I'll talk to her," I said, and followed.

When I went outside in the moonlight, I could see Sally running toward a car. It was fifty yards away, parked against the curb. I called after her, but she ignored me, opened the passenger door of the Mustang, and got in. "Damn," I muttered.

Even with my outstanding night vision I couldn't tell who was at the wheel. But I did see the vanity license plate that read HUFNPUF.

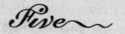

William

The fortified basement of Olivia's town house held a dozen or more coffins, all in a tidy row. It reminded me of the row of beds illustrated in the book "Goldilocks and the Three Bears" I used to read to Renee when she was a toddler. A twinge of pain shot through me like a stake when I thought of my darling stolen child.

I was to sleep in the coffin that had been recently vacated by the young woman whom Hugo had tortured and bled to death.

The sun was a couple of hours away and Donovan had still not returned. "We'll form a search party as soon as the sun sets," Olivia said. "Until then we have to get our daytime sleep and hope Donovan survived and found someplace safe to do the same. When we search tonight, I think we should stick together for safety."

"Do you usually go about in a pack?" I asked, already knowing the answer. I had showered and changed into a cream-colored Irish fisherman's sweater and a pair of gray woolen slacks.

"No," admitted Bree. We sat at a long library table with the other vampires awaiting instructions, standing back, as if trying to blend into the woodwork.

"I'll go out first," I said. "If I'm unsuccessful, then we'll section off the city and fan out."

"Why don't you want us out there with you, William?" Olivia asked.

"One of the last things Donovan said to me before we parted was that he could feel an approaching evil. The dark lords are coming. Maybe in their own form or maybe in another. We don't know. I think you should stay close to one another for now, until I can determine what we're dealing with."

Olivia ran an elegant, long-fingered hand through her platinum hair. I rose from the table and motioned for my topcoat. One of the vampires held it for me.

"You're going out now rather than wait for the next sunset? You can't find Donovan all by yourself. It would be like looking for a needle in a haystack," Olivia said. "You have only a short time to find him before sunrise and make it back."

"You should know better than to tell me what I can and cannot do. You forget, Olivia. Savannah may be my city now, but long before that, my city was London."

I prowled the streets adjacent to Hugo's rented house until I found a manhole in a secluded and shadowed area. I lifted its cover and lowered myself down, sliding the cover back into place behind me. I dropped into the sewer below, landing on my feet with a squelching sound. The noises of the street—lorry drivers making night deliveries—disappeared as suddenly and completely as did the horizon's first harsh glow from the approaching sun.

A new set of sounds replaced those produced by surface-dwellers: the gentle sluice of a distant subterranean waterfall, the faraway vibrating murmur of the nearest Underground train. And the skittering of the rats who called this place home.

I decided to explore the sewer tunnels beneath the area of Hugo's residence. If Hugo's gang had *disposed* of Donovan, the sewers would be the best and easiest place to discard the remains, where a body could linger indefinitely.

If a corpse ever were to be found by a human, it would most likely be discovered by a city water technician, or a flusher, as they were known. They only came to any given section of tunnel if a blockage impeded the flow of sewage. These hardy and fearless workers carried supplemental oxygen devices because of the noxious gases underground. Of course, we vampires had no such air quality concerns—except that the overwhelming stench offended my supernatural sense of smell to the point of madness. My vampiric senses could be a curse as well as a blessing.

I reached into my pocket for the flashlight I'd brought. Not even my eyesight could work in this pitch-blackness. Like a cat's, my eyes could amplify the smallest shard of light. But with no light whatsoever, I was as blind as the cockroaches that crept around my feet.

I rounded a bend in the tunnel and saw a crumpled human form. I trained the beam of the torch on the figure, relieved to see that it did not wear the clothing Donovan had earlier. I bent to examine the body, first checking the neck, naturally. There were no fang marks on the side that faced upward.

I turned the body onto its back so I could see the other side of the neck. The corpse of the unfortunate man emitted a sound that decomposing remains sometimes will—one last sigh from the lonely shell, left behind by its soul gone on to eternal reward or damnation.

I found the fang marks on the other side of the neck. Multiple fang marks, in fact. It had been a family meal. Something glittered in the beam of light, and I saw that the poor fellow still grasped a gold chain in one fist. At least I knew his occupation. The bloke could only be a modern-day "tosher," that is, an individual who braved the frightening and oxygen-deprived subterranean world to search for anything of value.

Such persons began their careers as mudlarks even while they were still children, going to the banks of the Thames at low tide to see what they could scrounge among the flotsam and jetsam. There were much easier ways of making a living, in my opinion. But who was I to judge? One of my many occupations was as a dealer in antiques. I could be said to trade in other people's castoffs as well.

I dusted off my hands and continued my search. I wouldn't have been surprised to find several such bodies. Hugo's party had been in London for days before I arrived. The surrounding area was home to a number of backpacker hostels and cheap hotels converted from old family homes, creating a continuous transient population: it was the perfect hunting ground. The occasional person gone missing might not be noticed right away, especially in some areas north and east of King's Cross renowned for the vices of drugs and prostitution.

I continued my walk, dodging the more disgusting items on the sewer floor as well as the sinuous tree roots growing down from the surface. I was fortunate indeed that I was in a section of tunnels that was high enough in which to stand upright. I would have hated to have to slog through the muck on my knees.

I paused at the sound of footsteps headed in my direction. There was something wrong with the gait of whoever approached; the footsteps were tentative, staggering as if the person were lame. A few feet and the individual would come into the range of my flashlight.

"I see torchlight. Who's there?"

"Donovan?"

"William! Thank the gods!"

When he came into view, he was doubled over. I could see that he held his arms tightly across his chest. When he reached me he collapsed into my arms. I leaned him against the cleanest section of wall I could locate and trained the beam of light on his chest.

There was a gaping hole directly over his heart. It was too deep and wide a wound not to have struck that organ. A piece of splintered wood adhered to his clothing, fastened there by the coagulating blood.

"Who did this to you?" I asked.

He tried to speak, but no words came out.

"How did you survive it?" I had never seen or heard of a vampire who could survive a wooden stake to the heart. I looked into Donovan's face and even by the dim illumination of the fading flashlight, I could see a fierce gleam in his blue eyes. By then he'd found his voice.

"You may have the voodoo blood. But I've got a few tricks up my own sleeve, mate."

Then he fainted. Dead away. If you'll pardon the expression.

Jack

Over beer and chicken wings at the little swamp bar I told Seth what I'd just seen. Actually, he ate the chicken wings and I drank. You can try until the cows come home to order rare chicken in a dining establishment and they simply won't serve it to you. Guess they're a mite worried about liability. I couldn't exactly explain to the proprietors why I was immune to salmonella.

"That Mustang belongs to Samson's oldest boy, Nate," Seth said. "According to my contacts hereabouts, his wife up and disappeared not too long ago. Maybe him and Sally are sweet on each other." Seth sucked some wing sauce off his thumb and forefinger. "Ah, opposable thumbs. That's one of the best parts about being a part-time human. Say, can you vamps shape-shift at all? Take the form of a bat or something?"

"No, I can't turn into a freakin' bat. Why would anybody want to turn into a bat? Those things are nasty. Have you ever seen one up close? They look like Chihuahuas with leather wings. Now that's just *wrong.* You've been watching too many Bela Lugosi movies." Seth had a thing for old horror flicks, the cheesier the better.

"Seriously, man, can vampires do anything really interesting?"

Seth and I had a running debate over which was the most awesome variety of nonhuman—vampires or werewolves. "Well, I might not be able to turn into a bat . . ." I looked around to make sure nobody was close enough to overhear us. ". . . but I *can* fly."

Seth went wide-eyed. "You're shitting me, right?"

"Nope."

"I gotta see this." Seth reached for his wallet and laid two twenties on the bar. "C'mon outside."

"Now, wait a minute. I don't want to oversell this. I can't fly like a bird or anything."

"Dude, you can either fly or you can't. It's like being pregnant."

"Well, that's the way I fly. A little bit. Really, it's more like I . . . hover."

Seth laughed so hard I thought he was going to choke on his beer. "Okay, so you can hover. I guess that's better than a poke in the eye with a wooden stake." He raised his beer bottle in salute.

"That's more than you can do, dog breath."

Seth lowered his bottle. "I should have taken a bite out of your hide the other night, but I don't like dead meat."

I started to counter with another of my witty rejoinders, but the words died on my lips when I realized who had just walked through the door.

Samson Thrasher. With a platinum blond Connie

Jones on his arm. Without thinking about it, I stood up. "What the—?"

Seth grabbed me by the arm. One glance at him told me he was as shocked as I was. "Chill out, Jack. She's gotta be working undercover. Don't blow it. You could put her life in danger."

It was all I could do to sit back down. But I realized Seth had to be right. It was the only explanation why Connie would be with Samson Thrasher. I hated the thought of her hanging out with the Thrasher pack, even if she was doing police business. "I thought you had them under surveillance. Why didn't you know?"

"It's the platinum wig," Seth hissed. "I saw a bleached blonde around the place now and then, but I wasn't close enough to see who it was, and I didn't think anything of it. I just figured one of the boys had a new loup-garou wife."

To prevent too much inbreeding, the Thrasher pack had often turned to a number of packs in Cajun country to find mates for their sons and daughters. A loup-garou is a Cajun werewolf. I suppose that a swamp dog is a swamp dog whether you're in Savannah or Louisiana. They evidently like to stick to their own kind.

"So much for keeping the Thrasher matter just between us monsters. What are we going to do now that the police are involved?"

"I don't know," Seth said. "I need time to think."

"Time's up, buddy," I said. I stood up and started toward Samson and Connie.

"Be careful, Jack. Don't say anything that might endanger Connie."

"Don't worry," I said, giving him a meaningful look. "I would never do anything to hurt Connie."

I sauntered over toward them. Two other male werewolves, each with a girl on his arm, had entered the bar behind the pack leader. One of the girls was Sally.

Samson didn't look much different from the last time I'd seen him, many years ago. He was tall and rangy with that wiry strength that always took you by surprise in somebody so thin. Especially when you had to fight them. He had shaggy gray hair, cut in a mullet. His eyes were different from Seth's; they were the pale blue-white eyes of an Arctic wolf. I always wondered how Samson came by those eyes that made you feel like you were staring into a mile-deep pool of water just on the verge of freezing.

Those eyes widened when he saw me. "McShane, you old grease monkey, you. I guess they'll let anybody or any*thing* in here these days. I'll have to speak to the proprietor about his lack of good taste and refinement. What brings you to my neck of the swamp?"

"Oh, you know what a social butterfly I am," I said. "I thought I'd check out the nightlife hereabouts."

Out of the corner of my eye, I noticed that Connie hadn't flinched from the time she saw me. She had a wad of chewing gum in her mouth and an expression of lazy boredom on her face. Man, she was good.

Samson tilted his head upward, put his nose in the air, and took a deep breath. He smelled another werewolf besides the ones he'd come in with. About that time the music on the jukebox stopped and when the folks on the dance floor sauntered toward their seats, Samson saw Seth, who raised his beer bottle in his direction and gave him a big, toothy grin.

"Who's your friend?" Samson asked.

"Him?" I said. "His name's Seth. He's somebody you should meet. So who's *your* friend? Aren't you going to introduce me to this fine lady?"

Samson inclined his head toward Connie. "This here little lady is Bitsy," he said. "Bitsy, meet Jack McShane."

"Bitsy?" I couldn't help it. I snickered.

Connie glared at me. "Pleased to meet you."

The music on the jukebox started up again. It was a slow dance. "Bitsy, would you like to dance while Samson here goes and introduces himself to my friend? I'm sure they have a lot to talk about."

I was strictly going on instinct. Since Seth had saluted Samson instead of sneaking out the back door, I could only figure that he had some plan up his sleeve, so I might as well invite Samson to meet Seth because he was going to whether I encouraged him or not. Besides, this way I'd get to talk to Connie alone.

Connie shrugged and smacked her gum, as if she didn't care one way or another. "Sure. Why not?"

"I'll be back in a minute, darlin'," Samson drawled. "Now, Jack, don't you try anything fangy, uh, I mean fancy, with my girl here while I'm gone, you hear?" Samson slapped me on the back a little too hard and laughed at his own joke before making his way over to Seth. The other werewolves and their girls followed him. When I looked after them I could see Sally steal a scared, wide-eyed glance at me, but she wisely said nothing.

I took Connie in my arms and guided her to the farthest corner of the little parquet dance floor. "What the hell are you doing here?" I demanded.

"I'm doing an undercover investigation. What are *you* doing here?" she hissed. "And Seth. What's going on?"

"Seth and I have reason to believe that the Thrashers are manufacturing crystal meth. So we're investigating, too."

When I mentioned the name of the drug, Connie's expression hardened into what I could only describe as a look of hatred. It was a little unsettling. "Seth's in law enforcement," she said finally, "so I can understand him being here. How did *you* get involved?"

"You see the little blonde with one of the Thrasher boys?"

"Yeah, Sally. Evidently she's the girlfriend of Thrasher's oldest. How do you know her?"

"She's one of Eleanor's girls."

"And?" One of Connie's delicate brows shot upward. She had learned all about Eleanor since right after she found out William and I were vampires. I had told her everything. Well, almost everything. She still didn't know about other nonhumans. But she was about to find out.

If she had known about Eleanor's operation while El was still in business—that is, before Reedrek burned her house down—I had no doubt that Connie would have raided the place for prostitution. That is, if the higher-ups in the police force, the ones who had turned a blind eye to the operation for so long, had allowed it.

Eleanor's place had been a favorite with politicians

and other powerful, rich guys since the day it opened. If the police had shut it down, they would have had a lot of explaining to do. Connie wouldn't have cared if they demoted her; she would have busted Eleanor and her gang anyway. That's how by-the-book she was. But none of that happened and now *I* was the one with a lot of explaining to do. Namely, why I was so concerned about one of Eleanor's charges.

"Well, um, you see, William felt responsible for Eleanor's girls, what with his sire burning down their house and destroying their livelihoods and all. So when he left for Europe he told me to take care of the girls."

Connie gave me a look that said she wished she had a wooden stake in her hand. "Do you mean to tell me that you have been babysitting a whole whorehouse full of floozies since William left?" She put her hands against my chest and pushed away from me.

"They're homeless," I said. "Where's your Christian charity?" I put my arms around her waist and gently drew her back to me. I just loved to feel that girl against me. And she always smelled so good, just like a woman should.

Connie glanced over to where Samson and his boys were talking to Seth, and my gaze followed hers. So far they were talking peacefully. I was glad the juke joint was packed tonight. Nobody wanted to make a scene in front of the human crowd.

"So, you're telling me you're here because the Thrashers have gotten this Sally, who you're supposed to be looking out for, hooked on meth?"

"Yeah," I said, glad that she seemed to have calmed down. At least for now.

"How did Seth get on this case? He's way out of his jurisdiction."

"Well, he—that is . . ." What could I say that wouldn't spill the beans on Seth's being a werewolf? It was his place to tell her, not mine. Although I must admit that having Connie know he was a monster, too, wouldn't bother me one little bit.

"What are you not saying, Jack? Whatever it is, I need to know."

She was right. She was putting her life on the line in this investigation in ways she didn't even begin to understand. I had no choice.

"This is not easy to explain," I began. I was relieved to see a guy feed another quarter into the jukebox.

"Spit it out. It looks like Seth is keeping Samson and his boys occupied for now, but we don't have much time."

"Seth's a werewolf," I blurted. "Uh, I mean, Samson's a werewolf. Hell, they're all werewolves."

Connie looked around her wildly. "All these people are werewolves? Wait a minute! *There's such a thing as a werewolf?*"

I glanced around to make sure nobody had heard her since her voice just went up an octave. "No, not all of them are werewolves."

I pulled her closer and she let me hold her. Much more of that and I was going to get turned on, and then I might have that little problem with bursting into flames that I did the last time I tried to get intimate with Connie. That might make a bit of a scene in itself. Not to mention set off the smoke alarms.

"Only Seth and the Thrashers are werewolves," I said. Holding her as I was, I could feel the small revolver she had in a shoulder holster under her jeans jacket. I was glad it was there for her protection.

"Seth's a werewolf?" Connie looked as stunned as if somebody went upside her head with a two-by-four. "All this time I've known him and he's a werewolf." She shuddered.

"Do you remember how I told you that vampires have to police themselves so that human beings won't find out about us?" I asked. "Werewolves are the same way. Think about it. It would be a bloodbath for people in and around the county jail and a disaster for all nonhumans."

Connie squeezed her eyes shut. "I can't believe this. First vampires. Now werewolves. What else is out there, Jack?"

"I'll explain all that to you later. What you have to know now is this: Seth and I will handle the situation with the Thrashers. The local police can't get involved. You need to go back to the city and stay there."

"I can't do that."

"Why the hell not?"

"Jack, I didn't come here to investigate the methamphetamine case. I came here to investigate a domestic violence matter that may have turned into a murder. You see Sally's new boyfriend, Nate?"

I looked at Samson's oldest as he slouched against the bar while his father talked to Seth. He had the mean, insolent look that the whole pack had. Being the son of the alpha didn't sweeten his disposition any. He had to help his father fend off challengers but could never challenge Samson himself. Well, he could, but then he would have to kill his own father. The Thrashers were a tight bunch, and I doubted if the other pack members would accept one of their own who offed his old man. "Yeah? What about him?"

"I heard through . . . informants that he was beating his wife on a regular basis. By the time I got down here to investigate, she had vanished. I tried to question the women in the extended family, but none of them would talk about what happened to her."

Alarm bells went off in my head. "It seems to me you've done too much already. Don't you know that the womenfolk will tell their men you've been asking after this girl? You've got to get out of here and leave all this to Seth and me."

"No way. I may be on the verge of being able to bring in the police."

"Bring in the police? Are you telling me you're doing this without any backup?" I couldn't believe my ears. "Do they even know you're here?"

Connie thrust out her chin in that way she had of letting me know that she was going to follow her own course no matter what anybody said. "Not exactly. I didn't have enough evidence to go on at first. But now that you tell me there's a meth operation, if I can go there tonight and see the beakers and other equipment, the lye, the cold medicine, the whole bit, I've got the probable cause to come back and bust them on drug charges. After Samson goes down then maybe the women will talk more freely."

"But the Thrashers can't go to jail," I insisted. "Remember?"

Connie grimaced. "Oh, crap."

I looked at her carefully. "You're mostly interested in the domestic violence part of this, aren't you? Do you do this often?"

"Do what?" Connie wouldn't meet my gaze.

"You know what I'm talking about. Do you go off on your own investigating wife beatings before making it an official police case?"

"Maybe," she admitted. "You have to do what you have to do."

"Well, I'll be damned," I said, putting a little swing in my dance step.

"What?"

"By-the-book Officer Consuela Jones, who sees everything in black and white, is a rogue cop. Who'da thunk it?"

Connie gave me a petulant look. "I guess you don't know everything, do you?"

"I guess I don't at that. But then, you never cease to surprise me." I also never ceased to be impressed with the woman I held next to me. Her determination and courage were inspiring. Throw in the brainpower and education and she was just one awesome female.

The music was coming to an end and the other couples were making their way off the dance floor and to their tables, leaving Connie and me on our own. Reluctantly, I took my hands away from her body and immediately felt like a cold-blooded creature again. Whenever she was in my arms, it was so damn easy to pretend I was a real, live boy, as Pinocchio used to say in one of the bedtime stories I read to Renee.

I was about to ask her what she proposed we do now when I saw Nate Thrasher raise a bar stool and break it over Seth's head. That took care of the what-do-we-do-now? question.

By the time I reached the melée, Seth, who had remained seated until then, had stood up. All six feet, four inches of him. The three Thrasher men went slack-jawed. I took advantage of that half second they remained motionless to lay out the youngest one with a punch square to the jaw. That brought Samson and Nate back to their senses, and the fight was on. Werewolves like to fight in wolf form, so I just hoped these guys could stop themselves from changing in front of all these humans. Talk about all hell breaking loose. And Seth didn't want Connie to see him like that. I looked into his eyes. He *desperately* didn't want Connie to see him like that. That twisted my gut a little bit, I don't mind telling you. If there had been any doubt in my mind that he had feelings for her, those doubts were gone. I put my romantic problems out of my mind since I had more pressing matters to deal with.

Nate swung; I managed to duck but not far enough, and the punch landed on my shoulder *much* harder than it should have. "Shit!" I yelled, and shook my arm to bring the feeling back into it.

Seth sidestepped a punch from Samson, which brought him to within a foot of me. "Jack, watch out! They're on meth!"

Double shit. When guys were tweaking on meth, they came on super-strong. Not only did the drug make them temporarily more powerful and aggressive, but it made them feel like they were ten feet tall and bulletproof. Luckily, I'm a vampire. I *am* all that, by God. I hauled off and hit Nate Thrasher in the gut so hard it knocked the breath out of him and made his face as red as a cherry tomato.

I took advantage of the extra seconds Nate's bad fortune gave me to pay attention to the humans in the bar. Some of the men were gravitating toward us. A couple of them had picked up empty beer bottles off tables and were holding them by the neck. Their reaction was only natural. Although I can't imagine that the Thrashers were popular hereabouts, they were probably regulars and Seth and I were seen as the interlopers. I had to do something quick.

I'd only practiced enthrallment, or glamour, or whatever you wanted to call it, a couple of times. But it had worked, and William told me I was some kind of prodigy at it. I'd never used it on a whole bunch of people at once, but I knew I'd better give it a try and it better be a success or me and Seth, and maybe Connie, would be in a world of hurt.

Nate had his breath back and was barreling toward me. As I braced myself, I concentrated on a message to the humans. *There's nothing to see here. Nothing to do. Go on back to your tables and focus on your beer and your women.* And then, just for the hell of it, I thought really hard: *Dance!*

I dodged Nate Thrasher's punch and landed one of my own on his cheekbone, which reeled him backward again, this time toward the door. It gave me a second to look around. The Thrashers were unaffected. Samson and Seth still struggled hand-to-hand. Connie stood to one side, watching the melée with her shooting hand under her jacket so she could draw her weapon if she decided it was necessary. The werewolf woman who had been with the youngest Thrasher was kneeling over him as he lay moaning.

It was no surprise that the werewolves didn't go under the spell. They were not human, after all. And Connie wasn't human either. I had seen her be enthralled by

Reedrek, but he'd had hundreds of years more than I had to practice. It figured it'd take more umph than I had as a novice to put her under my spell.

Sally and all the other humans were dancing like there was no tomorrow. Somebody had put another quarter in the jukebox. Elton John belted out, "Saturday Night's All Right for Fighting."

I paused a second too long gaping at the crazy scene and Nate Thrasher connected with a punch right to my jaw. I shook it off and came at him, knocking him down and half out the door. As we wrestled for the upper hand we rolled down the wooden front steps of the place and landed with a thud on the cold ground. By the time we scrambled to our feet, Samson had come flying out the door and landed next to us.

Seth jumped out of the doorway and landed on his feet next to me with the grace of the powerful animal he was. The youngest Thrasher had come around and staggered down the steps to help his brother haul their father to his feet. The female stood behind them. Connie came out to the top step, watching.

Now on his feet, Samson eyed Connie warily and then turned his attention to me. "Good job in there, Jack. How come our lady friend here didn't get bewitched like the rest of those humans, huh?"

I stole a glance at Connie and shrugged. "I reckon she don't feel like dancing, is all." Man, that sounded lame. Connie wisely said nothing.

Seth looked at Connie and back at me. He shifted his weight from foot to foot. I could guess why he was nervous. It wasn't that he and I couldn't take on three male werewolves and one female on our own. It was that whenever there was some real serious werewolf fighting to be done, they always shifted into their wolf form. That's what Seth anticipated right now.

I had no idea how long the spell on the humans would hold, so I decided I may as well press matters and see what happened when I rolled the dice. "So I take it y'all dudes got acquainted with old Seth here," I said. "So, boys, what's it gonna be?"

Seth spoke quickly, I guessed so he could put his own spin on matters since Connie was present. "These gentlemen and I have an appointment in a couple of days. That's when we'll settle . . . matters."

"When the moon is full," Samson put in. "We'll have it out."

Seth glanced at Connie again. "Until then, boys."

Samson looked at Connie as slyly as only a wolf can. "You coming with us, precious?"

After seeing that she was different from the other humans, Samson was clearly suspicious of Connie. He knew she wasn't a shape-shifter or vampire, but he knew she was something out of the ordinary. If he was curious enough and had the opportunity there was no telling what he might do to her to find out what. In any case, it was impossible for her to go with him now; I only hoped that she realized that. Earlier she'd said she would go over to Samson's to try to see the meth operation, but surely she'd give up that idea.

Connie shook her head. "No. I'm not going." She came down the steps to stand with Seth and me.

Samson didn't flinch, only looked from one to the other of us. I could see the wheels turning in his head. "I should have known you couldn't run Savannah all by yourself without William Thorne," Samson said to me. "You had to call in reinforcements. Had to get yourself a real man, a werewolf, to help you run the show. And some kind of witch woman whose skirts you can hide behind."

I felt like smacking him, but I wouldn't let him goad me into prolonging this fight with the humans around. It wasn't worth it. "Yeah, yeah, whatever. Just know that Jack McShane and his buddies are in the house."

Just for good measure, and because they'd pissed me off, I decided to see if I could manage another little show to impress them, something besides my glamourizing of the humans. I let out my fangs and concentrated on lifting off the ground. I spread my arms and raised one leg like in the kung fu movies, and sure enough, I rose a couple of feet and floated toward the werewolves.

Samson and his boys gasped. Seth said, "Dude, you *can* fly! That's better than the vampires in *Salem's Lot*."

"Awesome!" Connie breathed.

Determined not to show fear, Samson recovered quickly, belched out a forced laugh, and casually turned to go just like he was menaced by flying vampires every day. The others followed, all except for Nate, who turned to go back in the bar, presumably after Sally. I caught him by the arm. "Not a chance. We'll take her home." He shook me off with a nasty look but backed away from the steps and followed his father and the others.

When I settled to the ground and looked back at Connie and Seth, they were now staring at each other. Samson had called Seth a werewolf and Connie a witch within the space of a heartbeat. I didn't even want to know what kind of thoughts were passing back and forth in those looks, but I had a feeling I was going to learn.

I walked between them and put an arm around each of their shoulders. "C'mon, kids, it's almost sunup and Uncle Jack needs his beauty sleep. Tomorrow night we've all got some 'splaining to do."

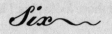

Six

William

I'd made it back to Olivia's with Donovan just before dawn. Postponing their sleep, Olivia's vampires had taken turns letting Donovan feed from them before he was put into his coffin to sleep. By my estimation, he would need at least two days' rest to heal that sucking chest wound. The stake had actually touched his heart, and as eager as I was to hear what he had discovered, my questions would have to wait. So when the next sunset came, Donovan remained in his coffin.

Olivia and I rose before the others. I had deposited my seven-hundred-dollar shoes in Olivia's trash bin and taken still another shower to try to remove the funk that I could still smell from my time in the sewers.

Afterward, she and I sat at the antique table in the basement lair next to the coffins. It was the first opportunity we'd had to talk alone.

"I've never seen anything like it," I told Olivia. "What kind of powers does he have?"

"I don't know of any extraordinary powers that he himself possesses," Olivia said. "But when we bathed him we did find a lorica tattooed over his heart."

A lorica is a kind of magic poem. A charm in the form of an incantation, if you will. "What did it say?" I asked.

Olivia recited from memory:

> "*O goddess Brigid, protect this warrior*
> *Make him invincible*
> *Make him victorious*
> *Make him immortal among immortals.*"

"You're versed in the ways of the Druid," I said. "Do you think the lorica is what saved him?"

"I believe so, yes. The stake went directly through the verse. It touched his heart but didn't penetrate it. What else but the lorica could have accounted for such a miracle?"

I smiled. Olivia was a student of Celtic tradition and an avowed pagan. Algernon had told me that his second-in-command took her religion seriously. But who was I to argue? I, who depended on voodoo-infused blood for my very survival. "What do you know about this Donovan?"

"I know that he's quite ancient. He was a Celtic warrior and fought the Saxons for most of his human life."

"That explains why he took the name 'Donovan.'" In the Celtic language, *Donovan* means "dark warrior" and *Baird* means "poet." Interesting.

"He's a lovely man. Makes us our tea every morning. I think he knew Alger back in the day. That's how he found his way to us. They had kept up a correspondence with each other for hundreds of years. He arrived here only days after I'd returned from Savannah. When he learned Alger had just been murdered, he was devastated."

"You said he was ancient. Do you know when he was made?"

"I believe he was made on the battlefield, just as you made Jack," she said.

It was common for male vampires to receive the dark gift on the field of battle and spend the day of their turning buried in the earth alongside their sires.

Vampires have stalked the shadowy corners of the killing fields since the beginning of time, drawn like sharks by the smell of blood. When night falls and the survivors have retreated with what wounded they can manage to carry with them, the blood drinkers come out to feed. The blood of the dead is an abomination, so they listen for the heartbeats of the ones still clinging to life and feed at their leisure until those hearts are still.

I must admit to being an old war dog myself. The sounds of armed conflict—the cannon's roar and the rifle's report—are a siren song. The fear is like nectar, the anger ambrosia. The sheer hatred of one human being for another stirs me.

Olivia looked toward Donovan's coffin as if she could see through the mahogany. "Alger said Donovan was mortally wounded defending one of the last Celtic strongholds on the northwest tip of Wales. Anglesey, I believe. I always suspected that Alger was a wee bit in love with him, but Donovan is a lover of women."

"Do you know that firsthand?" I smiled again. It had been my observation that Olivia herself was a lover of both men and women. Many blood drinkers don't discriminate when it comes to sex.

"I'll never tell." Olivia winked but then turned serious. "Anyway, I think it's good that we have some additional power to draw on. If he wrote a lorica that saved his life, Donovan could even be a shaman. Now we only have to wait until he wakes to tell us who staked him and what he saw when he followed Hugo and Diana."

"I'm afraid waiting is not an option."

"What are you going to do?"

"I'm going back to the house to talk to Eleanor. See how she fares and if she's found out anything about Renee."

"Do you want me to go with you?"

"No, you stay here." I stood up and put on my coat.

"I don't feel good about your going out alone tonight." Olivia stood with me and followed me to the door.

"Your colony needs you. I wouldn't want them to have to deal with the loss of two leaders in so short a time."

Olivia shuddered. Made in the roaring twenties, she was a relative infant by the standards of blood drinkers. And like my Jack, she had led a mostly sheltered existence until recently. The carefree flapper became a carefree immortal. Reedrek had put a stop to everyone's fun, and the youngsters had to grow up fast. Except for the glaring mistake she'd made in not telling me Diana lived, Olivia seemed to be rising to the challenge.

As I walked out the door into the dark mist, I felt myself wondering if any of us so-called immortals would live to be another year older.

I stationed myself in the little park across from the house Hugo and the others were using, far enough away so that my presence could not be sensed by another vampire—that is, unless the other vampire was my offspring.

Invisible in the dense copse of trees, I could feel Eleanor reach out to me with her mind, probing my psyche. I chose not to block her. Startled, I drew in a breath as she touched me.

It was as if she was gripping my cock and working it roughly. I was instantly aroused, my entire lower body tightening. My shaft stiffened as if she were kneeling in front of me, performing at her personal and professional best. I had to quickly open my trousers to free myself. I looked down, unable to believe that the lips, tongue, and teeth I felt so exquisitely were not physically before me.

As swiftly as she'd invaded my body, Eleanor barged into my mind, serving up image after image of our past lovemaking like a pornographic film. *The Best of William and Eleanor*. The time we fucked like animals in the midnight surf on Tybee. Me chained to her four-poster bed while she teased and tortured me in ways most men only dream about. She, riding me like a demon in the formal plantation garden as I met her stroke for stroke while the scorching fingers of the sun's first rays broke the horizon. Her begging for mercy as I pinned her to the deck of the *Alabaster* in the moonlight, probing every inch of her, first with my tongue and then with my cock.

And most intense of all, the night I told her I was a real vampire, not just another rich man with kinky tastes. She'd fucked me as no one had in five hundred years, showing me every move in her professional arsenal, bringing me to the most shattering orgasm I'd ever known. That same night she began her campaign to persuade me to give her everlasting life.

"It can be like this every night until the end of time," she'd promised. As soon as she played her old promise in my mind, a new promise resonated there. *It can still be that way, my darling. Take me home to Savannah and we can start all over again.*

As the film ran in my mind, the feel of her velvet softness gripping me deep inside her was as real as if she was clinging to me here beneath the shadowy evergreens. I let her lead me over the edge and came with a bucking fury.

Panting, I leaned against a tree and righted my clothing. I marveled at what Eleanor had managed to accomplish from afar. Perhaps I would let her amuse me in my off hours while I was here in London. If I was to rescue her, I would make her sing for her supper, as it were. I refocused my mind on the task at hand and waited.

At about the same time as the previous night, the evil little family came out of the house. My heart lurched when I saw my blond, inexpressibly beautiful Diana. It was impossible to reconcile the creature she now was with my memories of her as my human love.

And my son, reared under the influence of the wretched Hugo, was so malevolent I regretted saving his life with the gift of my blood. In fact, I had given Melaphia my solemn vow that I would return Renee to her even if I had to kill my own son to do it.

I had mourned both Diana and Will for five hundred years. Then, miracle of miracles, they came back to me, or so I thought. I now wished them as dead and buried as I had for so long believed them to be.

They walked in the same direction they had the night before. I thought to follow them, but I found I was moved despite myself by Eleanor's plight. When the three of them were out of sight, I went to the back of the row of houses and found my way to the cellar.

Eleanor was sleeping or unconscious when I entered. She had probably used the last ounce of her strength to minister to me in the special way she just had. In the dark, she looked much the same as she had the night before. At least she was still undead. I pulled the string attached to the overhead light and the bare bulb flickered to life. She stirred, blinking her eyes, and tried to stand. "William?" she said.

"Were you able to find out anything about Renee?" I asked.

"You ask me about Renee after what I just did for you? Is that all you have to say?"

"Thank you," I said. "That interlude was most enjoyable. Now, on to important matters. What have you found out about Renee?"

Her eyes suddenly focused on something behind me and she gasped. A hand spun me around just in time for me to see the head of an iron mace go spinning past my cheek. I felt the metal spikes bite painfully into the flesh just above my shoulder blade, forcing me backward and off my feet.

My back connected with the wall and Will was on me in an instant, his face inches from mine, pushing the point of a wooden stake into the flesh right above my heart. His golden red hair was vivid under the harsh light of the naked bulb.

"You," he spat. "You were going to let me, a fellow blood drinker, die rather than give up your precious little human."

"I knew Gerard could save you with his vaccine. And so he did."

"You knew no such thing. It was a gamble with my life." He pressed the spike deeper and I could feel the blood begin to seep beneath my clothing. Behind us, Eleanor began to sob.

"I wouldn't have let you die." It was the truth. I would have found a way to save him. If only he had stayed with me in Savannah and left Renee alone. But why should he? As far as he knew I was nothing to him.

"Bollocks! You would have sent me to hell to rot for all eternity. Give me one good reason why I shouldn't do the same for you."

I looked him in the eyes, and I couldn't imagine why he hadn't realized the truth the moment he met me. Will's eyes were not just the same as mine in hue, but also in what they held within. The rage sustained him just as it sustained me.

"Because I'm your father."

Jack

The night of the brawl, Seth went straight back to my place to crash. Sally and I took Connie to her car and followed her back to Savannah to make sure she made it home without encountering any of the wolves. As I was seeing her to her car, I told her she should come by the garage right after sundown the next night and I would explain the world of shape-shifters. Well, as much as I knew anyway.

While I had Sally alone, I read her the riot act about drugs, the Thrashers, and even prostitution while I was at it. I couldn't tell her they were werewolves, of course, but there was plenty I *could* tell her. She cried and denied everything, but I wasn't having any of it. I gave her the facts about meth—how it would ruin her skin and her teeth, make her look so old before her time that, if she insisted on staying a whore, the only johns she'd be able to attract were the lowlifes that hung around the bad side of town. I also told her what the drug would do to her internal organs, especially her brain.

The next night, I thought about my talk with Sally as I was tuning up an Oldsmobile. Only time would tell if I got through to her.

Connie showed even before the irregulars started to trickle in. I wanted the chance to talk to her before Seth got there, but he strolled in about the same time she did.

Well, now, wasn't this just peachy? I figured this would be one freaky group encounter session. I could just picture me as one of those TV shrinks. *Connie, Seth's a werewolf. How does that make you feel?*

Connie poured herself some coffee and sat down at the dinette table. She looked like she hadn't slept a wink. Seth jammed his hands in his khaki pockets and looked down at his Weejuns. Connie stared into her cup as if she was reading tea leaves.

"Don't everybody talk at once," I said. "Do the two of you have some things to ask each other?"

"Okay, I'll start," Connie said. She glanced at Seth. "So, you're a werewolf?"

Seth said, "Yeah."

"Have you always been a werewolf?"

"Pretty much."

Since Seth had all of a sudden become a man of few words, I added, "Connie, unlike vampires, werewolves are born, not made. That stuff about getting bitten by a werewolf and then turning into one is just something that happens in the movies."

Connie looked relieved. "So the business about the full moon and the silver bullets . . ."

"Well, now, *that* part's true," I said.

Seth rubbed the back of his head. "We have to . . . turn when there's a full moon. We don't have any choice. At other times, we can turn at will."

"Turn? Does that mean what I think it means?"

"Yeah." Seth looked away again.

"When he changes, he looks a little like Chewbacca the Wookiee," I explained helpfully. Seth gave me a look.

"I don't look *anything* like Chewbacca," Seth said.

"Oh God," Connie muttered. "Jack, do you have any aspirin?"

"Sorry," I said. "Vampires don't really get headaches. Except for hangovers, I guess. . . . Anyway, there is no aspirin around here."

"And I don't look anything like a werewolf in the movies," Seth said. "Not in the old ones, anyway." I guess I'd piqued his vanity.

"Relax, dude," I said. "It's not like the American

Kennel Club has a standard for good-looking were-wolves, but if they did I bet you'd win best in show."

Seth clearly didn't think that was funny, and he bared his teeth in that annoyed way he had. "Well, at least I have a *pulse,*" he snarled. "And I can go out in the sun, which is more than I can say for you."

Now, that was just hitting below the belt, if you ask me. "You can, but you probably shouldn't," I said. "You know what they say about *mad dogs* and Englishmen. Besides, how do you get that sticky SPF 15 sunblock out of your fur?"

"Why you pale, glassy-eyed sonofabitch. I oughta—" Seth stood up and came at me. I set down my coffee and took a step toward him.

"Stop!" Connie shouted, and as quick as the Sundance Kid, she drew her service revolver out of her shoulder holster and pointed it at the ceiling.

Seth and I froze in place with Connie still seated at the table between us. "Are those silver bullets?" I asked her. "Because if they're not, you're just going to piss him off."

"I'm already pissed off, and not at her," Seth said. "Besides, she's going to shoot *you,* asshole."

"Me? What'd *I* do?"

"*Shut,*" Connie said, "*up*!" She reholstered her weapon and got up from the table. Her chair made a screeching sound as it scraped across the linoleum, which I reckon made her head hurt even more, because she winced.

"One woman is missing," she said. "Another one is in serious danger, and y'all have just touched off a werewolf war. And now you're bickering about who makes a good-looking wolf and who can't go to the beach? Are you two crazy?"

Seth and I looked at each other. "You're right," I said. "Sorry." I reached out my hand and Seth shook it.

"Yeah. Sorry," he said. "What do you mean a woman is missing?"

Connie sat back down and so did we. She explained the situation with the domestic violence case she was investigating, skipping the part about going it alone. He asked her a couple of questions about the case, but I could tell she was eager to change the subject. Finally, she did. "All right," she said. "Tell me what's going to happen between you and Samson Thrasher on the night of the full moon."

Seth saw Rennie enter the far side of the garage and nod hello to us, and he lowered his voice a little. "We'll meet in the swamp and he and I will have a fight in wolf form. The winner will be the alpha wolf of the pack."

"That's what Samson is now," I said. Then Seth and I went on to give Connie the Werewolves 411. Seth covered pack structure and dynamics while I filled in the gaps about shape-shifters in general. She took it all in, asking a question here and there. She went wide-eyed once or twice, but didn't really flinch at anything. I've said it before and I'll say it again: The girl was tough.

"Jack, what else is out there besides vampires and shape-shifters?"

"Um, do you really want to know? You've got a lot to get used to already."

She rubbed her temples. "Maybe you're right."

"Are you okay?" Seth asked.

"I don't suppose I have to ask why you didn't tell me you were a—a werewolf when we knew each other in Atlanta."

Seth shrugged. "Most humans can't deal. I didn't want you to be freaked out. You already had enough trouble in your life."

Connie gave him a sharp look followed by a quick glance at me to see if I reacted to what he'd said. Seth's face went blank. Warning bells went off inside my head. What did he know about Connie that I didn't?

"What trouble were you going through?" I asked.

"Never mind," she said.

Seth quickly changed the subject. "Why did Samson call you a witch?"

"I'm not a witch," Connie said glumly. "I'm—I'm something else that's not human. We don't really know what."

"We?" Seth asked, looking at me. Was that a challenge in his eyes, or was it just my imagination?

"Melaphia's trying to help me figure it out," Connie explained before I could say anything.

"I always knew there was something different about you," Seth said, gazing soulfully at her.

I'd had about enough of the deep, meaningful looks between these two. Before I had a chance to change the subject, Connie went back to the original one.

"So what happens if you lose this fight for dominance?" she asked Seth.

He took a long sip of coffee. "I'm not going to lose."

"Cut out the macho bullshit," she insisted. "What happens if you *lose*?"

When Seth was slow to answer, I said, "It's a fight to the death."

Connie looked at Seth incredulously. "You're kidding me, right?" Seth shook his head.

"If Samson doesn't fight fair and the pack gets involved, I'll be there to back him up," I offered.

"Just the two of you? Against a whole pack? I'll ask you again: Have the two of you gone completely crazy?"

When she put it that way, Seth did sound like one loco lobo. Hell, I wondered if I was playing with a full deck myself. "Werm can fight with us." When I heard myself say that, I decided that Connie was right. I *must* be crazy.

"*Werm?*" Connie looked at me like I was a Martian.

"Hey, he saved your life, remember?" You had to give credit where credit was due.

"What's a Werm?" Seth asked.

"The only other vampire in Savannah right now. You'll meet him later," I explained.

"That's it," Connie said. "I can't let you do this. I'm talking to my lieutenant tomorrow."

"No!" Seth and I said in unison. Far across the garage, Rennie looked up briefly from his work, then wisely pretended to fish for a wrench in the toolbox.

"You can't do that," Seth said. "Werewolves can't go to jail, remember? You can set up a sting and bust Samson for the meth, but when the judge denies him bail and the full moon finds him in the city lockup, are you prepared to tell your fellow cops why they should switch to silver bullets or get their throats torn out?"

Connie winced. "I forgot. Again."

"We've thrown a lot at you tonight," Seth said. "I wouldn't blame you if you were getting overwhelmed. I would be, too." He reached out and patted her hand, then squeezed it for a few heartbeats longer than I was comfortable with, but I'd already acted like enough of a jackass in front of Connie tonight so I held my tongue.

"There's got to be a better way than a fight to the death," Connie insisted.

"Not this time," Seth said.

"All right," Connie said. "I won't bring in the police, on one condition."

"What?" I asked.

"I'm there with you."

Seth sat up straight. "That's not going to happen," he said. If Connie was there, she would see him turn into a werewolf. Seeing a shape-shifter turn is one hell of a sight. Seth knew that Connie would never look at him in the same way again. Part of me wouldn't have minded that. But I didn't want Connie there either, for her own safety.

"No way," I agreed.

"It's either that or I bust Samson right now and he goes to jail. You can get him out on bail yourself before the full moon if you want."

"And what if he doesn't make bail?" I asked. The full moon was only a couple of days away.

Connie shrugged.

Seth and I looked at each other. We both knew we couldn't just assume that she was bluffing.

"All right. But you have to stay out of sight," Seth said.

Connie smiled humorlessly. I could tell she wasn't agreeing to anything.

"At least promise that you won't go back there looking for the missing woman without us now that they suspect you have some connection to Seth and me. As bad as they treat their own females, they treat human women worse. These are *really* bad dudes, and you don't want them to get ahold of you."

"I get that," she said.

"Yeah," Seth said. "If you wait until I get control of the pack I'll intimidate them until somebody talks. Agreed?"

She looked from one of us to the other. "Agreed," she finally said. "Now I have to go to work."

We stood up when she did and watched her walk out the door into the night.

"That went well," I said.

"You're kidding me, right?"

I shrugged. "Neither of us has any bullet holes, do we?"

"Good point." Seth gave me an appraising look. "By the way, Jack, you don't have to worry."

"Worry about what?"

"About me and Connie. We were over a long time ago." There was raw pain in his eyes, so much so that I forgot my jealousy and felt sorry for my old friend. So they *did* have a thing going at one time. I wondered again what kind of trouble Connie had known in Atlanta, but I knew not to ask. Because of that one warning glance, Seth would keep her secret, whatever it was. He was a stand-up guy.

"Okay, well, thanks for telling me," I said awkwardly. "Sorry about the werewolf jokes."

Seth clapped me on the shoulder in that way we men have when we have to make some kind of physical gesture to another guy to indicate we've decided not to kick his ass. "I'm going to get some grub," he said. "Want to come along?"

"I'd better stick around and get some work done," I said.

"I'll see you later, then."

After Seth had zipped his jacket and walked out into the cold, I walked over to where Rennie was looking under the hood of a Lexus.

"Damn. What a night. Are my eyes glassy?" I asked. Hey, it's not like I can look in a mirror.

Rennie took off his glasses and wiped them on a shop rag so greasy I couldn't imagine how he was helping matters. He put them back on and blinked a few times. He looked carefully up at me.

"Your eyes are like limpid pools of wiper fluid," he said, and turned back to the Lexus.

I just love a grease monkey with a sense of humor.

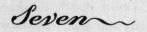

Seven

William

Will's face went slack with shock, and then his eyes filled with disbelief and suspicion. "What the hell are you talking about? What do you mean you're my father?"

"I am your mortal father," I repeated. "The one who gave you life. *Real* life. I am Diana's husband. I was there when she bore you."

"You lie! She would have told me!" He pressed the stake more deeply into my chest. "You'd say anything to keep me from draining that precious blood of yours and leaving your carcass for the crows."

"You were born in Derbyshire on the fifth of June, 1518, nine months to the day after your mother and I wed. Father Gifford was the parish priest who christened you," I all but shouted.

Will's eyebrows shot upward. "How—"

"Your mother and I were murdered when you were ten," I continued. "You were given to be raised by a couple named James and Juney Cecil."

"How do you know that?" Will dropped the mace, took a step backward, and blessedly lowered the wooden stake.

"I knew them both," I said. "They were in my employ. Juney was maid to Diana and James was one of my grooms."

"But—" Will started to protest.

"Fool!" Eleanor said. "Has it been so long since you saw your own image that you've forgotten what you look like? You're the very picture of him. I figured it out in Savannah. I thought you knew."

Will looked at me as though seeing me for the first time. "Why didn't you tell me before now? You had plenty of chances."

"Your mother forbade me."

"Liar! Why would she do that?"

"She claimed the price that Hugo demanded for giving you eternal life was that she never tell you of your real father."

Will looked far away, as if he was weighing the veracity of my claim against the events of his life. "Why? Why was he so afraid of you? He's afraid of you even now."

"Because this is the great William Cuyler Thorne," Eleanor said without irony.

"What's so great about him, then?" Will sneered. The young tough was back.

"He has dared to take on the dark lords," Eleanor said.

"How?"

I might have told him how I had been smuggling peace-loving vampires out of Europe and into the Americas for nigh on to two hundred years. That by doing so, I had cost the European sires the power that builds from their offspring feeding on humans.

I also could tell him that I was about to abandon this smuggling mission out of disgust that the most beloved of my own kind had betrayed me. But now was not the time, not when I had a chance to gain his help in rescuing Renee.

"Never mind that." I stepped forward and embraced him—I couldn't help myself—then I grasped his shoulders and held him apart from me, my face inches from his. "For now, just know that I am your father."

Will was clearly conflicted. He didn't return my embrace, but he didn't push me away either.

"How is Renee?" I asked him. When I saw his face soften at the mention of her name, I felt a glimmer of hope rise up in my chest. Did this monster who used to be my human child have any measure of compassion? Did he who had murdered dozens of peaceful vampires in a bioterror attack feel anything other than bloodlust? I remembered how he had murdered Sullivan, the trusted human of my closest western ally, by tearing his throat out. Could the same devil who did those things care about the welfare of a single human child?

"Renee is fine. For now."

"What do you mean, for now?"

"They have . . . plans for her."

I wanted to bellow with rage. At that moment I didn't care to imagine what vile use they planned for my dear child. But I clung to Will's having said she was fine—and the hint in his voice that he reserved some modicum of compassion for her.

Did I dare appeal to my son's humanity? When Reedrek had tempted Jack with the life of a dark blood drinker, I had bet my life that Jack still possessed the humanity that had inspired me to give him everlasting life all those years ago. And my undead offspring hadn't disappointed me. He hadn't "gone over to the dark side," as he'd put it, but rather had helped me save Savannah from the menace that was Reedrek. I decided to use the same appeal to Will.

"Help me get her back," I implored him. "I know that you care about her. I know that she's special to you."

"You must be putting me on," he said, an unconvincing sneer on his face. "She's nothing to me."

My heart sank and then hardened. If he would not help me out of love, perhaps he would be motivated out of hate. Was he his father's son after all? I thought of all the things I could tell him about Hugo and his mother and how to begin.

"I want to know why you left Mother and me to that fiend Hugo," he said, as if reading my thoughts.

"I didn't leave you. Until the moment you arrived in Savannah I thought both of you had died the night Reedrek made me a blood drinker. But before he spirited me away, he gave your mother to Hugo to be made into a vampire. You must know the rest."

"They waited until I reached adulthood and then they came for me," he said in a hushed tone. "And when they did, Hugo slaughtered James and Juney right in front of me even as my mother begged for their lives."

I shuddered. "Believe me, my son, if I had known that you still lived, I would have protected you with my undead life until God himself had seen fit to take your mortal soul."

"Well aren't you the hero? And then I suppose you would have ridden on a white horse to my mother's rescue and freed her from Hugo."

"I would have killed him, and that would have freed your mother, yes. I now believe she would not have let me."

"What are you talking about? She only pretends to go along with him. She hates him."

"Are you so sure?" I asked. "While you were unconscious from the plague in Savannah, I tried to kill him. After I allowed you to feed from my veins to see if my blood would cure you, we all assumed that I would be infected. I went to bite Hugo and infect him as well, but Diana stopped me."

Will's face registered shock at this news. I could see the wheels turning in his mind, trying to make sense of it. "She was probably afraid not to come to his aid. She's terrified of him."

"I can't imagine why. Hugo's bond as her sire came to an end after two hundred years; that's how it is with all our kind. She's only drawn power from him since then. In truth, she's more powerful than he is. If you had been conscious when they fought in my plantation house, you could not doubt it. As Jack would say, she wiped the floor with him, and I have the repair bills to prove it."

"Expired after two hundred years? They told me that a female vampire's bond to her sire never expires!"

"That's a lie. It works the same as it does for males. After two hundred years, you were both free of him."

As Will struggled to process what I told him, it

occurred to me that Diana and Hugo had done just what I had with Jack all those years. They had kept Will in the dark about the rules of the vampire game. In my case, I had been trying to protect my offspring. Hugo's little family had out-and-out lied, and their motive was more sinister. Diana and Hugo had used Will's innocence to control him.

I explained to Will how during sex female vampires draw power from a male blood drinker's seed in exchange for their forfeiture of the power of procreation. "They told you none of this?" I asked.

"No," he said bitterly.

"And you learned nothing from others of our kind? What of the Russian blood drinkers?"

"I don't play well with others. Never have," he said. The punk sneer was back in a flash and was gone just as quickly. "They told me nothing. They were a pretty remote lot for the most part, very independent of one another. Beautiful things, but not social. Suited me just fine."

I had seen Will charm his prey in Savannah and charm his way into Renee's heart for his own ends. But perhaps the charm was only skin deep, something he cultivated to use only when he needed it as a weapon. Despite all my hopes for whatever humanity he might have left, I realized I had no idea what he was capable of.

"So Mother is stronger than Hugo," Will said. "She said he would kill us if we tried to run away."

"She stayed with him all this time only because she wanted to."

"But why has she gone to such great lengths to convince me otherwise?"

"She wanted both of you. It was the only way she could persuade you to remain in the same place with Hugo, whom you so justifiably hated. I saw the scars on your back when you were ill."

"He beat me unmercifully," Will muttered. "If he weren't my sire and I wouldn't die in the killing, I would have sent him to hell by now."

"I don't doubt it," I said. "It seems that is one rule they did see fit to share with you, since it benefited them."

Will squeezed his eyes shut and massaged his temples. "So many things . . . are becoming clear now. So much that never made sense before."

I couldn't help but notice that Will had lost his tough working-class accent. I could sense that he was reliving his life in his mind, experiencing earlier memories, painful ones. "Yes, my boy, I would imagine so," I said soothingly.

"When I left London for Russia, I begged her to join me. Now I know that she could have come to me whenever she wanted and left him behind," he said. "I made several trips back to London to try to get her to come to Russia with me and she refused."

Something new and startling must have occurred to him because he looked up at me suddenly and cried out, "My mother couldn't have been in on the plot to kill me with the plague!"

"No," I said, and laid a hand on his shoulder.

"If she wanted me dead, she wouldn't have gone to the trouble of keeping me with her all those years."

"When she found out that Reedrek and Hugo had encouraged you to spread the plague, knowing full well that you would contract it, that's when she fought

Hugo so unmercifully. In her way, I think she loves you."

"But not enough to stop him beating and bleeding me all those years. And *still* she stays with him, knowing that he set me up to rot," Will said incredulously. "Reedrek and Hugo told me if I carried the plague to California that they would set my mother free, but they knew she was free all along. They said I was immune. Instead Hugo knew I would catch a pox that would have my flesh rotting from my bones."

"I think he wanted Diana to himself after all these years," I said. "He probably always did but didn't have the courage or the intelligence to get rid of you for good until Reedrek came along with a plan."

Will began to pace back and forth. I could feel his anger building as if it were a living thing. His fangs lengthened and his eyes became bloodshot. After a few moments he stopped, balled his fists, and let his head fall back on his shoulders. His bellow of rage reverberated through the cavernous space. Eleanor began to whimper from fear. As for myself, I let my son's pain and anger wash over me like a toxic rain.

His thoughts were so intense I could see them in my own mind. I closed my eyes and saw what he was projecting—the image of Hugo tearing into the throats of James and Juney Cecil, the sight of Hugo beating him with a lash, bringing more blood and bits of flesh with every stroke, bleeding him, starving him, isolating him in dank holes in the ground for weeks at a time.

I took Will's pain and rage and bonded it to my own until I felt our separate wills forge together as one. Then my scream rose above his. "Enough!" I roared.

The sound brought him back to himself and the parade of images stopped. Our gazes locked and I stared at him for several moments. "I'll ask you again," I said. "Will you help me? Will you help me to defeat them and get Renee back?"

He began to nod before he spoke. His eyes held not a hint of doubt or weakness.

"Yes," he said. "I will help you free Renee from them if it's the last thing I do."

Jack

I decided it was time for Seth to meet Werm, since I had tapped the Werminator, as he liked to call himself, to help us fight the werewolves. And also because I was in the mood for a good laugh.

So when sundown rolled around again, and after I'd hopped out of my coffin and showered, I called Seth on his cell phone and gave him directions to Werm's new place. When I got there, I was impressed with the progress that Werm and the ladies of the evening had made since the last time I saw it. The walls had been painted, the ceiling spackled, and most of the fixtures were in place. In fact, Werm was setting up the bar and uncrating liquor when I walked in.

"Let me pour you the first drink, Jack," he said and opened a fresh bottle of my namesake, Jack Daniel's.

"Don't mind if I do." I took a gulp of whiskey. "Say, are you sure you know how to tend bar?"

Werm laughed. "C'mon. My mom's a Savannah society lady, remember?"

"Oh, yeah. I forgot there for a minute." Savannah

society ladies are well-known for their alcohol consumption. Whether it's at a garden club luncheon, a tea party, a bridge game, or a charity social, the first rule of etiquette is that nobody's glass is ever allowed to be empty. The ladies often stagger away from the soirees tottering on their designer heels, their Sunday hats sitting crooked on their heads.

"I can mix anything from an appletini to a screaming orgasm," Werm assured me, "with my stirring arm tied behind my back."

"Here's to screaming orgasms," I said, raising my glass, "and to leaving the ladies shaken *and* stirred."

"I'll drink to that," Werm said. He poured a shot for himself, clinked his glass with mine, and gulped it. He was finally starting to drink like a man. When I first met him, he was into sherry—an old lady's drink, for God's sake. But the night I screwed up my voodoo ceremony, I'd gotten him to start swilling some real liquor. I was proud of him.

"The place is coming along real nice," I said, and poured myself another.

"Good thing, too, since opening night is tomorrow," Werm said.

I did a spit take, spewing a swallow of good whiskey out of my mouth and causing the four girls who were laying linoleum tiles to look my way and giggle. "That's only one night before the full moon," I said between coughs.

"Why? Is there a problem?" He finished the rest of his shot and refilled both our glasses.

I lowered my voice so the girls couldn't hear me. "In two nights we need you to go with us to fight the werewolves. I wanted some time to teach you some moves, do some sparring."

Werm looked at me blankly and then remembered what I'd said about training. "Oh, yeah. I forgot."

"How could you forget? Last time I talked to you, you were afraid a werewolf was going to chew your ass off."

"But, Jack, you said the other night that vampires are way tougher than werewolves."

I had to start paying closer attention to what I said to this kid. He actually listened to me. I looked at his spindly body. "You've got to postpone the opening."

"Jack, I can't. I've given out handbills all over town. The girls have been posting it everywhere. We've bought ad time on the radio, put the notice in the newspaper—"

To tell you the truth, Werm didn't look too disappointed about missing the conflict. In fact, he looked distinctly relieved. He evidently thought that I would let him out of his commitment.

"Damn. Okay. Well, I'm sure you'll do fine. Just remember to extend your fangs."

Werm's face fell, and his Adam's apple bobbed as he swallowed his next sip of whiskey. "Uh—okay, Jack, whatever you say."

"That's my boy." I gave him a guy's guy slap on the back that nearly caused him to drop the bottle of Jack. About that time the door opened and Seth came in. He got the attention of all four whores, who collectively sat up on their haunches and in unison thrust out their chests.

As Seth was introducing himself to the ladies, Werm asked, "Do you know that guy?"

"Yeah, that's my buddy the werewolf. Don't sweat it. He's not going to eat you."

Werm relaxed a little. "Good."

"You're too skinny anyway."

Werm took a swig straight from the whiskey bottle. "That makes me feel much better," he squeaked.

"Hey, man," I said to Seth as he reached the bar. I sat on one of the mismatched bar stools and patted the one beside me. Seth sat down as Werm seemed to get shorter and shorter behind the bar. If he crouched down any more, he was going to disappear altogether.

"Seth, this here is Werm," I said.

Werm nodded and mumbled something. Seth stared at Werm, who, since the painting and spackling were done, was back to his black leather duds. As usual, Werm jangled with so many silver studs and rings from various piercings, I was surprised he didn't set off all the metal detectors in the city. Then Seth turned his attention to me, and if looks could kill, I'd be werewolf chow. "So this is Werm, is it?" he said. "The one who's supposed to back us up in the fight?"

"Uh-huh. Stand up straight, boy," I directed Werm. "Let Seth get a look at you."

Seth said, "Can I have a shot of that JD? And by the way, son, you're squeezing that bottle so tight I think it's going to break right in your hand."

Werm straightened and got a clean shot glass. "Yeah, sure. Uh, you know, sometimes us vampires, we don't know our own strength."

"So true," I agreed.

"I'd shake your hand, Werm, but you've got too much silver on. I might get a burn."

Werm poured Seth's shot and refilled my glass again.

"Jack said it was true what they say about silver and werewolves."

" 'Fraid so," Seth said.

"So how do you kill a werewolf?" Werm asked. Seth nearly choked on his whiskey.

"That's not a very friendly question to ask a guy of the fuzzy persuasion right off the bat," I said. I wasn't exactly the Emily Post of the undead world, but damn, at least I could be tactful.

"I'm sorry," Werm said, "but if I'm going to have you guys' backs in a fight, don't you think I need to know a thing like that? I mean, Jack said it was bad form to get a gun with silver bullets."

"Jack can always be counted on to know the proper thing to do," Seth allowed, then took the bottle from Werm and poured himself another.

"I did, in fact, tell Werm not to pack a gun with silver bullets although I hope Connie plans to do just that. I certainly dropped enough hints to her on that very subject when we talked to her last night."

"As well you should," Seth agreed. "Incidentally, Jack, do you think you could see Connie again before the full moon and talk her out of coming? I don't want her to see me in wolf skin. And I *really* don't want her to see me change. Besides, if things get out of hand, we have to keep her out of danger."

"You heard me try to reason with her," I said. "You've known her longer than I have. You know how stubborn she is when she's made up her mind about something."

"Try again. Seriously, Jack. I've seen the way she looks at you. If anybody can get through to her, you can. Just give her some sweet talk. She'll come around."

"Okay. Okay." Actually, I was glad of any excuse to go and talk to Connie and this was a good one. If I was careful about it, I might even get Connie to talk about her relationship with Seth so I could get an idea if she still had feelings for him.

Besides, I didn't want her at the fight either. Too much could go wrong. If I absolutely couldn't talk her into not coming, maybe I could at least get her to load up on silver bullets.

"Where do you buy silver bullets anyway?" I mused. "It's not like the sporting goods department at the all-night Wal-Mart carries such a thing." The whiskey kept getting smoother the more I sipped.

"You have to melt your own silver and pour your own bullets," Seth said. "Can you believe that? Being a non-human in a human-oriented world is not for sissies."

We both looked at Werm. We couldn't help it. Thankfully, he didn't seem to notice. In fact, he was swaying like a small willow in a stiff breeze. A few more shots and he would be beyond noticing much of anything.

"When you're not human, it's hard to get your needs met by retailers," Werm observed. "Take blood for instance. *There*'s a product you can't just buy off the shelf."

"That would make our lives a helluva lot easier," I agreed. "Butcher shops aren't always open late."

"Let me see your fangs," Seth said to Werm.

"What?" Werm looked like his ninth-grade teacher had just called him to the blackboard to work an algebra problem in front of the whole class.

"Do it," I muttered, and downed my shot. "Do you have any tequila?"

Werm glanced over at the ladies to make sure they were not looking and timidly pulled back his lips to show his small fangs.

"Dude, you didn't tell me he was a *fledgling*," Seth said to me.

"Listen, this little guy's got *skills*." I took the bottle from Seth and poured myself another shot.

"What skills? Is he going to whine somebody to death?" He gulped the last of his drink and held out his glass for more. I poured.

"I can go invishable," Werm said, producing a bottle of tequila.

"You don't look invincible to me, little man," Seth countered.

"*Invisible*," I said. "I've seen him do it."

"How can you see him if he's invisible?"

I opened the tequila and drank from the bottle. "When he hides behind curtains I can see them sway. And when he pours himself a drink, you can see the liquor bottle move on its own. He crashed a big vampire convention a while back. I had to haul him out. Everybody thought I was crazy."

"No shit?" Seth remarked with admiration. "That *is* some skill."

"Damn skippy," I agreed, and passed the tequila bottle to Seth.

"Hey, let's come up with a plan to use Werm's invishability," Seth said.

Werm raised his hand as if he were asking permission to speak in class. "Should we make a plan for a fight to the death while we're drunk?"

"I come up with some of my best plans when I'm drunk," I insisted.

"Not to mention accidentally raising zombies," Werm observed.

Seth looked at me and blinked. "Say what?"

I waved and shook my head. "Nothing to worry about. Just a little . . . mistake."

"That's a doozy of a mistake, pal," Seth said.

"Huey. His name's Huey." Werm held out his glass for tequila.

"Huey's a zombie?" Seth said. "Well, pour me some plasma and call me a vampire. I thought he was looking a mite overripe around the cheekbones."

"He's ripe, all right," I said. "I gave him one of those little Christmas-tree air fresheners to wear around his neck. That gets him a lot of strange looks from the customers, but it keeps him springtime fresh. As long as he stays a fair distance from the customers they can't tell the difference."

"Melaphia cast a spell to keep him from rotting any more," Werm explained.

"This is some top-shelf tequila, little bro," I said. "Now, where were we? Oh, yeah, a plan. Let's see. Seth, we know that you can beat Samson Thrasher in a fair fight hands down, right?"

"Right," Seth agreed.

"But we also know that Samson doesn't fight fair unless somebody forces him. So let's say that once the fight starts and he tries some dirty trick like getting the other wolves involved, we do this . . ." I laid out my plan for Werm and Seth. When I was done, they both nodded.

Werm said, "That ought to put the fear of God into the Thrashers."

"After that, Seth here will be pack leader and they won't dare defy him."

Seth looked at Werm and me in genuine surprise. "Hey, that's actually a pretty damn good plan."

"*Hell,* yes," I said. "What did you expect?"

"From two drunk vampires?" Seth asked. "Not much, to tell you the truth."

"Oh ye of little faith and much body hair," I said, and shook my head.

Werm raised the near-empty Jack Daniel's bottle. "Here's to a cunning plan and a fair fight two nights from now. May the best wolf win."

I raised my glass and clinked it with the bottle. "Let the Wookiee win," I corrected. Seth gave me a sour look and issued a low growl.

"Don't start," he said, and clinked his glass.

William

"I will help you," Will repeated, and stood up a little taller. "But I wouldn't get my hopes up, mate. I doubt if we can reach her. And even if we could, you and I together aren't big enough to take on who's got her."

"The two of us together would be powerful," I said. "But what if I told you there were more of us? What if I told you we could muster a dozen more vampires to fight at our side? Could we mount an offensive to take her back?"

His eyes widened with interest. "Let me see those vampires," he said.

I led Will to Olivia's to meet the others and tell them what he knew about Renee. We dared not talk of the matter while on the streets for fear that our words might be sensed through Hugo's psychic connection to Will. While we were in the cellar, Will had used all his skill at blocking his thoughts so that Hugo wouldn't know what was going on. But I didn't want to risk conversation in the open where the distractions of the street might break Will's concentration.

Of course, Eleanor had protested bitterly about Will and me leaving her behind. I was able to extract her promise not to tell Hugo and Diana of the plan to free Renee, but not before I'd let her feed from me again.

I was aware of the risk I took in leading Will to the site of Olivia's coven, but Renee was my first responsibility. If I lost Renee, Olivia and her vampires—and everything else in this world for that matter—would not mean a whit to me.

Bree and another of the females met us at the front door and called for Olivia when they saw I had a stranger in tow.

"Is this who I think it is?" Olivia turned her surprised gray eyes to me.

"Yes."

"Do you know what you're doing, William?"

"He's going to help us get Renee back." That was not precisely the answer to her question, and she knew it.

Bree grabbed her mistress's arm. "Don't do it, Liv."

Olivia shrugged off the woman. "Come in," she said, and stood back to let us pass.

Will took in the genteel surroundings—the Victorian furnishings, the French Provincial draperies, the curio cabinets in the foyer brimming with Alger's priceless collectibles. "Isn't this posh, then?" he said, his manner of speech again that of a streetwise London twenty-something.

It seemed that Will had lived through so many eras that he didn't stick to a consistent style of speech. Of course, most of the rest of us had lived through many periods as well but we had solidified a style of our own that was ageless. My theory was that Will had adopted a punk persona as a defensive measure, its toughness providing him with some type of cover that he craved. I believed that the softening of his attitude toward Renee indicated that he still had that spark of humanity that his mother lacked. Of course, Iban, whose family Will had murdered, would probably disagree with my judgment.

Olivia sent the two women to prepare refreshments, no doubt a ruse to get them out of earshot. Ignoring Will, who was examining the portraits on the wall, she lowered her voice. "How do you know he will not lead Hugo and Diana and whatever vampires they might have at their beck and call straight back to us at the next sunset?"

"He hates Hugo," I said.

"Plus, there are no other vampires at our beck and call," Will said, eavesdropping casually. "It's just the three of us. Besides the one Hugo has tied up in the cellar for sport, and she's not much good for anything but sex." He looked at me pointedly. "Sorry. Dad."

"I am responsible for this coven and their safety," Olivia began. "This is the man who slaughtered Iban's entire colony! Plus, he murdered Sullivan."

"You make it sound so bad when you say it like that," Will said. He held up a hand when she started to answer back. "I only killed those people under extreme duress; now I've turned a new leaf. Don't worry, I won't bring dear old stepdad to eat your precious darlings. William's right. I hate Hugo, but I quite like the little one. She grows on you."

It was extraordinary that on the very same night I'd gone from wishing my son dead to believing there was hope for him. And it was all due to the memories of a skinny, dimpled human child. My heart was buoyed for my own nature as well. If there was hope of saving Will from evil, then there was hope for me as well.

"Has he fully recovered from the rotting plague?" Olivia asked me.

"I'm not going to infect you, old darling," Will said. "I'm standing right *here*."

Olivia regarded him like a mangy dog. She excused herself to summon her vampires into the parlor.

"Will has agreed to help us get Renee back," Olivia announced. "He thinks he knows where she is and who has her, and he says she's in danger. Tell us what we're up against."

Will looked around the room. "Are these your fighters? They don't look very butch to me."

They were on him so quickly I barely saw them move. Before I knew it Olivia was standing behind Will, her arms wrapped around him as tight as a vise, trapping his arms to his sides. Her fangs were unsheathed and poised against his jugular. The others, each with some type of weapon—wooden stakes, silver stilettos and daggers—surrounded the two, poised to strike at Olivia's command. It was an impressive display of speed and strength. I must admit I'd had my doubts about them myself. They didn't look to be a robust lot on the whole, but looks can always be deceiving.

"You would be wise not to ever question the abilities of my family again."

"Bitch," Will muttered.

"Son of one," Olivia hissed.

"Children," I said evenly. "Let us not forget the matter at hand."

"Leave off," Will muttered. Olivia allowed him to shake her off him and the others went back to their seats. They sheathed their stakes, sterling stilettos, and various other weapons, and the sheaths in turn disappeared into the pockets of custom-tailored jackets and the gossamer folds of flowing black silk skirts.

"They certainly seem on edge. Wouldn't you say, Will?" I said. When things had calmed down, I asked him, "Where is Renee? Who is holding her?"

Will straightened his black coat, smoothing the leather where Olivia's death grip had rumpled it. "All I know is that I overheard Mother talking to some guy about her."

"Some guy? Does this guy have a name?" Olivia demanded.

"Ulrich," Will said. "His name is Ulrich."

A frisson of dread shot through me as Olivia and I exchanged glances. Ulrich was well-known to both of us—he was Reedrek's sire. I wouldn't have thought it possible, but Olivia's usual alabaster complexion went even paler. And well it should, because if the legends were true, then we might as well be up against Lucifer himself.

"Did you meet him?" I asked.

"No. I only overheard him. I followed my mother one night without her knowing. She walked and walked through the sewers until she came to a passage that led straight down into the earth. I followed her, climbing on stones and vines for foot- and hand-holds for so long I thought we were going to into hell itself. I could even swear I smelled sulfur.

"Just when I was thinking of turning back, the passage expanded into a kind of room. I remained hidden down the corridor and listened to Mother talk to a man she called Ulrich. Do you know him?"

"I've never met him," I said. "But I've heard of him. He is your great-grandsire. And yours, Olivia, as I'm sure Alger told you."

"Then we're kissing cousins, as the American hillbillies would say," Will said, and pursed his lips à la Mick Jagger.

Olivia ignored him. "I have heard Alger speak about this Ulrich," she said. "Alger never met him either, but he was still afraid of him. He said that Reedrek was terrified of him, but that he also . . . loved him."

"He is said to be very seductive and charming," I recalled. "And very evil. Reedrek always spoke of him as if he was in awe of his power." He used to threaten me with stories about Ulrich, as if to frighten a child with tales of a bogeyman.

"He gave me the willies." Will shuddered.

"Was Renee there?"

"No. She was being held somewhere else, somewhere . . . deeper."

I felt something lurch in my chest. My poor child, so far underground. So alone—or perhaps not. My mind refused to account for the possibilities. "How do you know?" I asked him.

"I sort of . . . felt her somehow. I—I sensed she was nearby at least. I can't explain it."

I could explain it. Will and Renee were bonded by

the voodoo blood flowing through their veins. The vaccine that had saved him contained a highy distilled form of the blood that Renee had donated.

"She is . . . in danger," Will practically stuttered.

"Tell us exactly what you mean by that. What did Ulrich say about her?"

Will took a deep breath and blew it out. "She is due to be sacrificed on the night of the full moon."

Jack

Seth encouraged me to visit Connie while he volunteered to help Werm and the girls finish the flooring. I could just imagine what those tiles were going to look like after being put down by a drunk werewolf, but hey, if a floor that looked like a crazy quilt was okay by Werm, then it was okay by me.

If I remembered correctly, and that could never be taken for granted after a quart of whiskey with a tequila chaser, tonight was Connie's night off. With a little luck I might find her at home. I didn't trust myself to get behind the wheel so I decided to hoof it through the tunnels.

The tunnels under Savannah were left over from early in the city's history, when the city fathers decided to raise the street level as a protection from hurricanes. Historically, the tunnels were used by pirates, bandits, and cutthroats of all kinds to hide loot, evade the law, and shanghai men to crew the shadier privateers. They also make a dandy way for vampires to get around the city when it's daylight, or when they're too drunk to drive and they want to take a shortcut on foot.

The way to Connie's apartment took me right past the new hospital where good old granddad Reedrek was cemented up in the cornerstone. William had sort of turned him to stone or froze him, I guess you could say, but later wanted information out of him so he unfroze him. But then he forgot to freeze him back. And he'd been annoying me ever since whenever I got within shouting distance.

Reedrek was still trapped all right, but his mind was mobile enough to try to work his mojo on any underground passersby within range of his psychic abilities. I'd recently caught him trying to talk a sewer repair crew into busting him out of his granite tomb with their jackhammers. I'd nipped his little plan in the bud that time, but his potential for mischief still gave me the creeps.

Ever heard that old expression I may be crazy but I'm not stupid? That pretty much summed up Reedrek's state. Even though he was still a wily old bastard, the sensory deprivation was making him as crazy as a shithouse rat. The few times I had come near him since the repairmen incident, he was spewing crazy talk and riddles.

I tried tiptoeing past his resting place, hoping he wouldn't sense me. No such luck. "Jaaaackeeeee," he sang out. "It's your poor old grandsire, Reedrek."

"D'oh!" I yelped. We may not share the voodoo blood, but we did have the regular vamp bloodline bond. He was my gramps, and he could sense me if I was anywhere around.

"Hush up, you old coot," I said, and kept on walking. "I've got places to be and things to do."

"But so do I, my boy. In fact, my carriage is on its way even as we speak."

"So where do you think you're going, and who's going to take you there? Personally, I wouldn't be caught undead with you at an Alabama chicken fight."

"I'm to make a great sacrifice!" Reedrek said with enthusiasm. "At least I hope I make it. The carriage is running late. No matter. Leftover lamb is fine, just fine. Perhaps in a nice lamb stew."

"What the hell are you talking about?"

"Hell is right," Reedrek said, giggling. "Hell's bells! Ask not for whom hell's bells toll. They toll for thee and thine."

"Okay, I'm leaving," I said, and waved him off as if he stood beside me. "Have fun, wherever it is you think you're going."

"I shall! And I'll give the lamb a kiss for you!" Reedrek's terrible, screeching laugh sent chills up my spine. He was just trying to spook me. "I just love lamb," he said.

"Crazy bastard. Stop talking nonsense." I shook off the chill and walked on, determined to put the old devil out of my mind. I'd speak to William as soon as he got back about putting Reedrek back on ice.

When I got to Connie's place, I knocked on the door and waited to see if she'd answer. I couldn't help but remember the last time I was here: I caught fire when Connie and I tried to get romantic.

I heard footsteps on the other side of the door and knew that she was looking through the peephole to see who was there. I waved. She opened the door.

"Can I come in?" I asked.

"Do you remember what happened the last time you were here?"

"Yeah, I do." The memory of it almost made me sober up. But not quite. "But I need to talk to you."

"You're as drunk as Cooter Brown, but I want to talk to you, too. Who knows? Maybe you'll make more sense this way. Come on in."

I walked into Connie's cozy apartment and sat down on the sofa, as far away from the cross on the wall as I could get. I'd accidentally backed into it the last time I was here and come away even more scorched.

"You first," Connie said, and sat in a gliding rocking chair opposite me. She looked soft and cuddly in a pink cotton sweat suit.

"Okay," I began. Now that I was here I didn't know quite how to say it. "I really wish you wouldn't come to the werewolf fight."

She huffed an exasperated breath. "We went all over this. I'm coming and that's that."

"Yeah, that's what I told Seth you'd say."

"So you two are still talking about it. Conspiring against me, are you?"

"The thing is, he doesn't want you to see him change into a werewolf. It's kind of a . . . grisly sight, you might say. I guess he doesn't want you to see him as an animal." I lowered my voice to a conspiratorial whisper, trying to sound all sensitive-like. Maybe then she might volunteer something that would give me a clue how she felt about Seth. "It's just an awful, awful thing to see. He's afraid you'll never look at him the same way again."

"I thought you said he looked like Chewbacca," she said.

"No thanks. I never touch the stuff."

"Chewbacca, the *Wookiee*," she explained.

"Yeah, right. It's awful, really nasty."

"Chewbacca's actually pretty cute."

"What?" I demanded, horrified. "Chewbacca?"

"Why don't you admit it, Jack? You want me to think that Seth is gross now that I know he's a werewolf." She arched a dark brow in that way she did when she thought I was misbehaving. So much for her taking the bait.

"Um, well, no. The truth is, I don't want you in a dangerous situation."

"And?"

"And, well, I do admit I never wanted you to see what I looked like when I went all fang-faced. I figured if you got to see Seth do his werewolf bit, it might make me look better by comparison." I realized when I said it that I'd gone from trying to determine her depth of feeling for Seth to trying to determine what her feelings were for *me*.

Connie shivered, no doubt thinking back to the night Sullivan died and she saw me have a knock-down-vamp-out with Will. The night I had to admit to her what I was. "At least I finally found out the truth," she said. "Always err on the side of the truth, Jack, especially when you're dealing with me. Promise me right now. Never, ever lie to me."

"Uh . . . okay," I said. Now this wasn't what I'd had in mind at all. Connie hadn't revealed any of her feelings, and instead had gotten me to make a promise

I'd never meant to. When you're a vampire, deceiving people about who you are and what you're doing is something you learn early on. There were still things about myself and my kind I didn't want Connie to know.

"Cross your heart and hope to die?" Connie said.

"Very funny."

"Promise, then."

"Okay. I promise. But please reconsider coming to the fight. Seth and I can take care of unhuman business."

"Just like you took care of Will?"

I knew it was only a matter of time until she threw that in my face again. "I know you're tired of hearing it, but that situation is—"

"Complicated, I know. You keep saying that. In light of your promise, don't you think it's about time you told me why it's so damned complicated?"

I couldn't argue with that logic. She already knew so much I couldn't think of a reason not to tell her. "Will is William's son," I said.

"His vampire son or his real son?"

The way she put that stung me a little bit. I always felt like I was William's *real* son, even though we looked about the same age in human years. "His human son," I said.

Connie ran her hand through her hair. She looked beautiful and sultry even in sweats and without a drop of makeup. "Okay. I suppose I can understand now. You could hardly kill William's son and not get in trouble with your sire."

"That's pretty much the size of it."

She smiled for the first time tonight. "See there?"

"What?" I asked.

"You filled in the blanks for me, told me the truth. That wasn't so hard, was it?"

"No," I said. "I guess it wasn't, at that. I suppose I should have told you before."

"Damn straight. Is there anything else you want to tell me—that you *should* tell me?"

Yeah, plenty. I wanted to tell her how her hair shone like black diamonds by the light of the Tiffany floor lamp, or how she smelled like wildflowers.

"Jack?"

"Uh, there probably is, but I just can't think right now," I muttered. "You said you wanted to talk to me about something. What is it?"

"It's about what I asked you for awhile back. There's somebody in the afterlife I have to see, and I want you to take me to him."

"How do you even know that's possible?" I asked.

"I know that the afterlife, or the underworld, or whatever you want to call it, is very real. Melaphia has shown me more than enough to convince me."

"So why haven't you asked Melaphia?"

"Because she began to clam up when I started talking specifics. And you know how she's been out of it since the kidnapping."

"Maybe there's a reason she doesn't want to speak about it."

"Don't talk around this, Jack. I *know* you know what's involved in this. You've opened up to me about so much in the last couple of days, and the sky didn't fall. Can't you level with me about this, too?"

I tried to remember what Mel had said when I asked her advice. She had reacted strangely when I suggested telling Connie about what happened to William in the underworld. Why? Melaphia had just told me to stall Connie and tell her Mel had forbidden her to attempt a trip to the underworld. But for the life of me, I couldn't figure out why I shouldn't just keep telling Connie the truth. It felt right, and it felt liberating. Besides Melaphia's ancestors, I'd never been able to come clean like this to a human before—especially not one I cared about.

"Okay," I said. "The reason I don't want to let you do this is that William had to go there once to rescue somebody who wasn't quite dead and wasn't quite alive either."

Connie leaned forward in her chair, staring, as if she was listening to a particularly scary story around a campfire at the Girl Scout camp from hell. "How can that be? I mean, how can somebody be in a state like that?"

"It has to do with the process of making someone into a vampire," I said. "Let's just say a lot can go wrong. But that part's not important right now. What you have to understand is what happened to him after he went there."

Connie nodded. "Go on."

"First of all, when he left his body, it was like he was dead. I mean *really* dead. Mel and I couldn't wake him up. To this day I don't know how he ever figured out how to get his spirit back to this world and into his body. And I don't even want to think about him getting trapped in the place where he was. It was full of demons of all kinds. Things in the dark that reach out, and—"

"Stop!" Connie had put her hands to her ears.

Slowly, she smoothed back her hair and moved her hands to the upholstered armrests of her glider, which she clutched until her knuckles were white. "Do you mean everybody goes there? Even—even if they're good and pure and innocent?"

I thought about that for a minute. The only ones I knew who had been there were William, Eleanor, and Shari, vampires or vampire wannabes all. "I don't know," I said. "Now that I think about it, the only dead people I've talked to who complained about the place were, well, vampires."

Strangely, Connie brightened for a second, but then she looked troubled again. She tucked her feet onto the chair and hugged her knees, thinking. "When you were human, were you a religious man, Jack?"

"I was raised Catholic just like you," I said, glancing at Connie's little shrine to the Virgin Mary on a table in the corner. "And I reckon you could say I believe in God." I thought about how crosses and holy water burned my flesh. What stronger proof of God's existence was there than having the third-degree burns to show for it? "Yeah," I said finally. "I guess you could say I'm still a religious man. As much as a guy without a soul can be."

"Okay. Let's say that what they always taught us in church is right."

"Which part?"

"The part about how good people go to heaven and bad people go to hell. That would mean people who aren't bad could be satisfied with where they are in the afterlife, but people who are vampires—that is, damned for all eternity—end up in a place of torment, right?" she said, and added, "No offense meant."

"None taken," I muttered. Dang, there were some things a fellow just didn't like being reminded about, you know? "Yeah, I'm following you. So you mean that who you need to talk to was a good person and shouldn't be in a scary place."

"Yes, but there's more." The little crease in her forehead was back.

"What more?"

"I actually need to talk to two people. One is in heaven."

"Are you sure?" I asked.

"Absolutely sure," she said with finality.

"But the other?"

"He," she began, and her face changed. I saw revulsion and even, yes, hatred, in her eyes. "Is in hell."

"I have to ask you again," I said. "Are you sure?"

Connie's eyes told me she was no longer with me, not really. She looked like she'd gone to a faraway place and time, someplace that was her own version of hell.

Finally her attention snapped back to me and she looked at me with an intensity I'd never seen on her face before. "Oh, yes," she said. "If it's true there is a hell for those who are entirely evil, for those who deserve to burn for all eternity, he's definitely there."

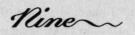

William

Renee was to be sacrificed. Fear was not an emotion I had often felt in my long undeath. It was not so much that I was so hard to kill; it had more to do with my ambivalence about my continued existence. But now I knew real terror for my beloved Renee. There were only two entities to whom a vampire would make a sacrifice. One was Satan himself. The other might be just as bad.

"The full moon is two nights hence," I said, trying to calm myself as best I could.

"Too right," Will said.

Olivia asked, "What did you overhear? What did they talk about?"

"Politics, believe it or not," Will said. "Evidently Mother is toadying up to this Ulrich fellow to try and move up in the ranks of some bloodsucking power structure. Ulrich himself is kissing up to those above him. They think that offering Renee as a sacrifice will be quite the feather in their caps with the higher-ups, maybe even get the Ulrich bloke a seat on some kind of vampire council. Does that mean anything to you, William?"

The *Council*. Just as I'd feared. I knew the day of my reckoning with them was coming, but I'd hoped it would be on my own ground, Savannah, with Jack and other trusted lieutenants at my side. Instead I must rely on those with uncertain powers and unknown loyalties, with Renee's life and Lalee's precious bloodline hanging in the balance.

"It is the gathering of dark lords," I said. "A thousand years or more ago, the most ancient and evil blood drinkers banded together to form an entity they thought they could use to rule over others of their kind."

"For what purpose?" Andrew, one of Olivia's vampires, asked.

"In simple terms, to force all blood drinkers to make as many humans into vampires as possible, so that they could take over the world," I said.

"They would enslave those of us who choose to live in peace and freedom, beyond the notice of humans," Olivia said.

"Or worse," I added. "If their numbers are great enough they could just as easily slaughter us all if we continue to be uncooperative."

"So these council members, they're the ones you also call the old sires?" Will asked. When I nodded, he said, "So it's because of them you started shipping to America those vampires who wanted to get as far away from the dark lords as they could."

"Yes. Late in the eighteenth century, I first went to the New World to make my fortune. There was to be an uprising among our kind against the old lords who had begun to enslave us. Many, like Alger, chose to stay and fight. But I'd had enough killing. For centuries, under Reedrek's thumb I was forced to slaughter humans indiscriminately and vampires in my own bloodline for retribution against every slight, real or imagined, to my sire."

"But the bloodbath never happened on the scale you and others were worried about, did it?" Olivia said. "Alger said so."

"That's right," I said. "But according to my contacts, their goals remained the same. Their minions made raids on vampire covens and colonies here and there, killing some outright, enslaving others."

"What happened to the all-out war they were planning, then? What have they been doing all this time?" Will wanted to know.

"No one knows for sure, at least nobody who's willing to tell. The prevailing theory—proposed by Alger, in fact—is that the Council thought that together, their power would be greater than each of them acting alone. But it didn't work out that way. They are still dangerous—don't mistake me," I said. "But there is a certain amount of infighting, and they were never able to summon an overwhelming force in numbers or power."

Olivia and Bree looked at each other. "William," Olivia began. "You've seen my journal, so you know about my ongoing project—the one where I document the lives of female blood drinkers, going back thousands of years."

I nodded. It was when Deylaud read Olivia's book that I had learned of Diana's existence as a blood drinker.

"We collect historical data through a network of contacts we've forged since Alger began the project before he made me," she continued. "We've only recently begun to put this information in a computer database."

I started to speak, but Olivia cut me off with a wave of her hand. She said, "Don't worry about it falling into the wrong hands. We've encrypted all the data and taken every security precaution imaginable, believe me. You're also aware of the wealth of research material that Alger collected on his own through the centuries."

I nodded again. My friend Algernon, in addition to being an unbridled libertine, was also, somewhat paradoxically, a scholar of the first order. He made copious notes throughout his long existence about myriad topics, mostly the history of blood drinkers and their origins.

"Just in the last couple of weeks we've started to enter all Alger's information in the database, so we'll be able to analyze it statistically and in other ways."

"What do you mean 'analyze the data'?" Will asked.

"We can make comparisons, draw inferences, construct models, make predictions . . . ," Andrew explained.

"Whoa, mate, what are you on about?" Will asked again. "How is all that supposed to help us?"

Intrigued, I said, "I can think of many applications. We can figure out which vampires through the ages have known one another, which ones would have been at the same place at the same time, determine what alliances may have been formed—"

"Exactly," Olivia said.

"Did Alger gather much information on the dark lords?" Will wanted to know.

"Yes," Olivia said. "Just a few days ago we found a cache of documents all about the Council."

I said, "I'm sure that Alger told me all he knew about the dark lords by the time of his death," I said. "We were very close. He wouldn't have held anything back from me."

"Of course not, William," Olivia said. Her eyes glistened as she spoke of her beloved sire. "Did you ever wonder why Alger agreed to come to Savannah when he did? After you had begged him to join you for more than two hundred years?"

"Yes," I said. "He hinted that he felt we were entering into a heightened time of danger from the old lords. As soon as he was settled in America, we were going to bring all of you over on the next crossing."

"That's true," Olivia agreed. "But it was more than that. He had just acquired the papers of another scholar blood drinker. It included research that goes back until almost—if you can believe it—the beginnings of blood drinkers on this earth. Some of this material is so ancient it's on papyrus and stone tablets, William!" She positively glowed with excitement now.

"What languages are they in?" I asked.

"Aramaic, Greek, ancient Celtic tongues, all types of languages. It will take some time to have it all translated. Particularly since we have to parse it out in so many lots."

"What do you mean?" Will asked.

"If we have to employ human interpreters, we cannot give too much material to any one—"

"To make sure no human is able to learn too much about us," I finished for her. "You seem to have this well thought out. I applaud you."

"Thank you, but most of the credit for caring for the material should go to Alger. He had his vampires through the years make duplicates of all the material as a backup in case it was torched or stolen by our enemies. When we found the stone tablets and the other really ancient stuff after Alger died, there was a notation that the material had already been copied. Alger even made rubbings of the stone tablets. He was taking the copies to you when he was murdered aboard the *Alabaster*. It was to be a surprise. He knew your love of ancient artifacts. He hadn't even taken the time to have any of it translated before he left. He thought you could help him with that."

I leaned forward in my chair. "No such papers were found on the *Alabaster* with Alger's remains. Reedrek said he'd stowed away on the *Alabaster* to murder Alger out of spite and stop my smuggling operation, but it may have been more than that. Perhaps Reedrek knew that Alger had important information about the Council that he didn't want to come to light."

"I expect what's left of those copies is at the bottom of the Atlantic by now," Olivia said.

"Why have you only now told me this?" I demanded.

"There was no time. You sent me back here to organize the Bonaventures so soon after you put Reedrek away, and then you assigned me to brief and dispatch spies to search out Hugo's vampires and determine if Diana was alive."

"Which you lied to me about," I said.

"Out of necessity," Olivia replied impatiently. "And then there was this crisis with Renee. You have so much on your mind, so much to deal with, I only wanted to wait until we had something of substance to share with you."

Olivia's gaze searched mine for something akin to the excitement she was feeling. "William, forgive me, but I thought you'd be more . . . enthusiastic about this discovery."

How could I tell her that I was beyond caring about vampire history and politics? She no doubt still expected me to transport her little coven to Savannah as soon as I got Renee back. I no longer gave a damn about her and her merry band of blood drinkers. I cared only about saving Renee. I barely cared about Will. I still needed Olivia's help, however, and this new revelation might mean she could provide even more aid than I'd dared to hope.

"I assure you, I don't lack enthusiasm. I'm just going through all the possibilities in my mind," I said. "Have you been able to decipher anything that will help us with the problem at hand right now?"

"I hadn't thought so until I heard Will's story just now about how Ulrich is trying to impress the Council with a—a sacrifice." Olivia glanced down at the floor. She couldn't bring herself to say Renee's name in such a gruesome context.

"But now?" I asked.

"We were comparing some of Alger's recent notes to some that he made around the time you first went to the New World. We think that he was trying to get to the bottom of the Council's resurgence—the feeling everyone's getting in their blood that some big event is on its way."

"The reason Alger decided to go to America when he did," Will said.

"Yes. Exactly." Olivia paused and took a breath as if what she had to say next would be difficult to explain. "When Alger himself began to get this—this feeling of . . ."

"Doom?" Will supplied.

Olivia snapped her attention to him. "Yes. Impending doom. That's exactly how Alger described it."

I appraised my son. He was much more intuitive than I had originally thought. Of course, he was five centuries old, much older than Olivia, and could therefore, like me, sense things younger blood drinkers could not. I too had sensed the approaching evil, as Donovan had mentioned the other night. At the time I had put it down to Reedrek's being in my life again after so many years, but now I was beginning to understand it was something greater than that.

"So are you saying there are similarities between the feelings vampires had two hundred years ago and the things that so many of us sense now?" I asked.

"Yes," Olivia said.

"So," Will wanted to know, "was there anything in those moldy old papers that shed any light on what the old demons are up to this time and what, if anything, makes them think they'll be any more successful than they were before?"

"According to one of Alger's more recent contacts," Olivia said, "the Council was learning to use their combined power to harness elemental forces."

"Earth, air, water, and fire," I muttered.

"And spirit," Olivia added.

Ah, Olivia, ever the pagan. "How do they know they'll be able to wield this power?" I asked.

"Do you remember when the last rogue country claimed to have tested those nuclear bombs underground?" Olivia asked.

"Claimed?" I said.

"Those were earthquakes, not nukes. According to this source of Alger's, the Council caused them."

The vampires in the room just looked at one another. Finally, Will said, "An earthquake? Doesn't that seem like a bit of overkill, luv, just to get a few vampires in line? And what would a blood sacrifice have to do with manufacturing earthquakes? What can the old bastards be about?"

"We don't know," Olivia admitted. "You're right, though, none of it appears to make much sense. Do you have any theories, William? . . . William?"

I barely heard her. The gravity of Renee's situation hit me hard. How did her sacrifice fit in with the plans of the old sires? And how in the name of heaven was I ever going to save her?

Jack

"So you need to talk to both of them? The one who's in heaven and the one who's in hell?"

"That's right."

"Do you mind telling me who these people are?"

"I'd rather not."

"How do you expect me to help you find them if you won't tell me who they are?"

"I have this . . . this feeling that once I get there they'll find me. Don't ask me how I know. I just do."

"Don't ask, huh?" I said. "It seems to me that this telling-the-truth business should go both ways. How come I have to spill all my secrets and you get to keep yours?" Now, I thought this was a reasonable question, but I'm a man. And every now and then I get reminded that what seems right and reasonable to a man seems like flat-out crazy talk to a woman. Connie looked at me like I'd just escaped from an asylum.

She started to say something sharp, I could tell. But she must have remembered she was trying to get a favor out of me, so she bit back whatever it was. Finally, she said, "I don't want to go into that. I just need you to do this for me. I can't tell you how important it is."

"Can't or won't?"

"Jack, don't make me talk about why I have to do this. I can't handle it. Just trust me."

"Like you trust me?"

She thrust out her chin and her eyes blazed. I felt like a fool then, opening up the way I did when it was clear that she didn't think enough of me to do the same. During the few tense moments of silence that followed, I begged her silently to say something, anything, to signal me that she would let me into her mind and her heart. But she said nothing, and the silence hurt more than any insult she might hurl my way.

Finally, I took a deep breath and said what Mel told me to say. "It's too dangerous. Melaphia forbids it."

"Dammit, Jack, are you going to let her tell you what to do?"

"Don't even start," I said. "You can't drive a wedge between me and Mel. She's just about the only family I have."

"That's more family than I have," Connie said, her eyes glistening. She got up and went to the door. Holding it open, she said, "Go home, Jack. And tell Seth that I *will* be at the fight."

I went to the door and walked out before I could say anything I'd regret. But I hadn't taken two steps when she spoke again. I turned back as she said, "Tell Seth this, too—tell him that whatever happens, I'll never consider him to be a monster."

What about me? I wanted to yell as she closed the door in my face. Sometimes it just doesn't pay to sober up.

When I entered the house, I heard screaming. I swore as I took the steps to the upstairs bedrooms two at a time. I burst into the room Melaphia had been using since Renee was taken and saw Reyha and Deylaud—in human form—leaning across from either side of the bed, trying to comfort her.

"What is it? What's the matter?" I demanded.

"They've got her!" screamed Melaphia. Her eyes were like those of a wild thing, and her arms flailed as if she were trying to beat back an invisible demon.

She shrieked again, and the twins, even though they were in human form, turned their faces to the ceiling and howled like the devil himself was after them. It was eerie enough to raise a fellow's gooseflesh and short hairs at the same time. Even a badass vampire's.

I turned on the light and joined Deylaud on his side of the bed. I put one knee down on the comforter and scooted next to Mel. "It's all right," I said. "William has gone to get Renee, remember? She's going to be fine." I said it to calm myself as much as to calm her. The sound of Melaphia's and the twins' wails had really rattled me.

"No!" Melaphia yelled. "It's never going to be all right. Not ever again!"

"Why? What do you mean?"

"I saw her." Melaphia stopped waving her arms and grasped my shirtfront, bringing my face close to hers. "She's not what she was."

"You had a nightmare, that's all," I insisted. I put one arm around her and gave her shoulders what I hoped was a reassuring squeeze.

"Not a nightmare. I saw her. I saw *it*."

Behind me I heard Deylaud lean against the wall and slump to the floor. I glanced around. "See to your brother," I said to Reyha, who scampered around the bed to her twin's side. It had obviously taken all his strength to change into two-footed form and make his way upstairs to come to Mel's side. He was as pale and wan as a ghost and he was panting, but his eyes were clear and frightened.

I turned my attention back to Melaphia. "What?" I asked. "What did you see?"

"She's one of *you*!" Melaphia turned loose my shirt and pushed me away. "She's a blood drinker! She is undead!" The look of horror and revulsion on her face made me back off from her. Hell, it nearly made me physically ill. And it hit me then as it never had before. This was what she thought of *me*. Why had I never known that the human I loved like a daughter thought of me as a monster?

I stood up and looked down into the faces of Reyha and Deylaud, as they whimpered on the floor behind me. They clung to each other as they stared up at me, their faces full of horror. They were as devoted to Renee as any dog has ever been to any child. It was not too strong to say they worshipped her. The look in their eyes broke what was left of my heart. I knelt beside them and tried to reassure them. "A bad dream," I said. "That's all it was."

Reyha nodded and reluctantly let go of her brother long enough for me to pick him up and put him in bed beside Melaphia. With no strength left, he was dead-weight, but at least he'd made it back into human form again. That was a positive sign. I pointed to the other side of the antique four-poster and Reyha knew what I wanted her to do. She scampered back around and got in bed on Melaphia's other side.

"Give me the doll," Melaphia said, and pointed to something on the pedestal table by the bed. It was the little doll she'd been making with beads. I handed it to her and she clutched it tightly. "Maman Lalee, help my child!" she said. "I would rather see her dead than a vampire. Please, sweet mother, kill her by your own hand before the demons take her to be one of them."

I didn't know what to say. I started to tell her that Renee as a vampire was better than no Renee at all. But the words sounded insane, even to me. Of course she would be better off dead, as I would have been had I really known the path I was choosing when William asked me on that battlefield if I wanted to live forever.

I wanted to tell her again that everything would be all right, and mean it, but I didn't know if it would. "I'll be back," I said. I went into the next bedroom down the hall, the one where Renee slept whenever she was staying at the "big house," as she called it. I unplugged the Alice in Wonderland night-light, which hadn't been lit since the night Renee was stolen. I took it back into the room where Mel and the twins huddled together under the down comforter, plugged it in, and turned it on. Then I turned off the overhead light and they relaxed a little.

I collapsed into a rocking chair in the corner, determined to stay with them until they were all asleep again. The little light glowed like it did the last night I read Renee a bedtime story. It just so happened that it had been *Alice in Wonderland*. Renee loved that one, although she found it scary at the same time.

I shivered, fighting an uneasy feeling. I was struck with the irrational need to get far away from this cozy little bedroom.

Melaphia still fretted. The twins were trying to snuggle with her, trying to make her feel warm and secure, but it wasn't working. I remembered my "talent" for bewitching humans—the one I'd only used a handful of times—and figured now was as good a reason to use it as I was ever likely to see.

I concentrated on making Melaphia calm and sleepy. *Go back to sleep,* I murmured to her mind. She quieted gradually, and after a few minutes she was completely still. It even seemed to be working on Reyha and Deylaud. A few seconds after the rhythm of Mel's breathing told me she was asleep, the twins' eyelids began to flutter closed.

As I watched them sleep, I didn't think I'd ever felt like more of an outsider, more of a cold-blooded imposter in the land of the living. It was clear that I was a demon even to the ones I loved the most. There was a built-in wall between us. The wall between the living and the dead. Between the good and pure and the ones who preyed on them. And those predators were me and my kind.

Looking at the three of them, I wanted nothing more than to curl up on the bed at their feet until the sunbeams came through the gap in the curtains and burned me to a cinder. Mel had said it, after all. I was better off dead. But my humans still needed me, and as long as they did, I guessed I might as well stick around, or try to anyway.

I went back outside to my Corvette and hopped in. There was nothing like a little physical work to get your mind off things, so I decided to head back to the garage since there was plenty of dark left. As I drove I wondered why I tried so hard to hang on to my humanity after all these years. I was a monster, a demon, but whenever I was reminded of that fact, it always came as some kind of surprise. And it always hurt. It was about damned time that I accepted what I was. Fangs and all.

Maybe accepting yourself as the evil dead would mean never having to say you're sorry.

Ten

William

"Will," I said, "you told me earlier that you could feel Renee's presence but that she was not there in the room where you overheard Diana and Ulrich. You said she was somewhere deeper. Did the passage continue past the room they were in?"

"The room was more of a cavern," he said. "I believe that if you kept on climbing down you'd eventually reach her. And them. I could feel them, too."

"The Council?" Olivia asked.

"Yeah. They smell like . . . hell," Will said. Then he looked at me a little doubtfully. "So, what's the plan?"

"I'm going there tomorrow night," I said. "You can take me as far as the room you spoke of. Beyond that I go alone. I don't want Diana and Ulrich to know you're working with me. If I find Renee and can't get her out myself, we'll make another attempt and you can come along. If necessary, all of you should be prepared to go with me that time. But tomorrow I will try to discover where they're keeping her and what their numbers are. If Ulrich has already delivered her to the Council, there may be many. If they're hiding her away from the Council until two nights hence, fortune may smile on me, and I might find her only lightly guarded."

"All right then," Will said. "Until tomorrow night." He turned to go; Olivia and I followed him to the foyer.

"Will you have any trouble slipping away from Diana and Hugo tomorrow night?" I asked.

"No problem," Will said. "I do have one question for blondie here before I go." He turned to Olivia. "You didn't trust me when I first came here tonight, and yet you spilled a lot of your secrets while I was around. Why is that?"

Olivia grabbed the front of his long leather coat, reached into the inside pocket, and brought out a bibelot that had been on the entry table when Will arrived, but which I now saw was missing from its place. I had been watching him the whole time, and I hadn't seen him pocket the trinket.

She set it back on the table. "I'll tell you why," she said, roughly letting go of the coat and shoving him a little at the same time. "You just don't look that hard to kill. And make no mistake: I *will* kill you if you double-cross us, William's son or no."

Will looked surprised but covered quickly with a laugh. He was still laughing when he closed the door behind him.

Olivia and I heard a hubbub from the other vampires and turned around. A ghostly pale Donovan stood in the entrance to the parlor, leaning heavily on the door-frame. "Who was that?" he asked.

"My son, Will," I said.

"Oh. His voice sounded so familiar, but I can't place it. I didn't get a look at him tonight or the night I followed him and the others. No matter. It will come to me."

Olivia rushed to him and put her arm under his shoulders. "You shouldn't be up yet. You need more sleep to recover."

"I can sleep when I'm dead," he said, and laughed at his own joke.

Olivia and Andrew walked him to a sofa and gently helped him sit. "Isn't someone going to pop the obvious question?" he asked. His face reminded me of marble, with blood vessels showing through like the matrix in the stone. But there was still a twinkle in his pale blue eyes.

"Who staked you?" I asked.

"Your lady wife, Diana," he said, and slumped forward in a faint.

Donovan came around well enough to feed off the other vampires and was put back into his coffin, but he wouldn't stay. As soon as the other vampires went to their own coffins, he crawled back out of his and insisted on joining Olivia and me. We helped him walk to the long table in the coffin room.

"Blood sustains me, but I was dying for tea," he said, and sipped the strong brew Olivia had just made.

"So what happened the night Diana staked you?" Olivia asked.

As if kidnapping wasn't enough evidence of Diana's evil, I winced at the thought of her unprovoked attack on a peaceful vampire.

"I was following the three of them," Donovan said. "And they slipped into an unused underground rail tunnel, then turned into the sewers. I lost sight of them around a bend, and the stench was so strong, I couldn't follow them by odor either. And then I got lost. Diana must have doubled back and come for me, because before I knew it, I heard a seductive voice behind me. When I turned around, she staked me in the chest."

"If it weren't for the goddess, you'd be dust right now," Olivia mused.

"As you say," Donovan said, raising his cup in tribute. "Praise Brigid."

"I shouldn't have let you go," Olivia fretted. "I keep forgetting you don't know the sewers like the rest of us do. We use them to get around the city when we need to move in the daytime or take shortcuts at night. When bodies started turning up there not long ago, we figured there was some rogue vamp activity in the area. It's not like a human serial killer could have been dumping bodies there. Any human without bulky oxygen equipment would have died of asphyxia going into those tunnels. Then we realized it was Hugo and the others. It's how we figured out where they were."

"All's well that ends well," Donovan said. "So what's been going on since I pulled a Rip van Winkle?"

Olivia filled him in: Will had agreed to cooperate, we'd discussed the vampire council, and our plan for rescuing Renee.

"What do you know of the Council of dark lords?" I asked him.

"What does anyone know of them?" he answered

cryptically. I wondered if he was being evasive or just philosophical. "I had heard the same as you, that they're learning to wield elemental power. But that's a tricky business and hard to control. The first time they tried to wield this power, they had some unintended consequences."

"What kind of unintended consequences?" I asked.

"Nobody I ever spoke to was ever able to say. But it did some damage to the Council as individuals and as an organization. They've been all this time repairing themselves, sleeping in the earth for rejuvenation, being fed from the blood of their minions. And now they seem ready to strike again, or try to."

"Strike how?" Olivia asked. "Isn't their goal still the same? To force all of us into making vampires and feeding off humans?"

"Yes, but I think they have a show of force in mind. Some way of flexing their collective muscle."

"Does anyone know exactly what they intend?" I asked.

"No, nobody I've talked to knows for sure. But many of the old vampires I've run across in my travels think that they planned this grand gesture as a way of getting our attention and making us afraid of standing up to them."

"Have you met this Ulrich?" I asked.

"No, but I've heard of him. The word is that he is trying to become the next dark lord. There are two vacancies on the Council, and he wants one of the seats."

"I've tried to remember everything I ever heard about the dark lords in my existence," I said. "Most vampires are ignorant, even some of the old ones.

Reedrek himself told me what little I know, but I never heard him say what it takes to be included in their ranks. Do you know?"

Donovan shook his head. "All I know is that it takes a gesture so evil it would make Satan himself sit up and take notice. And from what I hear of Ulrich, he's the essence of evil. He's been the hidden force behind some of the most gruesome chapters of history. I've heard it said he was the one who gave Caligula his ideas."

Olivia shuddered and glanced my way. "And now Ulrich wants to make an uber-evil gesture. Like sacrificing an innocent child?"

"Not just any innocent child," I said. "But a child with a power that they fear but do not understand." My gut was churning at the thought of it.

Donovan reached across the table and took my hand. His grip was as cold as the grave, but I knew his heart was sincere. "I give you my word, William, if there's anything I can do to help you find Renee, you can count on me."

"Me too, but you know that," Olivia said, and put her hand over mine and Donovan's. To my surprise I found that I was touched by their words.

"I thank you, my friends," I said. I just hoped it would be enough.

Jack

Back at the garage, I walked in to find an extra player at the card table, a woman of all things, and a werewolf woman at that.

As soon as he saw me, Jerry stood up. "Jack, this here's Wanda. Wanda, this is Jack McShane, the guy I was telling you about."

Wanda shifted her cards to her left hand and extended her right. "Pleased to meet you, Mr. McShane." She had a slight but pleasing Cajun accent.

"Call me Jack," I said, and shook her hand. It wasn't as soft as most women's, but that's to be expected from a shape-shifter. After all, when you spent part of your time running on all fours, well, you get my drift.

I looked at Jerry. "Does Wanda have a last name?"

"Uh, Thrasher," he said, and looked at the floor.

"I call," Huey said, throwing two quarters into the kitty. Everyone showed their cards. Huey, who only had one pair, lost again and was as surprised as ever, even though he lost every hand. "Durn," he said.

"Ms. Thrasher, why don't you and Jerry sit out this next hand?" I looked at Jerry and jerked my chin in the direction of the office. He took the hand of the lovely Wanda and followed me there.

"Don't tell me. Let me guess," I said when I was seated behind my desk. "You are Nate Thrasher's wife, right?"

"Estranged wife," Wanda corrected. "How'd you know?" She sat on the sofa across from the desk and Jerry sat down next to her.

"Just call it a hunch."

Wanda patted her hair and gave me a flirtatious look. "Are you really a—a vampire?"

Keeping my face as expressionless as possible, I looked to Jerry for an explanation. As I've said before, I'm no Emily Post, but Wanda's statement was a real breach of the unwritten code of unhuman etiquette.

Besides Connie and Seth, The V word was never spoken in my presence by anyone outside William's household who was not another vampire. I didn't want to come off as a nervous Nellie, but it just wouldn't do.

"Uh, honey pie," Jerry said, addressing Wanda, I hoped. "We don't call a v-a-m-p-i-r-e a v-a-m-p-i-r-e; it's not nice."

"Jerry," I pointed out, "I'm sitting right here. And I can *spell*."

"Oh," Wanda said, putting her hand against her vermilion lips. "I'm sorry. It's just that I've never met one before. A v-a-m-p-i-r-e, that is."

"Good. We can *all* spell," I said.

"She's a little nervous is all, Jack," Jerry hastened to explain.

She didn't look nervous. She looked hot to trot. In fact, she was looking at me like I was a big slab of rare sirloin on the hoof. "Miss Wanda, for safety's sake we don't talk about our nonhuman tendencies around here. Most of my customers are human, and we don't want to scare them off. You understand, don't you?"

Wanda nodded vigorously enough to make her blond curls bounce. She made the sign of a zipper across her lips and gave me a wink.

"Won't you excuse Jerry and me for a minute, darlin'?" I got up and took Jerry by the arm.

"Back in a minute, sweet cheeks," Jerry called as he followed me to the coffee area.

"Sweet cheeks?"

Jerry shrugged and I handed him a Styrofoam cup. "Aw, Jack, you know how it is."

I sighed, thinking of my last run-in with Connie. I

wished. "What are you doing here with Nate Thrasher's wife?"

"I had to get her away from there. He was beating up on her all the time."

Jerry held out the cup and I poured him some of Huey's finest brew, that is to say, coffee that tasted like tar-colored bog water. Or maybe bong water. I was beginning to wonder if he didn't use his zombie-flavored sweat socks as filters. I was also beginning to wonder if Wanda hadn't triggered the famous Thrasher temper by presenting for every swamp dog that came within sniffing distance. But all the flirting in the world didn't justify abuse. I just didn't want to see Jerry get hurt by a conniving woman or by a cuck-olded werewolf.

"I heard she's been missing for a while. Where have you been hiding her?"

"We've been staying at a friend's trailer, but the friend got nervous when he found out we were on the wrong side of the Thrashers, so we had to run," Jerry said. "How did you know she was missing?"

"Because Connie—Detective Jones—has done every-thing but drag the swamp looking for her. She sus-pected foul play. I've got to call her and tell her Wanda's alive."

"No, Jack, you can't! Nobody can know who Wanda is and where she's run off from . . . or who with."

"What about all your card-playing buddies out there?" I asked.

"They won't tell anybody."

"Look, Jerry," I said. "Connie infiltrated the pack, undercover. She even went out with Samson Thrasher.

She's risked her life to find Wanda. I've got to tell her."

Jerry took a sip of the coffee and made a face. "All right, but I have to ask you a favor in return."

"Oh, okay. What is it?"

"Can Wanda stay here until this thing blows over?"

"Here? At the garage? Geez, Jerry, isn't there anywhere else you can go with her?"

"There's nowhere else the Thrashers are afraid to go looking for her," Jerry said with a beseeching look. "They respect you, Jack. I know it sounds kind of backward, but that's why they want to take you on."

I sighed, remembering Jerry's admission that he liked to hang out at my garage because the Thrashers, who he was on the run from himself, wouldn't dare come looking for him here.

As I was thinking it over, Jerry said, "C'mon, Jack, it would only be for a couple of days. Word is on the street that Samson and your buddy Seth are going to settle things in two nights."

"Hmm. That's right. I'll tell you what, Jer. You come to the fight with me as Seth's backup and it's a done deal. She can sleep right in there on the couch in the office. I lock the doors in the daytime anyway, and if anybody tries to mess with her and you're not here, Huey can run them down and eat their brains."

Jerry looked sick. "Do zombies really eat people's brains? I thought that was just a wives' tale."

"To tell you the truth, I don't know. I do know that he tried to nibble a customer or two early on, before we broke him of it. If we actually sicced him on somebody, who knows? It might be pretty interesting to see what happened," I said. Who'd win a fight between a hungry zombie and a werewolf sounded like one of those stupid questions little kids asked one another, but it was still an entertaining one.

"I reckon it's about time I faced up to the pack," Jerry said. "It'll be a helluva lot easier with you and Seth there, too."

I clapped him on the back. "Sometimes a man has to take a stand, Jer. You'll be glad you did."

Jerry thought for a second. "Who else is going to back up Seth besides you and me?"

"Werm's going to be there with bells on," I said cheerfully.

Jerry looked down at his coffee cup. "Do you have anything stronger than this zombiefied coffee?"

Jerry and Wanda rejoined the card game after I told Wanda that a policewoman I knew was going to want to talk to her. She seemed fine with that. I called Connie.

"Jack, haven't we talked enough for one night? Do you know what time it is?" she asked groggily.

"I've got Wanda Thrasher here at the garage," I said.

"I'll be there in ten," she said, and hung up.

I hoped for all I was worth that finding Wanda would score points with Connie. I couldn't stand to leave things with her in the sorry state they were when I left her apartment. The other upside to finding Wanda was that now maybe Connie wouldn't feel like she had to come to the dominance fight. After all, working the Wanda case was her original excuse for going.

While I was waiting for Connie, I called Huey away from the card table. "There's something I want you to do for me, buddy," I told him. I put my hands lightly on his shoulders and looked him in the eyes. That was harder than it sounded as his eyes now worked somewhat independently of each other, kind of like some species of amphibian. You kind of had to sway this way and that in order to stay in his line of sight. Whenever I talked to him head-on, I felt like one of those Indian snake charmers.

"Name it, Jack. I'll do anything you want," Huey said, tracking me as best he could.

"You see that nice lady over there—Wanda, Jerry's girlfriend?"

Huey had to turn all the way around and cock his head to one side to see her. "Yep, I reckon I do."

"I want you to be her bodyguard," I said gravely. "Her husband is one mean sonofabitch and might want to come and beat up on her, but you do whatever you have to in order to protect her, all right?"

One of Huey's eyeballs did a U-turn back to me, and the other soon meandered over to see what number one was looking at. Curiosity, I guess. It was almost like they each had a mind of their own in addition to independent locomotion. "You can count on me, Jack. I'll protect that lady with my life."

"Good man," I said. Technically, of course, Huey had no life to protect Wanda with, but who was I of all people to quibble over semantics? Huey could be trusted completely to follow through with his commitments and that was the important thing. I gave the little guy's shoulders a final squeeze before I turned him back around toward the card table.

Connie showed up a few minutes later. Both pain and hope stirred inside me as she walked through the door. Even though I had found Wanda for her, I guess I still wasn't sure if she'd ever forgive me for refusing to be her conductor on the streetcar to hell.

I introduced her to Wanda and showed them both into my office so Connie could question her in private. When they came out, Wanda was dabbing her eyes with a tissue. Connie and I watched her go back to the card table where she sat by Jerry and put her head on his shoulder.

"So what happened?" I asked Connie.

"I tried to get her to press charges against Nate Thrasher, but she refuses." Connie glared in Wanda's direction in frustration.

"Not everyone is as brave as you are," I said.

Connie's attention snapped back to me. "What do you mean?" she demanded. Her gaze searched mine for a sign of something.

"I just meant that you were willing to go under-cover and risk life and limb to find her when you thought she'd been beaten up or worse. And now she won't even go so far as to press charges against Nate so he can't do that to Sally, or anybody else for that matter."

Connie visibly relaxed. "Oh," she murmured. "Well . . ."

"What did you think I meant?"

"Nothing. It's not important."

I had a feeling it was important. Very important. But if Connie didn't want to talk about it, she wouldn't, and that's all there was to it. Recent experience proved that.

"Jack, I want to thank you for finding Wanda for me. The case had become very important to me. It's very frustrating when a missing person seems to just vanish into thin air. Even though she won't press charges, I'm really pleased to have her disappearance solved."

"You're welcome," I said. "But listen, I'm sorry about what happened the last time we talked. I shouldn't have given you a hard time about something you're not ready to talk to me about—something you might never want to talk to me about. I didn't mean to pry. I'm just worried about you, that's all."

"I'm sorry for how we left things, too," she said. "I know you're just trying to look out for my safety. I'm going to quit bugging you about the afterlife thing. I mean, I still want to talk to them, but I'll work with Melaphia some more first so I'll better understand how to approach this. Maybe I can contact them with a medium, without us having to, you know, go anywhere."

I relaxed, knowing that she'd talk to Melaphia about things. She'd listen to Mel. Yep, Melaphia would straighten her out. But there was still the issue of the werewolf fight. "Now that you know where Wanda is, I guess there's no point in your showing up at the dominance fight, is there?" I suggested hopefully.

"Hmm," she said. "I suppose not."

Now I really did feel like a two-ton anvil had been lifted off my chest. "Good."

Connie pushed out her bottom lip in a mock pout. "I was kind of looking forward to seeing the show, though. I mean, how often does a girl get to see a bunch of guys change into werewolves?"

"You've got me there." She was angling for something, but I couldn't tell what.

"So how are you going to make it up to me?"

"Hmmm. What do you have in mind?" Visions of Connie shinnying out of her pink sweats danced through my head.

"Jack, stop playing dumb." She hit me lightly on the arm. "Werm's club is opening tomorrow night. Signs are posted all over town. It's supposed to be a pretty big deal. But you probably already have a date."

"Who? Me?"

"Yeah. You."

I cleared my throat. "Consuela, would you be my date for Werm's club opening tomorrow night?"

"I thought you'd never ask," she said. "If we're going to dance tomorrow night away, I've got to go home and get my beauty sleep."

I put my arm around her shoulders and walked her to her car. Unlocking the door, she said, "I'm really looking forward to our date. I got the night off by switching shifts with another cop. The entertainment should be very . . . interesting."

I barely heard her, high as I was on knowing that she not only didn't hate me anymore but had actually asked me out on a date. "Mmm-hmm," I murmured. "Very interesting."

She got behind the wheel and I gently shut the car door. She said something else, but the window was up and she'd started the engine just as she'd said it.

"What?" I called out to her as she was backing away from the garage.

She rolled the car window down a few inches and yelled, "Especially the female impersonator. See you at eight!"

The cobwebs finally cleared from my mind, and I stepped out into the street behind her as she drove away.

"Say *what*?"

Eleven

William

Will met me at Olivia's just after sundown. Olivia and all her vampires save Donovan, who had retired to a back room to recuperate, gathered in the foyer to see us off. "Are you sure you don't want me to come with you?" Olivia asked.

"Not this time," I said. "But be ready. If all goes well, I'll return later tonight with the knowledge of where she is and what it will take to get her out. Then I expect I shall be calling on all of you."

"Good luck," Olivia said, and stood on tiptoe to kiss my cheek.

"How about a wee snog for Willie boy, then?" Will suggested.

"Talk to me when you rescue Renee. Then who knows what you might get," Olivia said.

With that exchange, we set off and took the nearest entry into the sewer tunnels. I asked Will, "Did Hugo and Diana question you about where you were last night?"

"Nah. I'm my own man. They don't tell me where to go and what to do."

His answer sounded like youthful bravado. I decided to support his posturing. "I'm glad to hear it. I feared Hugo might still be trying to dominate you."

Will looked as if he would speak again but cut himself off.

"Have you thought about your future?" I asked him.

"My what?" He sounded slightly confused.

"When Diana and Hugo realize that you helped me steal Renee back from them, you'll be in serious jeopardy. You really should come back to Savannah with me," I told him.

A brief, bitter laugh escaped him. "What? And give up all of this?" He kicked at a lump of unidentifiable garbage and made an expansive gesture at the muck-covered sewer walls.

"I'm serious. Hugo is going to want to kill you, and your mother may not be able to protect you from him this time."

"If I go to Savannah with you, I'll have to follow your rules, won't I? I remember hunting with you there. You wouldn't let me kill anyone."

"You can still feed off humans, you just can't kill. And of course, you can't call attention to the fact that you're a blood drinker."

"Like I said, mate. I'm my own man."

"At least think about it."

Will seemed to be doing just that as we continued walking. Finally he said, "I imagine your man Jack would be thrilled if I moved into town to compete for Daddy's affections."

"Jack would adjust," I said. His mention of Jack reminded me of a more serious problem. At least three people were sworn to see Will dead. Two—Iban and Jack—were powerful vampires who, if they ever got the opportunity, would kill him on sight for what he did to Sullivan. The other, Melaphia, was the most powerful voodoo *mambo* in the hemisphere and would kill him for helping kidnap her baby. If that weren't enough, the human police officer Consuela Jones wouldn't hesitate to lock him up, knowing he would burn to a crisp in a jail cell when the sun came up. I couldn't very well blame any of them. But I still wanted my son. I had to think of a solution.

We walked awhile longer, the foul effluvia of a modern industrial city wafting around us. At last we reached an area where a profusion of vines and roots grew down from the surface and out from the sides of the tunnel as if we stood under a mass of vegetation. Will stooped and began to pull vines away from a depression in the floor of the sewer, which turned out to be a narrow opening leading to a pit.

"This is it," he said. "Do you want me to come with you to the cavern?"

"No. Hide yourself nearby, though. I'll call for you through the voodoo blood if I need you."

"You'll what?"

"We'll be able to communicate short distances without speaking. You'll know when it happens."

"Just like my sire can . . . unless I block his thoughts?"

"Something like that, yes. Now I must go."

I grasped the tree roots at the edge of the void and

lowered myself downward. Above me I heard Will clear his throat, and I looked up.

"Uh, good luck," he said sheepishly, as if any show of goodwill were a sign of weakness on his part. "I hope you find the little princess. That's what I call her—the little princess."

"Thank you." I held his gaze for a moment before I plunged onward.

I climbed down the narrow passage until the soil stopped smelling of rotten waste and began to smell of earth, though not clean, wholesome earth. There was an odor of a different kind of decay, something vastly more fetid, more poisonous. My rage built at the thought of Renee being taken to such a horrid place. And yet a sense of excitement began to course through my very blood. Will had told me he could sense Renee in the pit. With my stronger connection to her via the voodoo blood, I was beginning to feel as if she were standing right beside me. And the sensation of being near her was growing stronger the farther down I climbed.

At last I felt a firmness beneath my feet and realized I'd come to the cavern of which Will had spoken. I could hear the distant sound of an underground waterfall. But there was something else, too: Voices rose up from below me. Will had believed there was another opening in the earth leading downward from where I was standing, and that Renee could be found there.

It sounded as if at least two people were coming up from below. I hurried to hide behind a cluster of boulders that looked to be the result of some ancient, subterranean landslide. I harnessed the carefully honed powers of my mind and the strength of the voodoo blood to mask myself from detection and concentrated on blocking my outgoing thoughts, fighting to leave my mind open to any contact from Will.

With my superior eyesight, I could see through the darkness. Diana came into view, sending a series of conflicting emotions through me—longing, lust, rage. She was dressed in the modern style of sleek trousers and a clinging sweater. Her only concession to the fact that she was meters underground and not out shopping the tony boutiques of London were her heavy Wellington boots.

Beside her was a male vampire appearing to be perhaps forty human years old. I recognized him immediately and along with that recognition came a deep wave of revulsion the likes of which I had not felt in hundreds of years. It was the ancient blood drinker, my grandsire, known to me by another name. I wished that I had been able to kill him when I'd first tried, when I'd first had a chance.

"Your presentation went quite well, my dear," Ulrich said. "They could have eaten out of your hand."

Though he was perhaps better groomed, Ulrich looked much the same as he had when I'd last seen him. He had a grayish beard and shoulder-length brown hair that was also shot with gray. He was garbed in black from head to toe. Tall and thin with broad shoulders, he could have passed for a college professor, or perhaps someone in the arts. But I knew him to be a butcher and a sadist, the cruelest of my kind I'd ever met.

Diana beamed. In a different time, she might have been mistaken for a young Grace Kelly. Her golden hair flowed about her shoulders in a rich cascade, framing her classically beautiful face. She turned a gaze of adoration on Ulrich that produced a new wave of nausea in my gut. In spite of my disgust, I had the presence of mind to wonder as to Hugo's whereabouts. What could Hugo's role be in Diana and Ulrich's plan?

"Do you really think so?" she said, fluttering her long lashes. "How do you know?"

"I could *feel* it," Ulrich said. "Their power vibrates within me even now. Can't you feel it as well?"

Diana looked uncertain, but she seemed to know what answer he expected. "Yes," she agreed. "Of course. I can feel the power, too."

"Soon we'll be sharing in that power." Ulrich reached out and roughly pulled her against him. "With you at my side, we will be the most powerful force in the world of blood drinkers. Under our influence and command, we will use the vampires to rule the human world as well. There is no end to what we can do. No force will be strong enough to stop us."

"I can't wait for that day," Diana said. "I'd follow you into the depths of hell."

"That sounds like a plan," he said, and laughed.

"Tell me, do you think we will wind up being quite so . . . ugly as they are?"

Ulrich laughed again. "You and I could never be ugly. We will rule from this plane. We need not stay underground and tend the eternal fire like them. Perhaps you would like me to sample some of your beauty now."

Ulrich gave her a punishing kiss. As he groped her, she began fumbling at the fastening of his trousers. I had no desire to watch my wife have sex with another man. I turned my back to the boulders and tried to block out the sounds of their animalistic coupling.

My mind began to replay the images I'd so recently seen of Diana in her bath with a naked Hugo, and I concentrated on pushing them away. They were replaced with another unbidden memory, an older one, though so vivid that it could be happening before me. I did not want to see these things. It was as if I, too, could feel the power that Ulrich spoke of, the power that could only come from being so close to the dark lords.

Perhaps it was their collective evil that took me back to one of the most malignant and depraved episodes I have ever witnessed in my long existence.

The year was 1888. I'd grown weary of the hardships of war and reconstruction in my adopted city of Savannah. My offspring, Jack, had become self-sufficient in the years since I made him a blood drinker, and I'd trained him to manage my various business interests. So I decided to take a sabbatical from the war-torn South and all its political and social problems and return to the land of my birth for a change of scene. I much preferred the countryside when I came to visit England, but I had some business to transact in London, so I rented rooms at a fashionable address.

I was having a drink and a game of cards at a gentleman's club one night when I sensed a fellow blood drinker enter the establishment. The thrum of familiarity coursing through my body meant this was not just any vampire, but one of my own bloodline. I could tell it was not my sire, Reedrek, but I had no idea what this one's relationship could be to me.

Recognizing me as well, he sat down next to me and ordered a brandy. He reeked of the kill. He hailed me as kin, and introduced himself as my cousin.

"I've just had the most satisfying meal," he said. He was bold, taking scant care to cover his fangs as he drank. "I've something to show you, if you'd care to accompany me to Whitechapel."

I must admit I went with him as much out of curiosity as hunger, even though I had not recently fed. As we walked, the streets became more dingy with oppressive darkness and gloom. Men smoked evil-smelling cigars in the doorways of dimly lit shops. Bareheaded women clustered by twos and threes in openings to densely darkened alleys, shuddering against the damp and cold. Wretched-looking children darted in and out of unlighted passageways and up and down staircases. We passed a preacher stinking of rum who was being heckled by a few of the wayward youths thereabouts, and I remember a shoeblack waving his rag in a vain attempt to sell us his services.

"Where are we going?" I said finally. The sun would be up in a few hours' time and our walk seemed to be endless. If we were hunting, we had already passed up many suitable candidates. Any one of the adults we'd seen could have been easily separated from their friends with a few subtle, wooing words and a bit of glamour to go with them. A coin would separate some even faster.

"Have patience," my cousin said. After what seemed like hours, he led me around a corner and stopped in front of a dingy flat marked 13 MILLER'S COURT. As he opened the door he smiled and showed me in as if he were the host of a grand estate.

While Reedrek's protégé, I had been a rapacious killer of both men and women, yet I only took their life's blood to sustain me. I have killed out of hunger, out of pity, and out of rage, but never for sport. The scene that lay before me in Miller's Court was inexplicable even to one as savage as myself.

The room was awash in blood, gore, and body parts. What once was a young woman lay butchered and in pieces, barely recognizable as the remains of a human being. I looked to my host with utter disbelief. He smiled, exposing his fangs, which still bore bits of flesh. "Poor Mary," he said. "She was an Irish lass, lately of Wales."

"Why did you bring me here?" I asked. I knew it was not to feed, for the blood of the already dead is abhorrent to the vampire.

"For entertainment, of course," he said. "I thought perhaps you might have seen the newspaper headlines of late. I wanted to illustrate that your kin is a celebrity."

From time to time I am astonished at the depth of my lingering regard for humanity. It is both my blessing and my curse. It is what led me to make Jack McShane into a blood drinker when I saw him using the last of his life's energy attempting to save his fellow soldier on a blood-sodden battlefield. It has broken my heart as I held a perishing friend who refused my offer of immortal life. It was this unaccountable regard that now caused such an explosion of righteous anger that I laid hold of the savage vampire's lapels and led him outside. I dragged him into the nearest pitch-black alley and slammed him against the brick wall hard enough to crack a mortal's skull.

My fangs lengthened and my rage rose until a fine mist of blood began to emanate from my skin. I levitated off the ground and pressed my face close to his, searching his eyes for any sign of reason or sanity, much less humanity. I saw none.

"You swine," I spat. "You're Jack the Ripper!"

Jack

"Help, Uncle Jack!"

"I'm coming, Renee! Where are you?" I was running as fast as I could. A white rabbit came out of nowhere, running beside me. "Oh dear! I shall be too late!" it said, and disappeared down a rabbit hole in front of me. I heard Renee's cries again and realized they were coming from the hole, so I jumped in after the rabbit.

Down, down, down I fell, and the heat got worse the lower I fell.

I was headed to hell.

"Jack! Wake up. You're having a bad dream."

I opened my eyes to see Reyha's face looming above my own. She patted my cheeks gently. I let her help me out of my coffin and took some deep breaths.

"Are you all right?" she asked.

"Yeah, thanks. It was just a bad dream, like you said." Renee's voice and the feeling of her near me were so real I was still shaking. "You run along upstairs and check on Melaphia and Deylaud." She scampered up the stairs and I went to pour myself some blood and whiskey.

The liquor calmed my nerves, and so did the hot shower that I took once I polished off the whiskey. I told myself that the dream meant nothing and hoped with all my heart—if I still had one—that what I told myself was true.

I was glad I had something to distract me—I had a date, a real date, with Connie Jones. Of course, seeing a female impersonator perform in a goth nightclub that I helped finance would not have been my choice for a first date, but vampires couldn't be choosers. Not when it came to matters of the heart, that is. And not if the vampire was me.

I dressed up in black jeans and boots and a burnt orange dress shirt that matched my brand-new Number eight Dale Junior belt buckle. I went upstairs to check on Mel and the twins before I set off. As usual, they were at the kitchen table, the center of life in William's house.

"You look so handsome," Reyha enthused. She was still limping, but I noticed she had ditched the crutches.

"My, my, you surely do look good," Melaphia said.

"Thank you, ladies," I said with a little bow, happy that Mel sounded so normal. If she remembered implying that I was a monster the night before, she didn't show it. For my part, I was determined to put it out of my mind.

Reyha asked, "Where are you going all dressed up?"

"Werm is opening his nightclub tonight."

"I went over there earlier and blessed it for him," Mel said.

I was amazed to hear that Mel was getting out and around. As far as I knew, going to Werm's club was the first time she'd left the house since Renee was kidnapped. "That was sweet of you," I said. "I'm sure he appreciated that. What did you ask the *loa*s for?"

"I asked that the club be made safe—and profitable. I think Werm will particularly appreciate the profitability part." Mel had put on a colorful shirt and tied her dreadlocks back with a sassy red ribbon. She looked practically back to normal. The human mind has a great capacity to heal itself.

Deylaud looked better, too. Still in human form, he sat reading at the kitchen table. He looked up and smiled, then returned his attention to his book.

"How was your day other than blessing Werm's club?"

"Connie came to see us," Reyha said.

"She came to see Melaphia," Deylaud corrected.

Melaphia was working on what looked like a new beading project. The strange doll was gone. "Connie said she might talk to you," I said. "I put my foot down about that little trip she wanted me to make with her. She didn't take it well at first. I expect you backed me up—told her how dangerous it was—right?"

"We talked about it, yes," Mel said. "She told me she was going to be your date for the club opening." She looked up from her beading to fix me with a cautionary look. "Be careful, Jack. You know what I told you before."

"Vampires and goddesses don't mix. I remember."

"Don't do anything that you'll regret, like letting her hurt you. And I don't mean your *feelings*."

"I won't. I promise." I went around the table and

kissed everyone's cheeks, even Deylaud's. "I'll be home before I turn into a pumpkin. I promise."

Connie had really gotten into the goth thing for the night. She'd even put on some pale makeup, black eyeliner, and red, red lipstick. It was a pretty hot look, to tell you the truth. She wore a black sequined pants suit and a long red duster and red high heels. Be still my little bloodsucking heart.

When we got there, the joint was already jumping. A queue was even forming outside. Werm had set up one of those velvet rope lines like in the movies, complete with a bouncer with an earpiece and a clipboard. The sign on the front of the place read THE PORTAL. Whatever. When the doorman saw us, he immediately unhooked the velvet rope and motioned us in. Good for him.

Werm had said he envisioned that his club would be like Rick's Cafe in *Casablanca*. To me, it looked more like the alien bar scene in *Star Wars*. There were goths, gays, straights, punks, preppies, and, thanks to the irregulars, rednecks. And, just to round things out, vampires, werewolves, and one cockeyed zombie.

Jerry, who was a double threat as a werewolf *and* a redneck, had the delightful Wanda on his arm, and they were followed closely by Huey, who evidently was taking his bodyguarding responsibilities with dead—and I do mean dead—earnestness. He hardly took his eyes off Wanda. Actually, that wasn't quite true. His eyes wandered off Wanda with the same frequency that they wandered off everything else, but he was trying awfully hard to keep her in focus.

I caught the eye of Ginger, who was tending bar,

and bought all the irregulars a round. Tami, one of the other whores, brought out a tray loaded with amber bottles of beer. I handed one to Connie.

"I'm glad the working girls have found an honest way to make a living," she said. "I hope they don't go back to turning tricks, so I won't have to bust them."

"I hope so, too. But if worse comes to worst and you do have to wrestle Ginger to the ground, I want to be there to see it."

Connie laughed and swatted me on the arm just as Rennie walked up. "Police brutality," he charged. "You hate to see that."

"He wishes," Connie quipped.

"Who's minding the store?" I asked him. "I had no idea the whole gang would be here."

Rennie gave me a guilty grin, but not too guilty. "I decided to close up for a while. We wanted to come and stay for a couple of hours just to support Werm. It doesn't look like he needs any help from us, though. The place is packed."

"That it is. They're going to have to start turning people away at some point or expect a visit from the fire marshal. They must be close to capacity."

"And the entertainment hasn't even started yet." Rennie grinned. "Well, actually it has." He inclined his beer bottle toward the end of the bar where a tall, gorgeous blonde with an unusually large Adam's apple stood between Otis and Rufus, one arm linked through one each of theirs. The boys looked as happy as a couple of dead pigs in the sunshine.

"Don't tell me . . ." I said.

"Ain't love grand?" Rennie observed. "I hope she picks one of them to go home with."

"Don't you mean *he*?"

"Whatever."

"I hope they live happily ever after," I said.

Rennie sighed. "I want to be a bridesmaid."

"They'll make you wear a tacky dress you'll never want to wear again. One with those puffy sleeves."

"I hate it when that happens," Rennie agreed.

"Forget the wedding. I want to be a fly on the wall on the wedding *night*," I said.

"I'll drink to that." Rennie took a big swig of his beer.

"You two are awful," Connie said, laughing. Her laughter always sounded like music to me. She looked as carefree tonight as I'd ever seen her. She could have passed for a teenager. I made a mental note to thank Melaphia. Whatever she'd said to Connie must have been just what she needed to hear.

Connie inclined her head toward the dance floor. "Now there's something you don't see every day."

Jerry and Wanda were boogying the night away with Huey do-si-doing right along beside them. "Two were-wolves and a zombie cutting a rug?" I asked. "What's so unusual about that? I see it all the time."

"Uh-huh. You're a terrible liar." She studied the trio on the dance floor. "Zombies just don't have any rhythm to speak of, do they?"

"Are you kidding me? They're doing good if they're able to walk a straight line. Actually, now that I think about it, Huey's dancing will probably improve the more he has to drink."

"It sure couldn't get any worse."

The music changed and Huey modified his motions in an attempt to try and match the tempo. He looked like he'd been set upon by a swarm of invisible killer bees. "I hope his arms and legs are attached real good. I'd hate for his parts to go flying off. Halloween is over and people might ask questions if a finger wound up in their Jell-O shot."

"We're going to have to start calling Huey by his Indian name," Rennie remarked.

"What's that?"

"Dances with Werewolves."

"Hey, Rennie, what are Jerry and his date doing out in public? I thought he was bound and determined to keep her under wraps."

"He was," Rennie said. "But she whined and pleaded so long and loud that he finally gave in. The woman likes to party."

"Don't she, though?" By the look of her, she was already three sheets to the werewolf wind. She was almost as unsteady on her feet as Huey.

Werm came by with a small entourage of his goth friends. He had gussied up his usual black attire with an old-fashioned ruffled dress shirt and a long jacket that flared out from the waist. He looked like a cross between Prince and your garden-variety pimp.

"Wow, you look great," Connie said without a trace of sarcasm.

"Thanks," Werm said. He touched his cheek to hers and shook my hand. "Welcome to The Portal."

"Why did you decide to call it 'The Portal'?" I asked him.

"'Cause the first time Mel saw it, she said it was special. She thinks the ground it sits on has some kind of spiritual significance. She said she can feel it in her blood. Isn't that cool?"

"Yeah. Cool," I muttered. I barely heard him as he made introductions all around. What he said about Melaphia was kind of strange.

Werm moved on to greet other patrons and I finished off my beer. I couldn't much relate to the crazy music they were playing. Give me classic country anytime. Merle Haggard is my troubadour of choice. Marty Robbins was a close second, God rest his soul. I tapped Souxi on the shoulder as she moved past us with a tray of cocktails. I put a ten spot on her tray and whispered in her ear, "Ask the disc jockey to play something you can slow dance to. Something old and sappy." She gave me a wink and disappeared.

I set my empty beer bottle on the bar to the opening notes of Elvis's "Fools Rush In." "May I have this dance?"

Connie favored me with a flirtatious smile. "I'd love to," she said.

I took her hand, led her onto the floor, and pulled her close as Mr. Presley cautioned about fools rushing in. At least that's what all the wise men said. I'd been called a lot of things in my time, but wise wasn't one of them.

Maybe Melaphia was right about this being a special place. With Connie in my arms I could feel the pull of something elemental, something greater than the two of us. When she laid her head on my shoulder, I forgot all my troubles and just for a minute all was right with the world and rivers were flowing gently to the sea.

I held my woman's warm, vibrant, living body next to mine and something very much like happiness coursed through my undead being. No less an authority than Elvis Aaron Presley crooned that some things were meant to be. *Take my hand,* he said. *Take my whole life, too.*

When Connie tilted her face up to mine, I couldn't help falling in love with her. Forgetting myself, I gathered her closer and bent to kiss her. Just before our lips met, a force arced between us that drove our faces apart again. A thin blue flame sparked in the air in front of us for a split second and then was gone.

A few of the dancers nearby noticed, but they must have thought it was a bar trick, because they turned right back to their partners. Over Connie's shoulder I happened to make eye contact with Seth, who was standing at the bar sipping a beer and wearing a poker face. He'd seen it, too.

The music changed to something with a primitive beat like drums in the jungle, and Connie and I walked back to the bar trying to pretend we weren't shaken by what had just happened.

"What are you drinking?" Seth said casually.

"Beer," Connie said.

"I just love a woman of refinement and good taste," Seth said and held up three fingers for Ginger. He passed us our bottles and kept one for himself. "Who's that with Jerry?" Seth asked. Any new werewolf in town was always of interest to him.

"It's the woman I've been looking for." Connie lowered her voice and narrowed her eyes at him meaningfully.

"The one you told me about the other night at the swamp?" Seth asked.

"That's the one."

"Has she been with Jerry the whole time?"

"Yep," Connie said.

"I'll be damned."

"Uh-oh," Connie said. "Look who just came in."

That would be Nate Thrasher—with Sally on his arm. "That kid just doesn't have a dab of sense," I said. "I told her he was dangerous."

The music stopped and Werm jumped up on the tiny stage. "Welcome to The Portal. I hope everybody's having a good time!" The crowd cheered its approval and Werm waited for the noise to die down before he continued his introduction. "For our opening night, we have somebody really special to entertain us. Please give it up for the Lady Chianti!" The crowd cheered again and Werm hopped down from the stage.

"The Lady Chianti?" Seth asked skeptically.

"They say she's a poor man's Lady Chablis," Connie explained.

Speaking of poor men, I saw Otis and Rufus on the edge of their bar stools, clapping like a couple of lunatics. Otis put his thumb and index finger to his mouth and whistled. I'd bet the garage that their bar tab would wrap around the building twice.

"Where did Werm find her?" Rennie joined us again and set a plate of wings down on the bar.

"Double-damned if I know," I said.

"He looks so familiar," Connie said. "Oh, I know where I know him from. I busted him one time."

"For what?" I asked.

"Solicitation," Connie said, glancing at the barmaids meaningfully.

"Ouch," Seth said.

"Well, maybe he—she . . . whoever, has decided to go straight," I suggested.

The three of them rolled their eyes at me. "Or not," I said.

The lady, dripping with emerald green sequins and spangles, began by belting out some obscure Johnny Mercer tune that I doubt the twenty-somethings in the crowd had ever heard. Still they gravitated forward to get a better look at the performer, who was strutting from one end of the stage to the other, pausing now and then to fling the ends of her fluttering feather boa behind her.

It was right about that time that Nate got a gander of Wanda with Jerry, and Jerry got a good look at Nate looking at him and Wanda. What Sally was lacking in judgment she made up for in eyesight, and she spied all three of them. Poor Huey's googly eyes went every which way.

Seth and Connie and I just looked at one another.

"Oh, shit," we said as one.

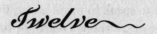

Twelve

William

"What did that helpless girl ever do to you?" I demanded.

The demon before me looked nonplussed. "Why, whatever do you mean, dear boy?"

"You didn't merely feed. You dismembered her." I peered into his eyes. I desperately wanted to understand the depths of his evil. This creature was one of my own kind. Was he the aberration or was I?

"I did it because I could," he said. "And because it amused me." He smiled broadly, showing a pair of stiletto-like fangs so long I realized he must be the most ancient blood drinker I'd ever encountered. I now realized why I'd seen a hint of his fangs in the public house. He wasn't just being careless. They were hard to disguise because they were large—and he was very, very old.

"Yes, I am," he answered my unspoken question. "Very old indeed. I walked these streets as a Roman centurion, boy. You do not wish to make me angry."

Did he dare to speak to me of anger, that which fueled me, drove me, sustained me? If he had never seen me, he had never seen anger. I seized him by the shoulders and hurled him backward once again. This time he struck the brick wall hard enough to crack the masonry.

He looked at me in shock. "What the devil?" he said. "Why are you so strong? You can't have been a blood drinker more than a few centuries."

I saw no need to enlighten him about my special gift and where it had come from. Though this most ancient vampire possessed the strength of ten blood drinkers due to his years, my voodoo blood, powered by my anger, made no worthy adversaries. He might kill me anyway. But since I cared little for my life, I might as well die fighting the kind of inhumanity I despised.

I pummeled him with my fists until his face dripped with blood. Still he caught me by the throat in one viselike hand and shook me like a cat shakes a mouse. "This grows tiresome," he said, and flung me out onto the street. He dusted himself off, his wounds already healing. He ran an index finger across a gash in his chin right before it closed, put his finger into his mouth, and sucked as an urchin would suck a stick of penny candy.

"You never answered me," he said in the tone of a schoolmaster. "Why are you so strong?"

I scrambled to my feet and launched myself at him. I hit him in the midsection and sent him sprawling back into the alley. I continued forward and leapt on him. My palm struck something hard and I felt the outline of a weapon inside his coat. He made to grab my wrists, but I was too fast for him. I had the blade in my hand before he could stop me.

"Is this what you used on her?" I asked.

He drew back his hand to strike me, but I blocked the blow and brought the blade down on his neck. Blood spurted from his carotid artery and he clutched at it with both hands as if he could stanch the flow.

As soon as I'd cut him, a searing pain doubled me over. I was swept up in confusion. He hadn't punched or kicked me. Luckily he was in no shape to take advantage of my distress.

I knew that his knife wound would heal as well, though not as quickly as the superficial cuts I'd inflicted on him. I was determined to sever this madman's head.

I drew back for the killing blow but he flung me away from him. His head lolled to the side like that of a ghastly doll. Before his body collapsed back into the dirt, I could see that his head dangled from just a small scrap of sinew. As I advanced on him again I felt another thunderbolt of pain. Then I heard behind me the cry of "Murder!"

I sprang to my feet and raced down the alley as best I could despite my agony. I did not look behind me. I could hear footsteps, but knew that no mortal could catch me even in my weakened state. When I reached the head-high wooden fence at the end of the alley, I vaulted it. Cries of "God save us!" echoed behind me as I continued running through the winding passages between the tenements until I was far away.

Now my thoughts were brought back to the present by a cry of pain from Diana. It was evident to me why I had been struck by sickness all those years ago outside that Whitechapel tenement. Ulrich, the demon known then as Jack the Ripper, was my grandsire. If I had succeeded in killing him, I would most likely have died. Had he been my sire, my death would have been certain. With one generation removed, I might have survived killing him, but I doubt if I ever would have fully recovered.

Diana screamed again. The sadistic monster she was having congress with was hurting her. In that moment I knew that the love for her that I'd carried with me for centuries had died a slow and agonizing death.

When I thought of her innocence on our wedding night, her eagerness to learn how to please me with her body, I was sickened. There was no way to reconcile the woman she was in life with the blood drinker she'd become. And why should there be? Weren't we all demons in the end?

I thought of myself when I was living. I'd had a kind of innocence as well. As a young man, my vision of evil was the antique, hand-illustrated picture of a serpent in the family Bible, inked by one of the monks at the local monastery. Later, when I met Reedrek, I came face-to-face with evil incarnate. But Reedrek himself was like an altar boy compared to his own sire. Ulrich was a Satan unto himself.

I wondered about we who are loath to hurt anyone beyond the temporary sting it takes to drink a human's blood, and those vampires who relish the kill enough to veritably bathe in blood. Clearly, the vampire Diana and I were not the same kind of blood drinker, and any dream I'd had of our reconciliation in undeath was pointless. Forging an alliance with Ulrich put her solidly in the camp of evil.

What troubled me now was not knowing with certainty on which side my son, Will, resided. He'd committed unthinkable savagery, and yet he'd shown tenderness for a small, defenseless human. I must watch him carefully.

As for Jack, my other "son," I knew without a doubt that he would retain his love for humankind even as a blood drinker. In the hundred and fifty years, give or take, since the night I first saw him, he had never disappointed me in that regard.

More screams brought my thoughts back to Diana. Where was Hugo, the vampire who had protected her for five hundred years? When they were in Savannah, they had been so inseparable that it had been difficult to get her alone to talk to her privately, but lately she'd appeared to abandon him in favor of her new benefactor. It seemed that my lady whore would open her legs for whichever male could help her to build her power and advance her ambitions.

When his grunts of release indicated their foul coupling was over, I peered back through the darkness. If I had any doubt this was the same blood drinker I'd nearly killed in the late nineteenth century, they vanished when I saw the deep scar along his throat.

"There," Ulrich said, zipping up his trousers. "That should give you an extra boost in power for the second part of your proposal to the Council. You should be able to 'knock them dead,' as the humans say."

"Thank you, master," Diana said, reclothing herself. "Your every touch is much appreciated. Do you really think the Council is amenable to my plan?"

"Yes, Diana. I think that as a vampire Renee's voodoo blood will benefit the Council immensely.

Think of the power I—I mean they—will be able to control. And more power is of vital importance since the discovery of the prophecy."

My first instinct was to vault the distance between Diana and me to rip her apart with my bare hands and fangs. That she had birthed the brainchild of sacrificing Renee to the Council drove me instantly toward madness. The horror of it nearly brought me to my knees. But I had to bide my time. I was able to overpower this monster Ulrich once, but I'd seen Diana display her own strength in Savannah, and even with the voodoo blood, I might not succeed in taking on both of them.

"The prophecy." Diana rubbed her arms and looked troubled by something. "When is this abomination supposed to appear in our midst?"

"The dark lords do not seem to know for sure. For all we know, the Slayer may already be among us."

Jack

Nate stomped over to where Wanda had fastened herself to Jerry on the dance floor. "Where in the hell have you been, woman?" he yelled. "And what are you doing with this sonofabitch?"

"I've been with Jerry. He knows how to treat a woman," declared Wanda. "He ain't always slapping me around like you done."

"And where do you get off calling my mama a bitch?" Jerry demanded. "She was one of your own people, and you treated her like dirt."

"I'll treat whoever I want however I want, and that goes double for my wife!"

"Not no more, it don't," Wanda said, standing tall. "I'm through with you."

Nate stepped forward, grabbed Wanda by the arm, and hauled her toward him. Behind him, Sally said, "Hey! Do you want to be with me or her?"

"Shut up, you cheap little hooker," Nate said.

Jerry started to go after Nate, but before he could take a step, Huey the bodyguard got between them, opened his mouth as wide as he could, and bit down on the biceps of the arm Nate held Wanda with.

Looking at Nate, I couldn't help but think: cheap hooker, fifty dollars; drinks at a goth club, fifteen dollars; getting bitten for the very first time by someone who *wasn't* a fellow werewolf? Priceless.

The look on Nate's face, sure enough, was something to behold. It was one thing to be bitten by a fellow wolf you were having a regular wolf fight with. But having a more or less ordinary-looking human put the bite on you with a set of normal *Homo sapiens* choppers had to be a new experience.

Nate shook him off, and Huey went flying backward, taking a big chunk of Nate's biceps with him. Nate roared in pain and Huey wound up knocking three or four clubgoers in different directions like so many bowling pins. That got the people *they* knocked over all riled up, and before you knew it, people all over the room were pushing, shoving, and punching.

Seth, Connie, and I started forward, pulling folks off of other folks and trying to calm people down. Out of the corner of my eye, I saw Sally pull Wanda's hair about the same time that Jerry landed a punch on Nate's jaw. On the other end of the room, I saw Rufus and Otis going toward the stage to rescue the lovely Lady Chianti from the unpleasantness.

About this time, I thought about the night I averted a massive fight at the swamp bar, and I wondered if the same thing would work here. But as I analyzed the situation I realized two things. One, in the swamp bar, I was afraid I was going to have to be a participant. And two, here in Werm's bar, I was just having too much fun as an observer. Besides, the main combatants were werewolves, and my glamour probably wouldn't work on them with all these people around anyway.

Otis and Rufus crawled up onto the stage. The lady reached down to give them each a hand, but Rufus, in his inebriated state, missed her proffered hand—as large and as strong as it was—and instead got a hank of her long, flowing hair.

To say that the lady flipped her wig over Rufus would not be an understatement. He came away holding up the hair of his lady fair like a knight showing off the favor he had been given by a noble maiden after winning a tournament. A drinking tournament maybe. As drunk as he was, it took him a couple of beats to figure out why he had a handful of hair. Perhaps in the melee he figured the lady had been scalped by a roaming band of wild Indians. Otis worked it out a little faster since he was on his feet on the stage by then and had gotten a closer look at the lady's face—and probably her five o'clock shadow—in the footlights.

Otis wisely excused himself and jumped down from the stage. The last I saw of him, he was staggering out the door, leaving the lady—as well as the bar tab—to the better man.

Chianti, whose real name I found out later was Eric, hauled Rufus to his feet, slapped her wig back on her head, and like the trouper she was, continued the show. By the time she started in on the high-leg kicks, Rufus had figured things out and was looking for a graceful exit. The younger patrons, who had crowded the stage earlier, were totally ignoring the fight behind them. Instead they attempted to form themselves into a mosh pit and regaled Rufus with shouts of "Dive! Dive!"

He dove. Right about that time the moshers decided to renege on their implied support, and poor Rufus went sprawling. Fortunately for him, he was so pickled I doubt if he felt a thing.

About that time, Werm materialized at my elbow. "Jack, do something!" he said.

"What?"

"You know. That glamour thing. Put the whammy on 'em. They're busting up the bar stools. We're losing money here. *Your* money."

That got my attention and made it worth a try. "Oh, okay." I thought about having people dance again, but I wanted to try something new, so I concentrated on a different command.

Don't worry. Be happy.

The disc jockey got my psychic suggestion right away and actually started playing the record. Dang, I thought. I'm good. People started calming down immediately and started swaying to the island beat instead of waling on one another. Who'd've thought he'd even have that song in his collection?

"Thanks, Jack. I owe you one," Werm said.

"That and a lot of green," I said.

I joined back up with Seth, Rennie, and Connie at the bar. "Everybody okay?" I asked.

"I'm fine," Connie said. "Much more fighting and I might have had to arrest somebody. It's funny how the brawl just stopped like that. Just like that fight at the swamp bar stopped before it had a chance to get going." She looked at Seth and me for an explanation.

"Don't look at me," Seth said. "I'm not the one with the undead mojo."

"It's kind of a vampire trick," I said. "I've only used it a couple of times. I just learned lately that I could do it at all."

Connie looked at me with something like fascination. "What are your other vampire tricks?"

I wiggled my eyebrows. "Play your cards right and you might find out."

Seth made a little snort of disgust. "I think that's my cue to leave. I've got to get my beauty sleep."

"Oh, that's right," Connie said, growing serious. "You have a fight tomorrow night. Are you sure I can't talk you out of it?"

"I'm sure," Seth said, laying a bill on the bar.

"Good luck then." Connie stood on tiptoe to give him a kiss on the cheek. "Break a leg. Or whatever it is that would be a lucky charm for a dominance fight."

" 'Break a leg' will do. Jack talked you out of going, I hope." Seth looked at me and I shrugged.

"He tried," Connie said.

"Connie—" Seth began.

"Okay, okay," she said. "I won't go."

Seth heaved a sigh of relief, which only proved to me that he didn't know Connie half as well as I did. If he thought she was staying away from the swamp tomorrow night, well, I had some of that swampland I'd sell him real cheap.

"Jack, can I speak to you for a minute? I want to go over a couple of things before I leave."

"Sure." I put my arm around Connie's waist and gave her a little squeeze. "I'll be right back, darlin'."

Seth and I stepped out into the cold night. Groups of young people clustered in twos and threes smoking and laughing in the parking lot. Seth led me to a spot out of their earshot.

"What the hell are you thinking, Jack?"

Seth's tone took me completely by surprise. "What the hell do you mean, what the hell am I thinking?"

"The electricity between you and Connie comes close to setting that place on fire, and an hour later you're joking about showing her your vampire tricks?"

"What are you getting at exactly?"

"I don't know what's going on between you and Connie but it looks to me like you're literally playing with fire. Something potentially dangerous is passing back and forth between you. I know you must be able to feel it because even I can. Hell, maybe even humans can, it's so strong."

"Of course I can feel it. Connie and I have something really special."

"Don't give me that 'something special' crap. Whatever it is, you obviously can't control it."

"What's your point?" By that time we'd raised our voices and the humans nearby were starting to look our way, maybe anticipating another fight.

"The point is, you're getting into something over your head." Seth lowered his voice again. "Listen,

Connie and you are both my friends and I don't want to see either of you get hurt physically or mentally. I know that she hasn't worked out . . . what she *is* exactly yet, and maybe that has something to do with what's going on. I guess all I'm saying is . . . for God's sake, Jack, be careful."

At that moment, all my frustration with being undead, my little affliction, as I like to call it, bubbled to the surface. The not being able to see Connie in the sunlight, the not being able to sleep with her—everything. "What's this really about, Seth?"

Seth narrowed his gold-green eyes. "What do you mean by that?"

"One day you tell me you're going to bow out where Connie's concerned and then the next you're coming up with excuses why her and me shouldn't be together."

"You *can't* be serious," Seth growled.

I'd heard werewolves start getting twitchy in the days leading up to the full moon. I could believe it. Despite the cold, Seth wore a short-sleeved polo shirt. I could see that the hairs on his arms were raised.

"I'm just saying," I said.

Seth took a menacing step toward me. Out of the corner of my eye I could see the humans back off, even though they were already a safe distance away. "If I thought I could get Connie to take me back, I would be with her right now, and there's not a damn thing you could do about it."

"Bullshit. She's into me, man. You're just jealous. You can't have her yourself, so you don't want anybody else to have her, especially not me. Especially not a *vampire*."

I think I may have forgotten to mention something kind of important about vampires and werewolves. They mostly don't get along. Jerry and Seth being friends with me is not the normal state of things. I don't know why it is, but in most cases we're natural enemies. I'd never felt that way about Seth until right then.

"I'm going to forget you said that," Seth said in a low, rumbling voice.

"Whatever," I said, showing fang.

"I'm going to leave now, before *I* say something I'm going to regret. But let me tell you this, *pal*. Don't show up at the swamp tomorrow night. I don't want you there. I don't trust you enough to watch my back, so just stay home."

I took a breath to answer him something snarky right back, but I stopped myself. This was serious. He couldn't go into that fight without a second. I wanted to speak out, tell him I was sorry, that I didn't mean what I'd said, but I couldn't.

It was a man thing. So instead, I watched my friend walk away, maybe for the last time.

"Fine," I said to his back.

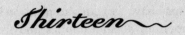

Thirteen

William

Prophecy? Slayer? I made a mental note to ask Olivia, the scholar, about the matter of a slayer in some prophecy. I didn't like the sound of a vampire slayer, but I would have to think about that another time. Right now, getting Renee back was my first and only priority.

"What about the matter of Hugo, my lord?" Diana said, reverting to a kind of speech I hadn't heard in hundreds of years.

"I take it you wish to be rid of him?"

"Yes, my lord," Diana said, her eyes downcast like a maiden's.

"The Council will be expecting an offering of food. We'll serve up Hugo. A human virgin is the traditional sacrifice, of course, but as we are making Renee a vampire, we'll substitute Hugo. He's old enough and powerful enough to satisfy their thirst. I'll go and summon him whenever the Council says it is ready. He'll come along on the pretense that you suggested."

"I don't know how to thank you, my lord."

Ulrich leered, his yellowed fangs flashing. "Oh, yes you do."

I almost felt sorry for Hugo. Almost. He had outlived his usefulness with Diana at long last, and she would serve him up like a suckling pig. Diana and Ulrich left, disappearing through a passage on the other side of the cavern. I had begun to follow them when my head suddenly rang with calls for help. The voices were not as strong as Jack's were whenever he contacted me through the psychic connection of offspring to sire. But thanks to traces of the voodoo blood and a familial bond, I could hear them. They vibrated with alarm.

Come back quickly! Fire! Help! I heard Olivia shout.

I'm on my way now, Will said.

Damnation, what could be happening? I had only a moment to decide what to do. I couldn't lose my chance to find Renee, but Olivia and the other vampires I was counting on to help me were in jeopardy.

The path to Renee led directly to wherever the old lords had ensconced themselves underground. That much I could tell. In fact, my sense of her was so strong that I was sure it would lead me straight to her. But Diana and Ulrich—and perhaps the lords themselves— were between me and her. I needed reinforcements, and the only vampires I could call on were in danger at this moment. I didn't have any choice but to go to them.

I climbed as quickly as I could, glad that I hadn't let Will go any farther with me. At least he was closer to

Olivia's house. When I got to the sewers I ran as fast as my legs would carry me.

When I reached the surface, I could see the flames shooting from the roof of the vampires' house and could hear the sirens. I thought it best to approach from the back garden. Still, when I got there, I had to elbow my way past half a dozen gawkers. Several of the vampires lay coughing on the grass and were being tended to by a number of people I'd never met, probably neighbors.

I met Will coming out the door. With one hand he held Donovan across his shoulder. With the other he beat frantically at his own head and shoulders, trying to extinguish the flames that leapt from his body and clothing. I threw him and Donovan to the ground, removed my coat, and smothered the flames. Donovan was unconscious. He was alive and breathing, but I could see serious burns on his extremities.

"I had to break him out of his coffin," Will gasped.

I turned to my son. His hair had burned on one side and was emitting a ghastly odor. The right side of his head, his neck, and his shoulders oozed with blood and charred, raw flesh. He must have been in enormous pain, but he gave no sign of it.

"Donovan's going to be fine. So are you, but you need blood to heal."

"There are more of Olivia's kin in the house. I think they're in the coffin room."

"You'll be fine here. I'll be back as soon as I can." Will nodded and lay back on the grass.

When I reached the back door, I could see flames down the hallway, but the door to the downstairs was clear and wide open. I ran down to the coffin room and found it engulfed in smoke. I could see the silhouettes of several of the vampires as they rushed around the room. One of them ran by me, his arms full of books and papers.

Through the smoke, I saw Andrew across the room. "What are you doing?" I demanded. "You've got to get out of here. The roof could collapse at any second."

"Did Will get Donovan out?" he yelled between violent coughs.

"Yes. Did you hear me? You must go." Andrew continued scrambling around in a small area in the corner. "Are you all mad? Everyone out!" I commanded.

The vampires save Andrew finally heeded me. They went running up the stairs, their arms laden with printed material. Some appeared to be carrying flat stones. This had to be the historical research Olivia had described earlier. They were risking their lives to save it.

"Where is Olivia?" I called. Andrew finally seemed to be moving toward the exit, dragging a trunk so full of material, the lid wouldn't fully shut.

"She's upstairs!" Some of the papers hanging from the trunk caught fire. Andrew didn't pause to extinguish them, but instead chose to keep moving.

I cursed and ran back up to the foyer. The flames were licking at the staircase leading to the next floor, although they had not fully engulfed it. I charged up the steps two at a time. "Olivia!" I shouted.

"Here! Help me!" Olivia's scream rang from the bedroom at the end of the hall. I could barely see the door for the flames. I crouched down and hugged my arms to my sides. When I pushed through the doorway, the heat wrapped around me as if I'd instantly plunged into the depths of hell.

Not even the keen eyesight of the vampire could penetrate the density of the smoke. Olivia was coughing on the floor—I *felt* her rather than saw her. I helped her to her feet, but she started in the wrong direction. "This way!" I yelled, hauling her along with me.

We were at the top of the staircase when a flaming rafter fell into our path. Olivia screamed again and I lifted her into my arms and leapt through the flames, coming to rest on the landing below. When we crossed the threshold of the back door, our clothes were on fire.

We circled to the front yard, where the crowd of onlookers had grown considerably. Firefighters had arrived as well. They wrapped us in blankets and doused us with water.

Will was busy reassuring a man who seemed to be the firefighters' captain; he was explaining that everyone was now out of the building. Apparently Andrew had organized the vampires in a tidy group on the lawn. Behind them was a much less tidy pile of the material they had saved from the house. Donovan, still unconscious, lay on the grass, covered with my greatcoat. A couple of the other vampires were watching over him.

I could see that none of the vampires had escaped injury. They huddled together and tended to one another's wounds. Some of them were moaning in pain. By my count, two of them were missing.

The firemen began to pump a great arc of water into

the house through a hole in the roof. Despite that, I doubted much of the structure could be saved. Olivia trembled and extricated herself from the throng of firefighters and their questions and came over to me.

"What happened?" I asked, lowering my voice to a pitch no human could hear.

"Hugo," she whispered. "Finn and Joseph heard noises a short while ago and went to investigate. Hugo was in the back garden with a bottle of petrol."

"A Molotov cocktail. Crude but effective," I muttered. There is little a vampire fears more than fire, as it is one of the few things that can kill a blood drinker. Inhaling smoke will sear our lungs just as it would a human's. The difference, of course, is that a vampire can heal much more quickly. But time, rest, and blood are required.

As I watched the little throng of injured blood drinkers, I knew that none of them would be of any use to me; not even Will could help me to get Renee back. I noticed Olivia clutching something against her midsection. It was a book. Of course. I should have known that was what drew her into the fire. She'd kept a genealogy book of sorts—the history of all female blood drinkers, her life's work.

She saw the direction of my gaze. "I couldn't lose it, William."

"I understand." I nodded toward the group of vampires. Finn and Joseph, I now realized, were the ones who were missing. "I take it Finn and Joseph fought with Hugo."

"He staked them. They're ashes now. Like Alger's house." Olivia's lip trembled.

"What happened to him after he threw the bomb?"

"The coward ran," Olivia said bitterly. "He dispatched Finn and Joseph first. But the house was on fire by then, and we had to save ourselves."

"And your research," I commented. Olivia nodded. "Are those old papers and tablets worth lives, then?"

Olivia looked me in the eye. "Yes," she said simply. "They are. Someday you'll be convinced of that as well."

I started to reply when I noticed that stretchers were being unloaded from ambulances. "You must be strong now," I advised. "You and your vampires have to convince the authorities not to take you to hospital. Tell them you have . . . religious objections, perhaps."

Olivia laughed, and there was hysteria in the sound. But the thought of having any of her people wake up tomorrow in a sunny hospital room jarred her into action. "I'll think of something. And then I'll have to figure out where we're going to spend the daylight hours."

"Don't you have a backup location?" All vampires maintained at least one—ideally several—backup lairs where they could get their daytime sleep if something happened to their primary residence. Not to have taken this lifesaving precaution for herself and her coven would be gross negligence on Olivia's part.

"Our old one was compromised just before Alger left. He assigned me the task of finding a new one, but I just never found the time. I'm sorry."

"You've no need to apologize to me," I said. "It's your own coven you've let down."

"What are you going to do?" she asked miserably.

"I'll have to go in for Renee alone. I will go back underground until the sun rises. Then, when the others are taking their sleep, I'll make off with Renee. I'll free Eleanor as well and go directly to the airport with them, where my jet is waiting."

"You . . . you're not going to come back and check on us? To make sure we've made it to safety and have found blood to heal and sustain us?" Olivia asked this as if she couldn't believe what she was hearing. "What if we need you? What if Hugo comes back? Worse, what if Ulrich and Diana come here looking for you and Renee? They know we're here, William. As you just said, we need time to heal. You've got to help us!"

"Do I?" I asked coldly. "After all you've done for me recently? You hid Diana's existence from me for your own purposes. And now you've committed the ultimate in unforgivable negligence by not making sure your own coven was secure, thereby rendering yourself and them useless to me."

Olivia's gray eyes widened. "What about what you've done to me and my vampires? Do you think I don't know how Hugo found us? Think about it. You must have been careless with Eleanor. How dare you speak to me of negligence! She sought your whereabouts through your shared bond, and she found you. You can feel her even now, can't you?"

"Surely Eleanor could not have been so foolish as to betray me to Hugo a second time." But even as I said it, I realized that I had been the foolish one for believing I could control her with the promise of rescue at my convenience. Even though Hugo had abused her, she'd thrown her lot in with him again and betrayed my whereabouts.

I had left the psychic portal to Eleanor's thoughts

open so I could enjoy the eroticism of her calls to me. That in turn left her with an opening to sense my presence. My lust, my Achilles' heel, had given her the opportunity to betray me once again.

Olivia turned away from me and rushed over to persuade the authorities to leave her people on their own. She would have her hands full finding a place to stay and transporting the vampires and the little mountain of papers and other research material to wherever they decided to hide. And then there was the matter of procuring fresh blood, never easy even under the best of circumstances.

Will staggered over to where I stood, clutching his wounded side. The pain of his injuries was setting in, and I feared that the burns to his neck and shoulders might only be the beginning.

"What do you want me to do?" he asked. His question astonished me since only a few hours before he had expressed reluctance to come to Savannah for fear that he might have to, as he put it, play by my rules.

"Stay with Olivia. Help her any way you can. Start with finding a place for her vampires to stay after the sun comes up."

"But what about Renee?" he asked. "None of them will be able to help you now. You only have me." Even as he spoke, he wavered on his feet as if a stiff wind would blow him to the ground.

"You can't help me. You'll do well to remain conscious until sunrise. You have to help Olivia get these vampires to safety. Especially Donovan."

Will looked back at Olivia and the other vampires, who were arguing with the emergency workers. After a moment he looked back at me. "I can't let you go alone."

"I must. This is my fight after all."

"But the old lords know you're here now. That must be why Hugo came here."

"And they're also convinced that I either died in the fire or am busy dealing with its aftermath. They don't know that I'm aware of their plans." There was no need to burden Will with the additional knowledge I'd gained.

Will swayed violently and I caught him before he hit the ground. I carried him gently to a stone bench and set him down. "In the course of your existence, you have lived in this city longer than Olivia. I'll wager you have forgotten more of its underground nooks than she ever knew. Help her to get the others to safety and I'll talk to you when night falls again."

Will nodded, and I could tell he was having a difficult time keeping me in focus. I wanted to bite into my wrist and let him feed from me, but there were too many humans present. They had important work to do, and I could not put them under my glamour. Will would be unable to follow me, and that was probably for the best.

I made my way into the misty darkness. I would secrete myself underground, as close to Renee as I could. Then, when my senses told me the time was right I would make my move. Woe to any vampire who came between me and the daughter of the greatest *mambo* in the New World.

But first I must accomplish another most necessary task. I needed to cure my case of denial once and for all.

Jack

I went back into the club. People were still not worrying and being happy. I, on the other hand, felt as low as a snake's belly. Rennie, sporting a big, silly grin because of my spell, came up and patted me on the shoulder. "What's wrong with you, man? You look like you just lost your best friend."

"Maybe I have," I muttered.

"Huh?"

"Never mind." Connie was dancing with Werm and Huey, and the warring werewolves were nowhere to be seen. While I was able to calm down all the human patrons with my spell, the trance didn't seem to have worked too well on the werewolves.

"Hey, Ren, where did Jerry and Wanda go? And what happened to Nate Thrasher, the guy who started the fight?"

Rennie shrugged. "I don't know. I wasn't paying any attention."

"Why don't you go back to the shop and see if Jerry took Wanda back there? Nate is out to get Jerry for messing with his woman and I just want to make sure they got away from him without any more trouble."

"No problem," Rennie said, draining his beer. "I need to go back and open up for business anyway. Besides, Huey needs his beauty sleep."

"Like that's going to do him any good." Huey could sleep as long as Rip van Winkle and not be any more pleasant to look at, but you still didn't want a cranky, sleep-deprived zombie on your hands. Now that I thought of it, most people didn't want any kind of zombie on their hands, or anywhere else for that matter.

But I had made my undead bed, and I had to sleep in it, so to speak.

Rennie waved for Huey to follow him, and the little zombie shambled out the door at his heels. I tapped Werm on the shoulder. "Mind if I cut in?" I said.

"She's all yours." Werm smiled and made his way back toward the bar.

If that were only true. It was a good thing they were playing an up-tempo tune, so I wouldn't be tempted to slow dance again.

"I've had a great time," Connie said as we danced.

" 'Had'? You sound like you're ready to go."

"Don't you have to get your rest so you'll be strong for the fight tomorrow night?"

"Uh—yeah. I guess so." I thought about that. I knew I had to help Seth, despite the fight we'd just had. The way I saw it, I had to be there now more than ever.

"So why don't we call it a night?"

"Yeah, let's do."

We said our good-byes and gave our congratulations to Werm. It had been a memorable opening night—despite the fisticuffs. Or maybe because of them.

"I've got to hand it to you, little buddy," I told him. "I was skeptical at first."

"No!" Werm feigned shock, then laughed.

"Wise guy," I said. "Anyway, now that I've seen the place, I'm impressed. You've done a great job, and I think this is going to be a nice little enterprise for you."

Werm looked truly touched. "Thanks, Jack. That means a lot coming from you. Who knows, maybe you'll even get your investment back."

"I'd better. I know where you live."

"Where does he live?" Connie asked.

"As of tonight, the basement of this place," Werm said.

"Listen," I told him. "I'll pick you up here at sundown tomorrow night. We've got a fight to go to."

Werm's face fell a little, but he recovered quickly. "Will do."

Connie and I left and walked to the Corvette. I cleared my throat when she started to open the door for herself. She stood back and rolled her eyes. "My, but aren't you the old-fashioned gentleman."

"You can take the boy out of the nineteenth century, but you can't take the nineteenth century out of the boy," I said. "Old habits die hard, I guess."

When we reached her apartment building Connie said, "Given what happened to us on the dance floor tonight, I think it's best that you don't come up with me. Okay?"

"I guess you're right," I admitted, disappointed.

She leaned her head against the seat and closed her eyes. "What are we going to do, Jack? How are we going to solve this . . . this problem of ours?"

I shook my head, unable to speak. I wanted to tell her that I would be happy to flame out forever in exchange for one night with her. But I couldn't seem to say anything. Connie seemed to understand. She reached out to cover my hand with her own, but stopped herself and sighed.

"Thanks for tonight," she said finally. "It was a really . . . memorable date." I started to get out and come around the car to open her door, but she was too fast for me.

"I don't need you to get the door," she said. "I'm an able-bodied woman."

"You can say that again," I said, almost managing a laugh.

"We'll talk soon. Don't get hurt tomorrow night, and keep an eye on Seth and Werm."

"I will," I promised.

She pressed the fingers of one hand to her lips and then waved good-bye with them. I watched her all the way into the building before I pulled away from the curb.

When I got back to the shop, Rennie and Huey were the only ones there. Otis and Rufus were probably too embarrassed to show their faces. I was more troubled by the fact that Jerry and Wanda were not in attendance.

"Have you heard from Jerry?" I asked Rennie.

"Not at all. Wanda neither," Rennie said. He was tuning up a vintage Plymouth Fury.

Huey, seated on a nearby stool, paused in his gnawing on a raw pork chop. "I'm sorry, Jack," he said earnestly.

"What for, H-bomb?"

"I didn't protect Wanda like you said. Her and Jerry got away."

"You did the best you could, man. Don't worry about it. I must say, you were looking bodacious on the dance floor tonight."

If the little guy had had any blood circulating, I would have sworn that he blushed. "Miss Connie was awfully nice to dance with me. I sure do like your girl-friend a lot, Jack."

"How do you know she's my girlfriend?" Although we were at the dance together, I'd never tried to get affectionate with Connie in front of the guys here at the shop.

"Why, shoot. I can tell by your face how good she makes you feel when she's around."

I must be pretty transparent if even a zombie could tell how far gone I was.

"What are you thinking where Jerry and Wanda are concerned?" Rennie asked. "Do you think that Nate did something to hurt them?"

"I don't know," I said. "There's nothing much we can do until and unless Jerry or Wanda contacts us for help. There's too much other stuff going on. I've got to go over to the house and check on Melaphia and them. Let me know if you hear anything from Jerry or Wanda."

Rennie agreed, and Huey waved good-bye. As I left, I saw Huey bite the bone in two and suck out the marrow. I was glad that his choppers were still in good working order after he took a plug out of Nate the werewolf.

I hopped back into the 'Vette and started over to William's. On the way my conscience started to bother me again where Seth was concerned. If for some reason an anvil fell on my head and I wasn't able to help him out tomorrow night as I planned, I wouldn't be able to forgive myself. The twins were taking good care of Mel like they always did. If I went to check on them now I would only wake them up. Besides, they knew I always had my cell turned on and they could call me if they ever needed help.

I decided to go to my place, apologize to Seth, stay the night there, and drop by William's on the way to pick up Werm to go to the swamp.

What could go wrong with that plan?

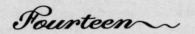
Fourteen

William

As I stood outside Hugo's house, I wondered at the
nature of time. Wasn't it only a few weeks ago that
the balance of my existence was laid out before me? I
would spend an eternity of erotic nights with my
beloved Eleanor, she who both adored and challenged
me. She who thrilled me.

Jack had come into his own and could carry on my
business interests and my efforts to aid other peaceful
blood drinkers. I could at last enjoy the fruits of my
long labors. My wish for eternal death had eased
somewhat, as had my anger at the world for the loss
of my human wife and son. How long had that ease
lasted? A day? Two? It was supposed to last forever.

Then Reedrek blew back into my life like the foul
breath of Satan on the wind, and everything turned to
ashes in the space of a mortal heartbeat. How many
human lifetimes had I spent trying to hold evil at bay?
What had it earned me? Nothing.

I entered Hugo's house through the back door. I

assumed that Diana was still underground with her current lover and mentor. As for Hugo's whereabouts I cared nothing. The next time I saw him, I would kill him. Diana would not be his savior again. She was poised to rise above his level, and he could only hold her back in her ambitions.

"Diana, is that you?" Hugo called from the cellar. "Come here right now. I have news."

I didn't need the element of surprise. By the time I entered the squalid room he knew by my scent it was me and not his lady. He was stunned to see me. Accustomed as he was to other vampires fearing him, he would never have expected another blood drinker to enter his home uninvited. He recovered his calm quickly. "You," he sneered. "I suppose you're here about the fire. Come to try to take your revenge, have you?"

Eleanor stood naked behind Hugo, her breasts rosy and red from his tender attentions. She looked even more shocked to see me, but unlike Hugo she had the good sense to look terrified as well. The room reeked of sex, and her condition looked much improved. He had provided her his seed and let her feed from him. No doubt as payment for her betrayal of me. I noticed that the room was like some sort of dungeon, full of weapons from ancient times. It seemed somehow appropriate.

I ignored him and addressed myself to Eleanor. "I see that Hugo has kept his bargain with you. He has strengthened you in exchange for information on my whereabouts. I congratulate you on the success of your transaction."

"William, I can explain!" Eleanor whimpered. She made a move to cover her nakedness.

"Why hide yourself from me now, you little whore?"

She gasped. It seemed strange that a brothel owner and avowed prostitute would act as if she'd been slapped in the face when called what she was. But I had never judged Eleanor until this moment.

She gathered what dignity she could and stood up straight, lifting her chin. Hugo stepped forward and spoke before she could. "I thought my message of earlier this evening was clear enough. You need to leave London now while you still can. Go back to your quaint river town and wait until you're called upon."

"Called upon?" I asked. "By whom?"

Hugo laughed—a nasty, grating, unhuman sound. "The old lords, of course. In fact, you'll have to leave right now. I'm late for an appointment with them."

"Oh?" I said. "For what purpose? Amuse me."

Hugo's lips trembled with rage. He was clearly not used to being mocked, and I sensed he couldn't fathom why I didn't show fear at the mention of the old ones.

"I have to assume you don't know who I'm talking about. I speak of the *vampire council*." He overenunciated the last two words as if he were speaking to an imbecile. "I am appearing before them tonight to introduce a plan that will put me in their favor and under their protection. Care to know what my plan is? Perhaps *that* would amuse you."

Behind him, Eleanor's entire body shuddered, and she uttered a little cry. "Be silent!" Hugo commanded and she stilled. He turned back to me and said, "My plan is to sacrifice your precious little Renee. The blood of virgins is especially nourishing to the old lords—and especially appreciated. When they find out what her magic blood can do, they will wish to thank me. In fact, an undead messenger just came and went." The smirk faded on Hugo's mouth when he didn't receive the reaction from me that he had anticipated.

"Oh? What did he look like?"

Hugo looked thoroughly confused. "He was tall, an ancient blood drinker with a gray beard. What could you possibly know of—"

"Tell me, where is Diana right now?" I asked.

"Hunting with that whelp of a son of yours, I suppose. How the hell should I know?"

"What if I told you that Diana had already presented your plan to the old lords as her own—with some modifications. And that she did so in order to secure a seat on the Council for her new lover."

"You lie! You'll say anything—"

"You had no idea those were the stakes, did you? You were willing to sacrifice Renee for the 'favor and protection' of the Council when you could have negotiated to become one of them. What a fool you are."

"All this is nonsense. Why, I—"

"Did this undead messenger happen to have a scar across his throat?"

"Well . . . yes." Hugo's face betrayed a flash of concern. He was beginning to get an inkling that perhaps I wasn't as ignorant as he'd thought.

"I gave him that scar a hundred years ago."

Hugo's mouth fell open, working like that of a great fish. I paused a moment to enjoy his reaction. "Who—who is he?" Hugo stammered.

"You seem to think you're an authority on the old ones. Tell me, have you ever heard of a blood drinker known as Ulrich? Ah, I can tell by your reaction that you have. Your visitor earlier—that was he."

I could practically see the wheels of Hugo's mind turning, trying to think of an explanation. "Of course," he said finally. "It makes perfect sense that the Council would send someone of his stature to issue their invitation."

"Does it really? Sending the most feared blood drinker on earth to serve as an errand boy? I think not. Let me tell you what I know to be true. Diana went behind your back to use Renee as a pawn to advance herself. Do you even know where Renee is being held?"

"Diana said she would find a place underground for Renee," Hugo said. "I'm not a nursemaid." He was still projecting a brave front, but I could smell his newfound doubt for his lady love. And his fear of me was growing.

"She has taken Renee to within an eyelash of where the old lords themselves reside."

"Why would she do such a thing?" he asked.

"You still don't understand, do you? Your plan is going ahead without you. But with one slight change. They plan only to sacrifice Renee's humanity. They will make her a blood drinker."

" 'They'?"

"Yes. As it happens, Ulrich is Diana's new lover."

Hugo was nearly stammering. "How would she have met him? She's with me most of the time, and I've never met him myself!"

"I've yet to discover that," I said. "I'm sure the answer will be fascinating."

"Why did Ulrich send for me?"

"So they can feed *you* to the old ones." I drew out my words slowly, enjoying every one, relishing the pure horror on his face.

For once Hugo was speechless. He began to back slowly toward Eleanor. "Is—is there really a seat to be had on the Council?" he sputtered. I could see rage and terror warring with each other in his eyes.

"Yes, only not by you, but by the man who cuckolded you by fucking Diana."

"I should have killed her," he muttered to no one in particular.

"Yes," I agreed, "you should have while you had the strength. But it's much too late now, isn't it?" Hugo nodded dumbly. What a pathetic display. I remembered the conversation with Olivia and her vampires in which we speculated how to take on Hugo and what his plans for Renee might be. Little did we know that Hugo was just a pawn.

"You were so pleased with yourself when you thought that all I ever cared about was yours. Diana, Will, Eleanor, Renee. Now you have nothing, and you've done me a favor in the bargain. You've shown me that Diana and Eleanor were not worth the having."

Eleanor put both fists to her mouth to stifle a cry of pain. She tried to reach through to my mind in order to beg my forgiveness. She projected images of happy times together, of mind-shattering sex, but I blocked her as I should have done from the beginning. Hugo was standing even with her now. In a sudden movement, he grabbed her and held her in front of him, thinking to use her as a shield.

"Did you hear what I said before? I said Eleanor is

not worth the having. If you think to use her as a hostage, you are a bigger fool than I took you for."

He pushed her away from him and turned as if to run. I was on him in a space of time too brief to be measured, pushing him to the floor with so much force I heard his backbone break. Eleanor screamed.

"As for Will," I continued, "he is mine. He's the one who led me to the place where they are keeping Renee. He allowed me to learn of Diana's plan for you. Renee will be mine in a matter of hours. So you see, you have cost me nothing." I looked at Eleanor. "Nothing of value, anyway."

Hugo made his move for me, but I had already anticipated it. He tried to hurl me aside with a sweep of one powerful arm. I rose to my feet in a move too fast for him to see, and as he blinked, wondering how he'd missed me, I cuffed him on the ear as a headmaster would an unruly schoolboy. Enraged, he dove fangs first for my legs, as if to rip away my kneecaps.

"I tire of this," I said, and hauled him to his feet. "Stand and fight like a blood drinker if you can."

Bellowing with rage, he came forward and swung a meaty fist at my chin. I dodged to my right and he connected only with air. His momentum took him to the wall where the weapons and implements of torture were hung. He grabbed an ax and smashed it against the wall, breaking off the head so that only the jagged wooden handle remained.

"Over the last five hundred years I've heard your name spoken on far too many occasions." He balanced the newly formed stake in his hand.

"I'm not surprised to hear that my wife still thought

about me while she was mated to you. The comparison doesn't flatter me overmuch. Is that why you forbade her to speak of me to Will?"

Hugo gritted his teeth and feinted to his right. I didn't go for the fake. "I didn't want to hear him whining about his father."

"I'd imagine the boy would rightly conclude that any male would be a better father figure than you." He drew back and charged me, but I sidestepped, sending him sprawling. He roared in pain, and there was desperation in the sound. No matter how quickly vampires healed, he still would not survive to be whole again, and on some level he knew it.

Hugo had built a reputation throughout Europe as a powerful and widely feared blood drinker, but he was no match for me on this night. Then again, his chosen female had, like a parasite, sapped every ounce of power from him that she could. Now that he could do nothing more to enhance her chances of survival— or her upward mobility in the hierarchy—she'd made plans to dispose of him.

I circled him so that I was once again facing Eleanor. "Do you see this, my dear? Do you see the blood drinker with whom you have twice cast your lot? Behold Hugo in all his glory, owner and despoiler of all that is mine. What do you think of him now? Can you possibly explain why you put your faith in him? Why you put your very existence in his hands?"

She only whimpered, red-tinged tears running down her pale cheeks. "Answer me!" I shouted.

By that time, Hugo had made it to his feet, and with what looked to be the last of his strength, threw the ax handle toward my chest, jagged end first, like a spear. It was a desperate gesture. I easily caught the spike in midair.

"You disappoint me, Hugo. I expected a better fight out of you. But then, what can you expect from a blood drinker who uses women to get what he wants? Not to mention one who throws bombs at those of his own kind and then runs away like a coward." I took an unhurried step toward Hugo, who frantically looked around him for an escape.

"And you, my dear," I said, addressing myself again to Eleanor. "What can you possibly be thinking right now, knowing that you bet on the wrong horse, as Jack would say? Knowing that your benefactor is about to die?"

I closed the distance between Hugo and myself and plunged the stake into his heart. With a bellow of defeat, his body disintegrated into a heap of dust. The room was dead silent for a moment.

I looked at Eleanor, the stake still in my hand. "Ashes to ashes," I said philosophically. "Dust to dust. And good riddance to bad rubbish."

Eleanor only stared in shock.

"So, why did you do it?" I asked her. "Why did you trust him and not me to protect you?"

I could see that Eleanor was trying to calm herself, but the rapid rise and fall of her beautiful breasts betrayed her panic. "When I left Savannah with them, it was because I was angry at you for neglecting me when Diana came to town. After she came it was like I ceased to exist."

"So you said when the shells showed me you and Hugo on the plane. And the second time? Even though

I said I would come back and give you your freedom, you betrayed my whereabouts to Hugo. Despite the fact that he beat you, abused you, and bled you from the time you left Savannah with him."

Once again I concentrated my psychic awareness on Eleanor's thoughts to detect any falsehood immediately. And again I felt nothing from her mind. Eleanor took a deep breath. "He knew you were in London. He said he smelled you on me the first time you came here. He said if I sensed you through my offspring bond and told him where you were staying, he would save me."

"Save you from whom?"

"From Diana. He said Diana would be able to seduce you, and then she would destroy you. And next she would kill me, so she wouldn't have to compete for Hugo's attention. He promised he would save me from her."

"Do you know me so little as to think I would get involved with Diana after she kidnapped Renee and ran with you and my son? Do you really think I'm that stupid?"

"She is beautiful, and you are a man." She shrugged and sniffed. "And you love her."

"What a fool you are." I felt sorry for Eleanor then, sorry enough to consider, just for a moment, letting her go. But she knew too much about me and the few I held dear. And she had demonstrated weakness, disloyalty, and poor judgment. Still, after all she had meant to me, and for all the times she had pleasured me beyond words, I decided to give her a sporting chance.

I tossed her the stake I still held and unblocked my mind. Recognizing the chance in her own mind, and being the opportunist that she was, she flooded my consciousness with sexual sensation even as she tucked the stake under one arm. The memory of her every caress washed over me. The combined feel of every time she had taken me in her mouth or between her legs and wrung from me the most exquisite and agonizing pleasure hit me all at once.

I wondered if Eleanor realized the danger in opening one's mind to outgoing signals. The consciousness is a two-way street.

"Before you come closer," I said, "swear to me again that you did not reveal Renee's value to Hugo and Diana."

"I swear it." She came toward me, licking her lips. When she was within an arm's length, she went down on her knees, and unfastened and lowered my pants. She put her cheek against my bare flesh and licked along my shaft until I was rock hard. Standing again, she shifted the stake to her teeth as a flamenco dancer would hold a rose. She put one hand on my shoulder and locked one leg around my hip. Raising herself on tiptoe, she grasped my cock in the fist of her other hand and put me inside her.

With her legs locked around me, she rode me, taking all of me with every stroke. The feeling was so intense, and my rage so complete I failed to notice her take the stake out of her mouth. I pulled her against me and kissed her, savoring her taste, like wild berries and cream. She freed her mouth from mine just enough to whisper, "Please forgive me, my love. All I want is for things to be the way they used to be between us. Take me back to Savannah, and we'll live happily ever after."

"It's so tempting," I lied. I laid a line of kisses down her neck as I savored the feel of her silken warmth around me. Her heat reminded me of the sex we'd shared when she was alive. She'd adored me. I had hoped when I made her immortal that we would be equals.

Of course, if she'd been my mate for eternity, she would eventually have become stronger than I, just as Diana had with Hugo. But I hadn't cared, because I trusted her. I thought I would have no need to kill my mate as so many males did when their females became strong enough to threaten them. I waited five hundred years for someone who I would not mind becoming more than my match. If conflicts arose, her power would only be an asset to me. Or so I reasoned.

But the struggle with the old lords had intensified, and to survive, I couldn't afford to have a lover I could no longer trust. Or one who could not size up a situation and make the judgments that would lead to our survival rather than our destruction. I might have given Eleanor a chance to redeem herself if not for the lie she'd just told me. She had offered up Renee as food for demons, and for my own self-respect I must prove to myself that I *could* kill her, even though I had loved her.

My own thoughts had temporarily crowded out the images with which Eleanor filled my mind. But she regained my attention when, in her desperation, she included the wrong image in the mix. I saw us in one of our more acrobatic trysts on her boat-size bed, and it reminded me of the little game we liked to play.

The game where she tried to kill me.

I could feel myself climbing that exquisite stairway

toward sexual release and heard myself groan. Like any attentive lover, Eleanor recognized the signs of my climax, and I felt an easing of the pressure on my left shoulder.

She raised the stake as high as she could over our heads, and I bit down on her throat at the same second that I climaxed in wave after wave of satisfaction. I made no move to block the stabbing stroke. I didn't have to. My fangs tearing the flesh of her neck and locking onto the blood vessels there shocked her entire system and the blow glanced off my shoulder. I sucked her blood as if I was starving, as if I had lain in the earth a hundred years without a meal.

I tasted my own blood, that with which I'd animated her such a short time ago, and its magic filled me. My body rose up involuntarily and floated above the floor, and I took Eleanor with me. We floated there in a dance both gentle and brutal, and I sucked until I felt her life force begin to fade.

I raised my lips from her throat and saw her panic-stricken eyes, like those of a mouse in the jaws of the cat. "I'm sorry, my dear," I said, and before delivering the killing bite, added, "I'll see you in hell."

Jack

When I got to the mini-storage unit that I usually called home, I waved at Tom, one of the gatekeepers I paid handsomely to guard my daytime resting place. He raised his hand in greeting, pressed the button that opened the automatic iron gate, and waved me through.

I pulled into my usual parking spot in front of my

unit and saw that Seth's truck was already there as expected. I knocked on the reinforced metal door and let myself in. Seth was sitting in front of the television watching the late movie with a beer in his hand.

"What's on?" I asked.

"*The Wolf Man*," he said.

"You're kidding me, right?"

"Nope. Look here." He motioned me to sit on the couch next to him and pointed at the screen. Lon Chaney Junior was talking to Claude Rains. "Lon Chaney Junior is supposed to be Claude Rains's son. What is wrong with this picture?"

"I don't need my super-duper vampire sense of smell to know that you're drunk," I said. "That's *one* thing that's wrong with this picture, what with you in the fight of your life tomorrow night."

"No, no. I mean in the movie."

I hoped I wasn't in for a long, sodden lecture about accuracy in werewolf pictures. As he'd asked, though, I studied the pair of long-dead actors. Chaney was about a foot taller than Rains and had the look of a boxer who'd been punched in the face too many times, a natural-born ruffian. The fine-featured Rains was built more or less like Werm.

"There's not much familial likeness there," I observed.

"Dude, they don't even look like they're the same *species*," Seth slurred.

"How many beers have you had?"

Seth looked at me blearily. "Don't worry. I'll buy you some more."

"That ain't the point. Do you really want to go into a fight to the death hungover?"

"No problem. Tomorrow, I'll just have some hair of the dog. Or in my case, *wolf*." He issued a wheezy laugh and wound up in a coughing fit.

I took the empty beer bottle out of his hand. "You've had enough. You've got to get some rest."

He sighed. "I guess you're right. I want to see the next part with the Gypsies, though. Then I'll turn in."

"Why do you want to see the Gypsies?"

"I like Gypsies."

"Dude, seriously . . ." I felt like I was talking to a two-year-old. I'd seen Seth drink some very tough guys under the table. Werewolves, as a species, could hold their liquor. He must have really tied one on.

"Don't you like Gypsies?" He held one hand out, palm up. "Cross my palm with silver," he said in a bad Eastern European accent. "And I'll tell you everything you want to know. Or whatever the line is."

I went to the bar where the kitchen began and threw the bottle into the trash. "Look. I came to apologize. I didn't mean that stuff I said earlier. I know you were just trying to look out for Connie and me."

He waved his hand in the air in front of him. "Oh, I know that. Fuhgetaboutit."

"I'll be there tomorrow night backing you up like we planned."

He belched. "I know that, too."

"Listen, I hope the fight we had wasn't the reason you tried to drink all the beer in Savannah. 'Cause if you go to this fight seeing double, you're not going to know which Samson Thrasher to go after. And if you go after the wrong one, I'm going to feel responsible when you get your ass chewed up and handed to you."

"No, man, that's not it." He picked up the remote

control and turned the television off, Gypsies or no Gypsies. "It's . . . the thing with Connie."

"I thought you just said the thing with Connie wasn't it," I said, confused.

"It's not our fight about Connie that made me want to get pickled. It was the thing that happened in Atlanta. It kind of came back to me all over again."

I went back to the couch and sat down beside him. "What *did* happen in Atlanta between the two of you?"

"It wasn't between the two of us," he said miserably. "But I still think it was the thing that drove her away from me."

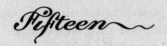

William

When I reached the cavernous room where I'd overheard Diana and Ulrich, I leaned against the wall and closed my eyes. I summoned every ounce of power I could muster to get a sense of any nearby vampires. I was aware of the old lords lurking somewhere underneath me. This far underground, I would not be able to sense when the sun rose and the other vampires went to their rest.

I had left Eleanor's bloodless body where it lay. It had already begun to decay, and I now felt a void where she had once existed as my offspring. I felt empty despite having consumed her blood nearly to the point of drunkenness. Sadness—one of the emotions I had long thought myself incapable of—washed over me when her body at last released its grip on undeath. I'd dispatched my beloved Eleanor to hell, and I found that part of me wanted to die with her. My old fascination with my own destruction had returned.

I vowed to myself that there would be no other thoughts of Eleanor this night. Not when Renee was within my grasp. My sense of her was as strong as it had been the night before. In fact, in the stillness and the absence of waking vampire activity, I could swear that I heard her calling me.

Uncle William, she said. *Please, take me home. I want my mama.*

I'm coming, my heart, my mind projected. Her little voice seemed to fill the void inside me.

I found a passage leading downward. Stones that had been worn smooth by centuries of contact with uncounted hands and feet protruded from the earth on one side of the narrow hole. Was this the path that untold supplicants used to reach the dark lords? I couldn't help but wonder how many had descended never to rise again. Using the stones as hand- and footholds I continued downward.

As I continued, the unrelieved blackness began to give way to a tiny glint of light from below. I sensed I was coming to another room of sorts. I found myself in an enclosure with lit torches set into holes dug in the earthen walls. Blades of all kinds hung in rows from spikes set between the torches—from broadswords to rapiers to falchions to dirks. At the end of the little cavern Renee sat in a simple wooden chair.

I practically flew to her. "Renee, are you all right?" She didn't move, and I saw when I approached that she was tied to the chair.

"I am all right now," she said. "I knew you would come. Either you or Uncle Jack or both."

She still wore the school uniform, now dirty and torn, that she'd been kidnapped in. Her hair had escaped its barrettes and colorful bands. But her brown eyes shone brightly and were unafraid.

I ripped the ropes in two with my bare hands, freeing her arms. "Are you all right?" I asked again.

"Hungry," she said. She winced and struggled to bring her arms forward. I gently massaged the feeling back into them, and as I did I saw to my horror that they were covered with cuts and fang marks.

"Who did this to you?" I demanded as she encircled my neck with her injured arms.

"Diana and the one she calls Ulrich." I felt her little body shudder as she said his name.

I hugged her and cursed silently. Diana had no doubt offered up Renee's precious blood to ingratiate herself with her benefactor. With Will having redeemed himself and Hugo and Eleanor rotting in hell, my rage intensified and focused on Diana.

The awareness of the true depth of Diana's evil settled into my bones like poison. It was as if a veil was lifted from my eyes so that I could see her for what she was. I finally understood that every trait that I prized in her as my human wife—goodness, compassion, loyalty, and the boundless capacity to love—had died on the night she was made into a blood drinker. What was left was nothing but a beautiful yet evil shell. When she'd come to Savannah, in my happiness at seeing her again after so many centuries, I had tried to fill that shell with my cherished memories of the love of my human life.

I'd been as great a fool as Eleanor. I only hoped that I had wised up, as Jack would say, in time to be spared her fate. And in time to spare Renee any more suffering. I silently vowed that Diana would pay with her undead life if it took me until eternity to exact my revenge.

"Where is Mama?" Renee asked, pulling back from me enough to look into my eyes.

"She wanted to come," I said. "But I asked her to wait in Savannah until I brought you back. Someone has to take care of your uncle Jack, you know."

Renee smiled. "And Deylaud and Reyha."

"That's right." I managed a smile I hoped would not betray my fears. I had no idea if her beloved Deylaud yet lived.

My hearing picked up a noise from the direction I had come. I turned my head toward the sound, almost like rain.

"What is it, Uncle William?"

"We need to fly, little one. Hold tight." Renee put her skinny brown arms around my neck and pressed her face into my shoulder. I picked her up and hurried to the passageway that led upward, but before I could get there, the pitter-patter had become a roar, and earth and rocks showered down from the passage, filling that side of the cavern floor. Renee gasped as I scanned the roof of the enclosure for another path. There was none.

But there was one leading downward.

In fact, someone had taken the trouble to construct steps on this section of the downward path. Crude handholds had led me down to this point, but from here the way was more refined. Could it be that only a select few made it to this lower level? What had happened to those where Renee was being kept who were not so privileged? I had no time to ponder the meaning of this. I looked behind me as the earth around the upward passage caved in, partially filling the room with rubble. Renee heard the rumble and whimpered.

The crude staircase leading downward was our only way out. I hoped it led to somewhere other than hell.

Jack

"It was awful, Jack," Seth said mournfully.

"My God, what happened?" I was starting to get a case of the creeps.

"When I first met Connie, she had just divorced her husband, Alonso."

So there had been a husband. I thought back to the moment in Melaphia's little garden when I watched the ceremony that Connie was participating in. The naked ceremony. I'd noticed what I was pretty sure was a cesarean section scar on Connie's abdomen. I always wondered what had happened to that baby, but of course I couldn't ask.

"She had a beautiful four-year-old boy." Seth let his head fall against the back of the couch and took a deep breath.

I didn't like the sound of this. Not one little bit. But I had to hear the rest. "Keep going, buddy," I urged Seth on.

"We met at the academy, like we said that night at your garage. After that training class I taught, she went back to Atlanta PD, and I went back to my job running the force in my town. But I couldn't get her off my mind, Jack. I looked her up."

"You dated?"

"Yeah. For a few weeks anyway." He rubbed his

eyes, not like he was sleepy but like he was seeing something in the past that he wanted to go away. Far, far away.

"What happened then?"

"Alonso, that's what happened. He had threatened Connie when she left him. They were living in D.C. at the time, and he was going to Georgetown. His family was a wealthy one who'd come here from somewhere in Latin America, and they insisted he go to law school. Alonso's parents had even planned a trip to the United States when his mother was pregnant so that Alonso would be born here."

"If they were so wealthy, why did they go to so much trouble to make sure he was born a U.S. citizen?" I asked, confused.

"Connie said they wanted to see their son become the first Latino president of the United States. Connie said Alonso was bright, but the stress of Georgetown Law, not to mention the pressure his parents put on him, got him down, and he started taking something. Connie said she never knew what it was. He was too good at hiding it. When she confronted him, he said he could handle it, that he only took it to help him cope."

I thought about how Connie had reacted when I told her about the Thrashers making methamphetamine. She looked mad enough to spit nails. "Go on," I said.

"See, they had gotten married right after she graduated from high school, and nine months later, when they were undergrads, Connie had his baby. She took a break from her own college career to be a full-time mom. She said everything was good at first between her and Alonso. It's an old story, I guess." He sighed.

"When did the abuse start?" I found myself balling my hands into fists and tried to relax. I couldn't stand the thought of Connie being victimized.

"I think it was after he got his bachelor's degree and moved on to law school and he started with the drugs. Evidently it was a pretty wild scene. Connie didn't put up with it for long, of course. She tried to make it work for the kid's sake. But Alonso ran out of last chances the night he put her in the hospital. She had him arrested and moved back to Atlanta with little Carlos. That's when I met her. She'd just joined Atlanta PD."

I rubbed my eyes, hoping to get rid of the image in my mind of Connie being brutalized by a man she loved. No wonder she was on the edge of going vigilante on the Thrasher domestic violence case. I think she told me one time that fighting domestic violence was the reason she joined the force. Seth's story explained a lot. I motioned for him to continue.

"He left her alone for a while. I think his parents put the fear of God in him. They knew that they could get a first offense expunged from his record, but a second one was dicey. The parents agreed to help her get a quickie divorce in exchange for her agreement never to tell anyone about the abuse. They were all about their son's future political career. Connie was glad to agree in order to get Alonso out of her life as fast as possible. So she thought she was in the clear. Then something made Alonso snap. Maybe it was the drugs. Maybe it was something else. I'm not sure she ever figured it out."

You know how you feel when you're driving along and you come to a car wreck? You don't want to look, but you can't help yourself. Right now I didn't want to hear, *really* didn't want to hear the rest, but there was no turning back. "Go on," I heard myself say again.

"One night we got back to her apartment after a date. The babysitter left; I hung around for a while and then said good night, both of us thinking everything was normal." Seth covered his face with his hands. "Right after I left, Alonso forced his way into the apartment."

"What happened then? I need to know," I said gently, not knowing if he would continue without prodding.

"Alonso had a gun."

William

I ran for the steps with Renee cradled in my arms. Down and down I ran until I came to still another cavernous room. The stench of old death was worse there, but that was of no concern compared to what I was staring in the face. Or should I say *who*.

"Good evening," Ulrich said. "How nice it is to see you again after so many years. More than a century, isn't it?" He fingered the scar at his throat. As old as it was, it should have been snow white, but the scar was a dark wine color. No doubt because he had recently fed from Renee. Diana stood behind her lover, looking as beautiful as ever.

"Hello, William," she said in a sultry voice.

"How dare you speak to me after what you've done to this child," I said, ignoring Ulrich. "After the way you betrayed me."

"Now, now, don't be rude," Ulrich said. "We can all be civil here, can't we?"

I scanned the room for a way out. The earthen ceiling was higher than the previous chamber's, and the walls had a number of lit torches imbedded in them. The light cast eerie shadows on the dirt floor. In the far corner I saw another passage leading farther downward. I could no longer hear the landslide up above, but that did not necessarily mean that it had stopped.

"William is a very reasonable man," Diana remarked. The obsequiousness in her voice sickened me. "And ambitious in his own way. Perhaps we can come to an understanding."

Renee had begun to tremble in my arms. "Look at me, little one," I said. She did as I asked, her wide, frightened eyes staring up into mine. "It's time for you to go to sleep now, and sleep until I wake you. All right?"

I focused my mind to deliver the glamour. If she chose to use the force of her voodoo blood, she might be one of the few humans on earth who could thwart me, but of course she did not. She would obey as much because she loved me as in response to the glamour of the vampire.

"All right, Uncle William. I'll go to sleep now and sleep until you wake me."

She was asleep in seconds and I refocused my power on shielding my thoughts from my grandsire, who was regarding me quizzically.

"That was a nice touch," he said. "I remember your . . . fondness for and sensitivity to humans."

"I'll listen to your proposal," I said as evenly as I could. I would subdue my disgust and get one or both of them talking enough to allow me time to formulate a plan. If I could get Ulrich to open up to me, perhaps I might discover a weakness. "But first I want information," I continued. "For my own edification, you understand."

"Why, of course," Ulrich said genially. "We have nothing but time, we vampires. That is our richest gift. Is it not, my dear?"

Diana nodded and smiled demurely. "Ask us anything, William. By all means."

"Why did Reedrek come to Savannah after leaving me alone for so many years? He said he'd wanted me to make more vampires to strengthen the bloodline. I believe his arrival had something to do with the plague that Will was sent to spread among the western vampires. Were you behind all that?"

"Yes, I was, I am loath to admit," Ulrich said with an expression of disgust.

"Why do you say it like that?"

"Because it failed." For the first time, the old demon showed his temper. "That senile Reedrek and the imbecile Hugo botched the plan when they deliberately allowed Will to become infected."

"Hugo was always jealous of my son," Diana said. "When Reedrek came to him with the plan, Hugo saw an opportunity to get rid of Will." Despite her gentle tone, her eyes flashed with hatred for her mate. Or rather her *former* mate. I wondered if she sensed that he was dead. He was her sire, after all. The nearness of the old lords might have distorted her perceptions. Even though they were asleep their combined psychic strength created a low buzzing in my own head. They were very near now.

Ulrich waved a dismissive hand as if he cared not at all for Diana's domestic problems. "What Reedrek told you about strengthening the bloodline was merely a cover story. What you could have accomplished in that regard, even if you enlisted the aid of your offspring, would have been only a—what is the modern phrase?"

"Drop in the bucket," Diana provided helpfully.

"Yes. A drop in the bucket compared to the kind of power that is in play with regards to my becoming one of the old lords."

"So that's what this is all about?" I said, leading him further into conversation.

"Oh yes, my boy. I tapped Reedrek to help me achieve that goal but he proved woefully inept, as you know. How clever you are to have trapped him in the cornerstone of that new building. It's one of the more creative ways I've come across for a vampire to neutralize his sire without suffering harm to himself."

"Thank you," I said dryly. "So Reedrek and Hugo hatched the bioterror plot themselves, did they? I would have thought that was too sophisticated for them."

"You're quite astute, my son," Ulrich said. "However, I cannot take the credit for the idea. The plot was the brainchild of our brilliant Diana here."

Diana took a deep breath and managed a smile. She clearly would have preferred that Ulrich not mention that part. She was clever enough not to deliberately antagonize me. She needn't have worried. There was nothing she could admit to that would make me hate her any more than I already did for kidnapping Renee.

I telegraphed that hatred to her. The force of my

rage made her take a step back. I savored the moment when she realized she no longer had any power over me.

"So Diana is the mastermind?" I said.

She gathered her composure with some effort. "While we were in Russia, I sought out a former nuclear scientist who was willing to engineer a virus—for a price, of course."

"I'm curious. What sum did he demand, if you don't mind me asking?"

"By the time he realized who and what he'd gotten involved with, he was happy to settle for his life."

"I'm sure he was. You must have known there was a market for a bioweapon like that," I observed.

"I knew the old lords would value such a weapon, yes, but I didn't know how to approach them."

"Or how to negotiate with them?" I looked from her to Ulrich with meaning.

"It just so happened there was an ancient and learned vampire in our Russian coven who put me in touch with Ulrich," Diana said.

"Was his name Vanya, by any chance?" I thought of the vampire who was almost clever enough to escape my killing rampage.

Diana's expression betrayed only the slightest hint of—what? Shock? Anger? "I suppose you killed him." It was a statement rather than a question.

"You suppose correctly. In fact, I killed all of them," I said. "And torched the house for good measure. But continue with the story, if you please. It's positively fascinating. I assume you kept Hugo in the dark about the fact that you were ultimately behind this little project."

"You assume correctly," she mocked. "Why should I share with Hugo the spoils of *my* plan?"

"Indeed. He was only your sire and the one who gave you the strength and protection to survive far longer than most females ever do."

"He was a monster," she spat. "He abused both me and my son. He didn't deserve any consideration."

I ignored her. "At some point you had to get Hugo involved to help carry out the plan. But I'm getting the story out of order. What happened after you contacted Ulrich?"

"I enlisted the aid of my offspring Reedrek," Ulrich said, taking up the tale. "He had done little enough for me lo these hundreds of years, so I gave him a chance to redeem himself in my eyes.

"I decided that Reedrek should approach his offspring Hugo and ask for his help. Reedrek and Diana let Hugo think that Reedrek was the mastermind and that she knew nothing."

"What did Reedrek promise Hugo for his cooperation?" I asked, having already heard the answer from Hugo's own lips right before I'd killed him.

"Merely the favor and protection of the old lords," Diana said.

"Not a council seat," I supplied, remembering how shocked Hugo had been to learn those were the real stakes in the game.

"He never dreamed such a thing was possible," Diana said. "At any rate, Hugo was hardly Council material, I think you'll agree."

I had no idea what Council material was, but I wasn't going to admit my ignorance. "So you double-crossed

Hugo and then Hugo and Reedrek double-crossed you by allowing Will to travel with the virus in such a way as to become infected himself."

"Yes," Diana said bitterly. "We set off for Savannah in the sailing ship and Will was supposed to meet us there after he infected those in the west."

"Which he did."

"Yes," she said tersely.

"Of course," Ulrich said, "she had no idea that her sire and grandsire would make such a dog's breakfast of things, endanger her beloved child, and get Reedrek encapsulated in granite in the bargain."

Beloved child? I nearly pointed out that Diana was incapable of loving anything, but I kept my thoughts to myself. Will was merely a possession to her.

It made me sick to recall how, while in Savannah, Diana had pretended she still had feelings for me as long as it had suited her purposes. Having cast in her lot with Ulrich here in London, she no longer bothered to keep up the pretense. For that, I could almost—but not quite—respect her.

"I wondered how you and your mate knew to hide your intentions the night you sailed into Savannah. I assume that Reedrek was able to project a warning to Hugo before you reached the harbor," I said to Diana.

"Our arrival was supposed to be a celebration of victory over the New World vampires. Instead, Hugo had to bluff and say we came just to make sure Reedrek was put away for good."

"When did you become aware that you would be meeting me, your mortal husband, in Savannah?" I kept my face as neutral as possible.

"Right before Reedrek sailed on ahead of us. He finally put a name to this legendary vampire whom the old lords wanted to defeat. You can imagine my shock."

"I'm not sure I can," I said. "I could imagine how my human Diana would have reacted to the thought of being reunited with me after such a long separation. But you? The creature you have become is a mystery to me."

She opened her mouth to reply but glanced at Ulrich and decided against it.

"Did the old lords consider the biological attack a success because you were able to wipe out the California colony?"

"At first, yes." Ulrich smiled a brittle smile. "But when word came that your scientist trumped our scientist by devising an effective cure so soon, well, let's just say it was a bit of a black eye. Diana knew that, so in order to redeem me in their eyes, she devised a new plan."

"I believe I know this part," I said. "When she learned that the vaccine was based on Renee's mystical blood, that's when she decided to kidnap her and bring her here to you. If you made such a rare gift as Renee to the old lords, not only would they overlook your little failure, but there's no telling how they'd reward you."

"Yes, but of course Hugo still didn't know of my existence. He thought he would be getting the glory." Ulrich laughed heartily.

"And instead you invited him here to offer him as food to the vampire council."

"Well, he *did* want to go before the dark lords,"

Diana said. "And in a *way*, he was to become part of them."

"Your powers of rationalization are positively astonishing, my dear," I said.

"Sarcasm doesn't become you," she said, showing fang. "I think you would do well to consider your situation before you antagonize us."

"What difference does my manner make? You're going to feed me to the Council in Hugo's place anyway."

"We would not use you as mere food, William. Perish the thought," Ulrich said. "You are more of a prize than that—a prisoner of war, let's say. Diana, how shall we make the presentation? You are my idea woman, after all."

Diana looked at me, and this time she was all sweetness and light. It took me a second to realize that she was trying to use glamour on me. Of all things, she was trying to appear most like her old human self, the Diana I used to know and love. She was trying to seduce me. Her eyes shimmered like sapphires, and her hair shone like spun gold. Oh, she was good. Her cheeks seemed suddenly as rosy as those of any warm-blooded human maiden.

"I believe I know exactly how we should present William as a gift to the Council," she said.

Jack

"The evil bastard shot Carlos in his sleep," Seth said, resting his head in his hand. "The poor little guy never knew what hit him. And then Alonso turned the gun on himself. Connie said it was all over in seconds.

When I heard the call on the scanner in my truck I raced back to the apartment, but there was nothing I could do. Carlos and Alonso were dead."

"He killed his own son?" I said, horrified. "Was it one of those ugly 'if I can't have my son, you can't either' kind of custody deals?"

"No, not really. I don't think he wanted the kid. I think he just wanted Connie to suffer for leaving him."

"So he murdered her child in front of her." Poor Connie. I reckoned I must still have a heart, because it was bleeding for her.

Something clicked in my mind. What had Connie said about who she wanted to see in the underworld? Somebody she thought was in a good place and somebody she thought was in hell. I didn't have to wonder who she was talking about any longer. If she wanted to make sure her boy was in paradise and his murderer was being eternally tortured in the fiery pit, who could blame her?

"Oh, man," Seth said. "I can't believe I unloaded all that on you. Listen, you can't tell Connie I told you what happened in Atlanta, okay?"

"Okay," I said.

"Swear?"

"I don't know what good an oath from a vampire is, but if it makes you feel better, I swear."

"Cross your heart and hope to die?"

"Dude."

"I keep forgetting."

"You are so wasted."

"You think?"

I sighed. "We've got to get some sleep now or we're going to be wolf meat tomorrow night."

"All right. Do you want the couch?"

"Nope, I keep a spare coffin in the rafters. I'll sleep up there. Oh, but I need to ask you something. I have to go by William's tomorrow night just long enough to check on Mel and the twins. Do you have to change right after sundown or can you put the fight off until I get there?"

"I'll get a mite twitchy, but I don't absolutely have to change until the moon is high," Seth said. "I'll stall until you get there."

"Excellent." I jumped up on a bar stool and pushed up one of the tiles in the suspension ceiling. Then I remembered something else that had bothered me about the story he just told me.

"Seth," I said. "What happened after the murder-suicide? I mean, when you first started talking about it, you kind of made it sound like it ended your relationship."

"It did," Seth said mournfully, pulling off his boots with some drunken difficulty.

"Why? Did it put her off men in general for a while, or what?"

"No, it wasn't like that. It was more like—no matter how I tried to assure her that I didn't pity her, she was convinced that I did. She was convinced that everybody who knew what happened pitied her. That's why she moved to Savannah, so she could start fresh where nobody knew her and how her son had been murdered. That's another reason why I'm warning you not to let her know that I told you. It could ruin your relationship with her, too."

Now that's what I call a pal. "Thanks for looking out for me, man. I really appreciate the warning."

"Damn," Seth said. "I think I'm sober. I need another beer."

"No, you're not, and no, you don't."

"Oh, okay," Seth said peevishly.

As I climbed into the rafters under the tin roof that got so nice and warm in the daytime, I wondered how I would ever get to sleep after that horrifying story about Connie. Even vampires have bad dreams.

I heard Seth turn the television back on. Strains of Gypsy violins wafted up to me as I settled myself in my spare coffin. Before I closed the lid, I heard a drunken Seth mutter along with the dialogue.

"Even a man who is pure in heart
and says his prayers by night
may become a wolf when the wolfsbane blooms
and the autumn moon is bright."

Sixteen

William

"Tell me, what is your idea, my dear? I am keen to hear it," said Ulrich, as if he were still a gentleman in Victorian England and Diana had just proposed throwing a garden party instead of a grisly sacrifice to Satan's demi-demons.

"Perhaps we could persuade William to come over to our way of thinking and become one of us."

My mind went back to the night I'd first met Ulrich and I saw the brutally dismembered Mary Jane Kelly, the last victim of Jack the Ripper. What other atrocities had he committed through the centuries? Before the advent of the newspaper, such crimes would have become only the stuff of legend and nightmare, passed down from father to son and mother to daughter around bucolic campfires. The bogeyman of old went by many names. I would wager that for many a long-dead villager, one of those names was Ulrich.

Did I ever want to be that kind of monster? The blood-soaked memory of that crime scene was so vivid

I lost control of the thought, and Ulrich picked it up as if I'd telegraphed it directly to him. He wasn't disturbed by it in the slightest. In fact, his face split into a ghastly smile, revealing his saberlike fangs.

"That's it, my dear boy. Savor that splendid memory. I know I do. This is what we are made for, we vampires. We who have been robbed of life should be dedicated to its wholesale destruction. We sow terror among humanity. We are the architects of nightmares."

I felt his glamour wash over me like a lilting tide, seductive and appealing. While Diana's glamour had had little effect, Ulrich's sang to me through my very blood. His ancient power was many times stronger than hers, and his skill for glamour had doubtless been honed to a blindingly sharp edge over thousands of years. I held fast to the sleeping Renee as if she were a talisman. "B-but we don't have to do evil," I stammered.

"You misunderstand me, my son," Ulrich purred, coming closer. "Evil is not what we do. It's *who we are*. This charade you've been living ever since you won your independence from Reedrek is a fool's game."

"A fool's game," I heard myself repeat. My thoughts were not my own. Ulrich plied my mind with vivid images and delightful sensations, all involving blood, buckets of blood. I tried to remember when I'd last fed. Was it from Eleanor? I couldn't recall.

"Feel your hunger," Ulrich said. "Rejoice in it. Your hunger is your gift."

He stood right in front of me now. His breath smelled like the grave. Why was he stoking my hunger like this? What would it gain him?

"You know what you have to do," he whispered in my ear. Then he reached down to stroke Renee's hair. He wanted me to make Renee a vampire.

Jack

I was showered and dressed and out the door the minute the sun went down. Seth had slept late, taken a lot of aspirin, and had drunk a lot of some sports drink. He assured me he was totally over his bender and waved me off into the night.

"Don't start the party without me," I said on the way out.

"Yeah, yeah," he agreed.

When I got to William's, there was nobody in the kitchen. Concerned, I went to the den. Nada. Alarmed now, I heard a noise coming from the back veranda that faced Melaphia's little house. Maybe she'd gone home for some of her things and taken the twins with her. I exited through the French doors onto the veranda and saw Deylaud and Reyha standing mesmerized by the scene they were looking down on.

From the height of the veranda, you could see into Melaphia's little garden. I drew up short and froze when I saw what the twins were gaping at. Melaphia writhed like a wild thing. She wore a silk robe of too many colors to count and had tied a blue kerchief around her head. It was the exact shade of blue that warded off evil spirits—voodoo blue, the faithful called it.

She'd built a fire in a brazier, and the flames were licking at a number of offerings she'd put on top.

Some type of burning herb created blue smoke and an intoxicating aroma. She danced back and forth to a rhythm only she could hear. The smoke followed her every motion like it was listening to her and obeying. She chanted and prayed, both in English and in languages I didn't recognize. Languages I didn't think even Melaphia knew, not on a conscious level anyway. Somehow she knew them through her blood.

She paused and cocked her head to one side, then broke into hysterical laughter and started dancing again a few moments later. I couldn't tell who or what she was listening to, and I was glad about that. My nerves were so shot, I didn't know if I could stand that dark knowledge on top of the tragic story I'd heard the night before.

Deylaud and Reyha were rooted to their spot on the porch, unable to take their eyes off the show. They clung to each other, afraid but not knowing of what. They could sense the power, though, just as I could. Whatever genie Mel was conjuring up, I just hoped she knew how to get it the hell back into the bottle when she was through with it.

My God, I hadn't checked on them last night. How long had this been going on? The twins were so incapacitated they would have been unable to call me.

"Great googly moogly," I heard myself whisper. Melaphia was dancing so hard, I was afraid she would collapse. I didn't know what to do. Should I go out and stop her before she fainted or fell onto the fire and hurt herself? Or would trying to calm her just make things worse? I kept watching and waiting, afraid to leave until this ceremony, whatever it was, had played out.

I didn't have much time to get to the fight if I was

going to watch Seth's back. He was counting on me. But I couldn't leave Mel alone. I could tell the twins could not help; it was like they were hypnotized. Damn, what should I do?

Call Connie. It was all I could think of. I knew that she would take care of Mel. And there'd be the added benefit of insuring that Connie didn't show up at the werewolf fight, where she'd only be a distraction to Seth and me. I only hoped I could reach her before she left for the swamp.

I flipped open my cell and dialed Connie's number. "Hello?" she answered.

"Connie, it's me. There's something awful wrong with Mel, but I'm going to have to leave right away to go back Seth up. Can you come over to William's and look after her? Deylaud and Reyha are useless. I think they're scared or in a trance or something."

"Jack, is this a ploy to keep me away from the fight?"

"No. I swear it on Maman Lalee's grave. Will you come?"

Connie didn't hesitate. She knew a serious oath when she heard it. "Of course I will. I'll be right there."

I raced back to the porch, feeling all prickly, my flesh tingling and popping like when you shuffle your feet across the carpet and then touch the wrong thing. The twins were more frightened-looking than ever. Whatever was happening, they felt it, too.

Melaphia twirled, her colorful robe billowing around her with each rotation. Then she stopped dead. She looked heavenward, reached into the pocket of the robe, and removed something.

It was the strange little beaded doll.

Connie was there in a matter of minutes. I met her at the front door and motioned for her to follow me.

"Jack, what on earth?"

"Come see for yourself."

She followed me onto the porch and stopped short. I had to take her hand to lead her to the edge where she could see better. The twins were still where I'd left them, but now they were wailing, a hair-raising sound that within seconds turned into the howls of the canines they were.

Connie looked at me. "Jack, what the hell?"

"I don't know what's going on," I said. "For all I know, Mel might be in danger."

"I'd say somebody sure is." She pointed to Mel. "Unless I miss my guess, that's a voodoo doll."

Mel held the doll up high, and I could see that her other hand held something sharp. It was one of her beading needles. She squeezed her eyes tightly shut and muttered something in a tongue I didn't recognize. Then she opened her eyes and shrieked with crazy laughter.

And plunged the needle into the doll.

William

Ulrich touched Renee's forehead, and I felt her stir in my arms. "Don't," I said weakly, "touch her." I would never have thought that with my power I would be vulnerable to glamour. But I had never met as ancient a blood drinker as Ulrich. I now realized that he and

Diana were combining their glamour, and it seeped into me like an insidious toxin.

"You know what you must do, grandchild," Ulrich murmured seductively.

"No. I won't." I tried to think of a reasoning that could convince them to spare her. "You would kill what you don't understand. You know only of the mystical ways of ancient Europe. Renee carries a powerful magic from places you have never been. The voodoo blood must be preserved."

"Of course," Diana said. "But think how much more powerful her blood would make her as a vampire."

"You don't know that," I insisted. "You could be killing the goose that laid the golden egg." I looked down at Renee, loath to describe her in those terms. "Keep her alive, let her grow to adulthood, and utilize her blood sparingly so it will last." I was grasping at straws, and Ulrich and Diana knew it.

"Nonsense. She must become a blood drinker herself. Think of the havoc that kind of hybrid could wreak with the world. But I grow impatient." Ulrich locked eyes with me. I tried to close mine, but they remained open despite my best efforts. I was becoming weaker.

"You won't catch me unawares a second time," Ulrich muttered. He grasped me by the arms as if to wrench Renee away from me. As he did, a loud rumble came from above and a rivulet of loose dirt tumbled down the steps that Renee and I had just descended.

"The earthquake should have stopped by now," Diana said.

"Did you cause the cave-in?" I asked.

"The old lords wanted to make sure you did not escape. Ulrich and I could have accomplished that, but they wanted to impress you with a show of force. Over the centuries they have learned to call the elemental forces."

"So they manufactured an earthquake," I said.

"Yes," Diana said. Her confidence seemed to be waning, however, and she dropped her part of the glamour. Something was wrong. A thunderous crack came from overhead and she flinched.

"But this part is not their doing." Ulrich looked above him and lost concentration on his own glamour. Still holding Renee, I took advantage of his lapse to back as far away from him as possible. And as far away as possible from the stairway.

A high-pitched whine like the howling of wolves came whistling down the passage from upstairs. It was strange, yet familiar. Renee stirred despite her promise to sleep. The sound was calling out to her.

"Mama! Deylaud! Reyha!" she cried, her eyes opening wide.

The rivulet of earth falling down from the level above became a river. A boulder caromed off the walls and came straight for Diana. She screamed and dodged it, losing her balance. Ulrich caught her in his arms before she fell. The mammoth rock came to rest directly in front of the entranceway leading to the level below, cutting off the only exit that wasn't caving in.

If I wasn't so afraid for Renee's safety, I would have laughed at the panic on Ulrich's and Diana's faces as Ulrich backed up against the far wall, still holding her in front of him as if to shield himself. They were powerful enough to burrow their way out of many landslides, but they were both becoming concerned that a power had been unleashed that even they could not claw their way free of.

Just then a primal scream split the air. Renee's face lit up with recognition and delight. If what I now imagined was afoot, never in my half a millennium had I seen such a display of mystical power. And I knew in my bones that this was not the doing of Lalee. This remarkable cataclysm was being caused by Melaphia.

Tumbling end over end down the stairway amidst the rocks and dirt came the broadsword I'd seen hanging from the wall above. It shone like Excalibur, traveling in slow motion. Its hilt struck a stone on the floor of the cavern and it took flight, changing trajectory and sailing directly toward Ulrich and Diana. The metal sang like a siren as it made its flight.

Diana ducked her head to escape the blade an instant before it pierced Ulrich's throat precisely over the scar from my century-old blow, pinning him to the wall.

The falling dirt and debris closed the space between us as Diana screamed, "Damn you to hell, Thorne! You won't stop me from getting my due!"

The last thing I saw was her formerly beautiful face twisted by hatred and horror. The last thing I thought before I lost consciousness was how the magic of the shells may not have been able to work from across the sea, but the magic of a *mambo* robbed of her baby surely could.

Jack

"I'd hate to be whoever that doll represents," Connie said, wincing.

"Me too. It looks like she's working some kind of strong mojo on somebody. William says Mel is the most powerful *mambo* in the hemisphere. Maybe on earth. I've seen her do some amazing things when she gets all worked up, and I've never seen her as worked up as she is now."

"Is that so?" Connie knew that Melaphia was a *mambo*, of course. But she still looked at Mel now with a new kind of respect.

"Look, I can watch Mel and make sure she's all right," she said. "You go on to the swamp. And make sure you and Seth come back in one piece."

"No problem," I said. "I'll be back in a few hours." I tried to sound nonchalant, like a werewolf challenge fight was no big deal, even though either Samson Thrasher or Seth Walker wouldn't survive the night.

"Okay, Jack, I got it. You only went over it three times. This isn't exactly rocket science, you know," Werm said.

"Pardon me for being overly cautious. It's just that Seth's life is riding on this plan," I told Werm. I'd picked him up at the club, and on the way to the swamp I went over what I wanted him to do, ad nauseam to hear Werm tell it.

Tonight Werm was wearing so much silver that he looked like a poor man's Mr. T. I wasn't sure even that would help him if a werewolf got close to him, but who knew?

"Are you going to be able to run with forty pounds of silver around your neck?" I asked.

"Don't worry. I'll be able to run like a scalded dog if a werewolf gets after me," Werm said.

"Have you been practicing your invisibility?"

"Yeah, I can control it pretty well now."

"Please tell me you haven't been practicing in the locker room at the YWCA."

"Would I do that?" Werm pretended to be offended. "Like William might say, being blood drinkers doesn't mean we can't be gentlemen."

"Uh-huh."

Werm had discovered quite by accident that he could go invisible when he got embarrassed, usually by a female, but now he had learned to do it at will. All vampires have their own unique power to some extent. But those of us with the voodoo blood have super-duper revved-up powers, or so William says. William can do lots of things, like what he calls remote viewing with the help of the magic shells Lalee gave him. I needed to practice my flying skills, which I hadn't been doing much of just lately. All these abilities can come in right handy, as you might imagine.

Anyway, it was Werm's invisibility that gave me my bright idea at the bar the night me and him and Seth got drunk. I hoped it would enable Werm to help me and Seth—potentially a lot—without actually having to get involved in the fight. I mean, the little guy would have to learn to fight sometime, but preferably not when somebody else's hide was on the line.

"We're here," I said.

"We're in the middle of nowhere," Werm said.

"We can't exactly drive right up to the place. We've got to sneak up on it."

"Oh, okay. Sure."

"Be on your toes. Seth said he'd stall as long as he could, but we're running late so the wolves may already have changed. They should all be at the clearing where the fight's going to be, so you might not need your invisibility at all, but if they're not, just remember their sense of smell is top-notch."

"Oh, man, I didn't think about the smell thing. You mean that even though I'm invisible they might be able to *sniff* me out?" Werm sounded every bit as concerned as he should be.

"That's about the size of it." I found a place to pull the 'Vette off the side of the road between two cypress trees and parked.

Werm got out of the car and came around to my side. He slung the bag I gave him over one shoulder. "What'll I do if that happens?"

"That's what fangs are for." I clapped him on the back. "No more talking. Their hearing is pretty good, too, but their night vision is nothing to ours. Speaking of night vision—you see that path right there?" I pointed at a small trail worn bare by the tread of many wolf paws. He nodded. "Follow that and you can't miss the place."

He looked up at me. "Wish me luck."

"Good luck, man. You'll do just fine. When you do your thing, come straight back to the car. I'll meet you right here when it's over."

"Uh, Jack?"

"Yeah?"

"What if one of us runs into trouble and isn't back in time to get to Savannah by daylight?"

I realized I had been lazy in teaching Werm how to be a resourceful vampire, but what with marauding grandsires, rogue vamps, rotting plagues, kidnappings, and so forth, I just hadn't had the time. "If you can't find any light-tight shelter, then I'm afraid you're going to have to dig yourself a bed and lie in it. That's what we call old school, son."

Werm looked doubtfully at the swampy ground, gave me a wan smile, and started up the trail. When he was out of sight, I put my nose in the air, sniffed for werewolf, and set off through the swampy woods. Before long I began to see a flicker of light in the distance. A bonfire at the fight site, I guessed. I adjusted my direction about the time the wind changed and I smelled werewolves close by. *Very* close by.

Two pairs of golden eyes came out of the undergrowth. The larger one gave off a low growl. The smaller one, a female, I guessed, eyed me with great interest. Being outnumbered by werewolves was bad enough. But it was the dark thing rising up out of the swamp behind the wolves that had my undivided attention.

I was at the place where the boggy bushes and loblolly pines gave way to the pools and prairies of the actual swamp. The light of the full moon shone on the water, casting reflections of the overhanging cypress trees and creating eerie shadows of everything else. But the thing slogging toward me wasn't a shadow.

I blinked. Damnation, it must be the creature from

the black lagoon. It was dripping with swamp water and muck, rotting vegetation streaming from its outstretched arms as it lurched toward me. The wolves paid it no mind. They must have been immune to whatever power this being possessed.

I'd fought vampires, witches, shape-shifters of all kinds, even a fey creature or three. But I didn't know how to fight this thing, because I didn't know what it *was*. If I bit it, exactly what would I be biting into? A vampire needs to know these kinds of things. People think that having superhuman strength and a good pair of fangs will get you out of any situation, but everything's relative. When you meet up with a creature with unknown powers, things can get interesting.

As it kept coming, I shifted on my feet. There was nothing to do but unsheathe my fangs, try to look really scary, and prepare for the worst.

"Is that you, Jack?" the thing asked in a watery but familiar tenor.

"Huey?"

"I can't see you too good. I got mud in my eyes."

Huey couldn't see too good under the best of circumstances with that little semi-detached roaming eyeball problem of his, but now that he was covered with muck, he was profoundly visually challenged.

"I can see that," I said. I walked closer and let the two wolves sniff my hands for solidarity's sake. Then I reached into my back pocket for my bandanna and mopped the mud out of Huey's eyes.

"Thanks. I accidentally fell in the swamp and mired up to my neck just about. Wanda and Jerry pulled me out."

The big male werewolf gave a friendly *woof*, and the female wagged her tail. I should have known it was Jerry and Wanda. The Swamp Thing, also known as Wanda's faithful bodyguard and my pet zombie, gave me a big grin. I guess I should have realized who he was, too. But hey, even vampires get spooked now and then.

Huey said, "Jerry and Wanda were afraid to come back to the shop after the dance. Jerry said that Nate might figure out where Wanda was staying now that he knew she was with Jerry. Jerry came by the garage a little bit ago looking for you and said I could come with him and Wanda tonight. I'm going to bodyguard Wanda and help you and Jerry in the fight with the bad wolves."

"Well, that's real good of you, Hugh-man," I said. "The more the merrier." It did make a certain amount of sense. I mean, Huey was already dead, so it's not like he could get killed . . . again. If he took on some damage, we could probably just patch him up with a needle and nylon thread like we did with his old wounds.

"Here," I said. "Let me help you get some of that off." I wiped him with the bandanna and some pine straw until he wasn't so weighed down with muck. "That looks better."

"It's all good," Huey said.

Jerry *woofed*, pawing at the ground.

Huey looked at Jerry. "Yeah, we'd better go."

"Can you understand him?" I asked Huey.

"Sure. Can't you?"

"Not a *woof*. But I'm glad you can." So zombies could speak werewolf. At least this one could. Who knew? "Jerry, you and Wanda lead us to the fight site."

Jerry and Wanda took off and I followed at a trot. Huey tried to keep up, but it looked like he would just have to follow our trail and do the best he could. He couldn't run much better than he could dance.

Within half a mile or so we stopped at the edge of a clearing. Two huge wolves—one Seth and the other Samson with the ice blue eyes—were circling each other. In a ring around Seth and Samson were the wolves of the pack—six females and eight males by my count. I wondered which one was which. For Sally's sake I wanted to take a big bite out of Nate, and I wouldn't mind teaching the one named Leroy a thing or two for stalking her.

Seth the wolf looked in my direction and nodded his huge head. Then in a flash he lunged at the throat of the blue-eyed wolf. Samson twisted, but Seth was able to sink his teeth into the nape of his neck. The two wolves went rolling and writhing in a solid mass of fur and fangs until I didn't know where one wolf ended and the other began.

Samson was finally able to wrench himself free of the death roll; he came up limping and bleeding from the back of the neck. One of the big males in the outer circle started howling. I can't say how, but I knew this was Nate. He was probably urging his father on.

While Seth still had the advantage, he lunged again. Samson tried to dodge him, but Seth latched on once more, this time a little nearer the front of Samson's throat. *Way to go, you fuzzy bastard,* I silently cheered my friend.

Seth must have had a tighter hold on Samson this time, because he started waving his head violently, shaking the other wolf like a rag doll. That's when Nate and one of the other big males, a red wolf, stepped in. They left the circle and the red wolf nipped at one of Seth's rear ankles. The move distracted Seth just enough for him to lose his grip on Samson, who was able to squirm away again.

"Time to join the party," I said to Jerry and Wanda. As one, we stepped out of the cover of the forest and into the clearing. All the wolves stopped and looked at us. The diversion allowed Seth to put the bite on Samson again, but Big Red got back in the game quickly and bit down savagely on Seth's flank.

I dove onto Big Red and put a headlock on him. I felt like I was riding a bucking bronco as he leaped into the air to try to shake me off. The second time he leaped I arched my back and landed on my feet, forcing him onto his back legs in front of me. I sank my fangs into the side of his throat and felt his blood run free.

The wild, gamy taste of werewolf hit my tongue and stunned me for a moment, sending primal images through my mind. I'd almost forgotten the flavor of this mythical beast that, like my own kind, had been the stuff of nightmares since the dawn of humanity. Biting down harder, I no longer tried to capture the rising font of blood, instead choosing to savor the tang of feral flesh, losing myself in the primitive taste.

A yelp from Jerry brought me back to myself. I released the red wolf who, if not already dead, soon would be. I looked toward Jerry. He was outflanking the Nate wolf, who was trying to work his way to Samson's side. Wanda was holding off all six females, who had backed off from the circle. Their hearts didn't seem to be in the fight.

Samson and Seth were locked in another death roll. I charged the two wolves who were trying to enter the fight on Samson's behalf. One ran off, and the other one whined and wouldn't make eye contact. It seemed like Samson wasn't popular with all the males—at least not popular enough for them to willingly spill their blood for him. I bared my fangs and roared as loud as I could, and the timid one fled behind the first.

I tried to get closer to Samson and Seth and so did one of the two remaining males. The other wolf did a screen move on Jerry and freed up Nate to go for his former mate, Wandawolf. Unfortunately for Nate, this was the moment Huey finally burst into the clearing. Despite my earlier efforts, Huey still pretty much looked like something out of a Japanese horror movie. Nate hesitated long enough for Huey to lunge onto him and put the bite on him much as he had the previous night.

Huey rode Nate into the woods like a rodeo cowboy, the zombie's formidable choppers firmly clasped onto the flesh between Nate's ears. Jerry lunged for the wolf circling him, and Wanda, having neutralized the females, joined her new mate. I grabbed the wolf trying to get the drop on Seth and bit him deeply between the shoulder blades. He ripped himself free of my fangs and arms as I spit out a mouthful of his fur. He wheeled to face me again and this time he was *real* mad. He pawed at the ground like a bull. Frothy foam dripped from his muzzle, which looked as wide as a cinder block and just as tough.

Out of the corner of my eye I could see that Nate was back from the woods, having bucked Huey off somewhere. He was heading straight for Seth.

Where the hell was Werm?

Seventeen

William

When I regained consciousness, I had no idea how much time had passed. The scent of the soil reminded me of my homeland. Only there was something evil in it, too. Then I sensed a human and smelled blood. Renee.

I remembered then and opened my eyes. Alarmed for her safety, I quickly determined that she was still in my arms; an air pocket had formed around us, but we were buried in darkness. I couldn't tell how much time had passed, and I didn't know how much oxygen remained for Renee in the little space. At least I wasn't using any. Renee's breathing was regular, and I sensed that she was asleep and unharmed.

When she awoke I would use my glamour once again to keep her from being frightened by our predicament. My natural instinct was to start digging. I could dig myself out in the fullness of time and reach the surface as a leathery, starving husk of a creature. I could recuperate at my leisure, but as far underground as we were, my digging would do Renee no good.

I would hold her until she breathed her last breath and weep while the human I loved so desperately died in my arms. Then I would abandon myself to the earth to rest with her remains forever. What a tragic waste. Renee was the most promising mystical being I had encountered in half a millennium.

I couldn't let that happen. I closed my eyes and focused my mind with the power of every drop of blood, every bone and sinew in my body. I called out to my kin on this continent—but most of all I called to Will. I felt my call rise through the earth. The soil throbbed with its vibrations.

By the power of the voodoo blood, save this child.

Jack

The wolf I was facing lowered his body and leaped, just as an explosion shook the earth hard enough to throw me to the ground, the wolf landing awkwardly behind me. The other wolves seemed stunned by the concussive blast. Though Samson's cabin was a quarter of a mile away, the light of the fire that consumed it was clearly visible. Unfortunately for Samson, the sight distracted him just enough for Seth to deliver the killing bite to his neck.

Nate and the remaining pack wolves could only slink away in horror.

Jerry, Wanda, and Seth lay down in the clearing,

panting. Huey came slogging back out of the woods. "What happened?" he said. "What'd I miss?"

I pointed toward the blazing meth house. "Werm came through for us," I said. "He blew up Samson's cabin."

"Hmmm, doggies," Huey remarked.

The three wolves thumped their tails on the ground. Wanda licked a wound on Jerry's shoulder and he nuzzled her head.

"Ah, puppy love. Come on, Hugh-man. Let's let the werewolves do whatever they do on nights when the moon is full and bright. Me and you will meet up with Werm at the Corvette and go to the house."

"Can we ride with the top down?" Huey asked hopefully.

"It'll be cold, but what's a little chill to two vampires and a zombie?" I said.

Huey patted his mud-soaked head and asked without a trace of irony, "Do you think it will mess up my hair?"

"Buddy," I said, "you don't have much hair to begin with, so I wouldn't worry about it. I would recommend that you hold on real tight to your eyeballs, though."

When I got back to William's after dropping off Werm and Huey, everything was blessedly quiet. The light in the foyer was on, so I went upstairs and found Deylaud and Reyha watching over Melaphia, who was sleeping peacefully in the guest bedroom.

"Is Mel okay?" I asked.

"She's fine," Deylaud whispered.

"What happened after I left?"

"Connie stayed and watched over Mel until she was finished with her ceremony," Deylaud recounted.

"Or whatever it was." Reyha shivered.

Deylaud continued, "Then Mel quieted down some, but she was still in magic mode. She and Connie talked a long, long time out in the garden."

"Then Mel calmed down some more," Reyha added. "She came up here and went right to sleep. Connie said she thought Mel would be fine, so she went back to her apartment."

"Good," I said, relieved. "It sounds to me like Connie was able to talk Mel down from whatever voodoo high she was on. I assume the voodoo doll was for whoever is holding Renee."

"We were afraid to ask," Deylaud said. "We didn't want to get her all worked up again. But that seems to be a good assumption."

Reyha said, "Connie said to tell you to come by her apartment when you got back, no matter how late it was."

"Okay," I agreed. I figured she wanted to hear how the fight turned out and make sure Seth and I had survived. There was still plenty of time before daylight. "You guys call my cell if there's any more trouble."

They nodded and I said good night. I headed off to Connie's through the tunnels, enjoying a great sense of relief. The fight had gone my way. It would be a while before any of Savannah's other nonhuman kingpins wanted to stir up trouble with yours truly.

And the latest crisis with Melaphia was over, at least for now. I hoped with everything in me that whatever magic she'd worked with the voodoo doll would help William free Renee.

William

My call reverberated around the little cell in which Renee and I were imprisoned. It had gone upward and outward, hopefully to resonate in the minds of Olivia and Will, spurring them to action and serving as a magnet to draw them to our location. But the call also found its way downward. There was no controlling its path. I felt the earth roil and grind beneath us, and I knew that if Olivia and Will did not hurry, something else might come up from down below to claim Renee and me.

I closed my eyes and wished, not for the first time in my long existence, that there was someone or something to which I could pray.

The noise began as a breath, then grew to a whisper. Before long it was a pulsing roar. Something was coming directly toward us.

But was it coming from above or below?

Jack

Connie came to the door barefoot. She wore only a black satin bathrobe. *Nice.* "C'mon in." She gestured toward the couch. I sat, only then realizing how tired I was.

"So, how'd the fight go?" she said. "It looks like you came out without a scratch." She sat beside me, resting one arm along the back of the couch and drawing one leg up under her. The robe fell open to reveal long expanses of smooth, shapely thigh. I tried to be a gentleman and not look, but hey, I may be dead, but I'm also a guy.

"Fine. Um, do you mind if I take off my jacket? It's kind of warm in here."

"Please do," she said. I tossed the leather bomber onto the arm of the wing chair. "Is Seth okay?" she asked.

"Yeah. He's pack leader now. He killed Samson."

"Half of me thinks I should arrest him."

"Don't think of it as Seth killing a human being. Think of it as a wolf killing another wolf, a bad wolf, in a fight that's part of the natural order of things."

"You make it sound simple."

"It's not." I sighed. "Nothing about being unhuman in a human world is simple."

"I'm starting to understand that."

"What do you mean?"

"Jack, I learned so much from Melaphia tonight." Connie's eyes lit with an intensity that made me sit up straight.

"I was going to ask you about that. What happened after I left?"

"Melaphia finished the ritual with the voodoo doll. After that she was fine, but not back to normal exactly. She was still alive with magic. I started asking her questions about who and what I am."

"I thought you already worked with her on that. Once you found out you were something more than human, I know you had at least one ceremony to find out what you are."

" 'Something more than human.' That's a nice way of putting it. She did work with me a couple of times, but then she clammed up. It was like she didn't want to talk about it anymore."

"Well, after Renee was kidnapped she withdrew from everything and everybody."

"This started before Renee was kidnapped. But for whatever reason, she opened up to me tonight like never before. She gave me a world of information in a short period of time. I think I know what I have to do to be at peace with events from my past that I've never learned to deal with."

I thought about the stuff Seth had told me and I was glad for her. The thought of Connie being haunted by tragedy made me so sad. "It sounds like whatever Melaphia told you was as good as therapy."

"Yeah. There are a few things I have to work out, but I think I'm going to find a new way to experience life. And that's not all. Mel gave me suggestions on how to develop my power and control it."

"Oh, yeah. I guess you'd need to know that, what with being a goddess. Control is important with power. I mean, after all, that's why you and me can't . . ." I hesitated, awkwardly groping for the right word.

"Be together?" Connie suggested.

"Yeah." I shifted uncomfortably, my body tightening at the thought of what lay under the incredible shrinking bathrobe. Not only was the gap creeping open from the bottom, but it was also sliding apart at the cleavage end.

"Uh, Connie, speaking of that. If I didn't know better I would say that you're teasing me right now. Given the fact that I can't touch you without catching fire and I can't bear to look at you half naked without touching you, don't you think that's a little mean?"

She swung her free leg back and forth and chuckled low in her throat. "Ooh, that *would* be mean."

"But you're not mean," I said. "You wouldn't tease me like this unless—"

She looked at me, and the light in her eyes thrilled me to my cold, hard core. "With what I know now, I think we can do it, Jack. I think we can make love. I've made . . . preparations." She pointed to her little altar where a red candle still burned. She'd made her plea to whatever entity she thought could help us.

She didn't have to tell me twice. If she was mistaken, I didn't care if I burned alive as long as I was loving her while I did it. "Let's do it," I said, reaching out for her.

"Wait a minute," she said. "I have to make sure the prayers and chants are going to work. I don't want to hurt you. This is important to me."

Connie got up from the couch and moved to stand right in front of me. Then she untied the satin sash and let the robe slide off her shoulders, revealing her to be completely, gloriously naked underneath. If she wasn't a real goddess, she'd *still* be a goddess, if you know what I'm saying. Venus herself had nothing on Consuela Jones. She took my breath clean away.

"Are you aroused?" she asked.

"Are you kidding?"

She gave me a quick up-and-down glance. "Okay. I guess you certainly are. Here goes, then."

Slowly, Connie raised her hand, palm out. I did the same. We both held our breath and brought our hands together. When we touched, I felt her warmth, her strength, her passion. But not the wrath of God.

"I'm not electrocuted," I said.

"And you're not on fire," Connie agreed.

"Not in a bad way, anyway."

Wordlessly we brought our other hands up, touched our palms, and wove our fingers together. I'd touched women more intimately before, but never with such depth of emotion. It was like we were already one.

After a moment I stepped closer to her, picked her up, and carried her to the bedroom. I set her on the bed and stripped off my shirt while she undid my belt and pants. While I kicked off my boots she laid a line of kisses down my belly that had me shivering all over. When she got my jeans down, she took hold of me in both hands like she'd just found a treasure she'd been searching for for a long time.

With a quick look up at me, she tasted me and I arched my back, trying to keep myself in check. "Wait a minute, honey. I've been waiting so long for this I might have some control issues of my own."

I laid her back on the bed, and she linked her arms around my neck. "Jack," she said in a breathy whisper. "I want you to know that whatever happens later, even if something goes wrong, you mustn't blame yourself. Promise?"

"Sure. Promise," I said before I started kissing her. She sighed and I held her still closer. I released her lips and laid a path of kisses down her neck and collarbone. She arched her back, aching for her breasts to be touched. I obliged her, kneading them gently, and framing one nipple between my thumb and forefinger. I took the other one in my mouth and sucked, drawing a sharp moan from her.

She reached down and touched me with long, sure strokes until I was wild with wanting her. I moved lower, deliberately out of her reach, and she opened her legs for me. I gave her bottom a gentle squeeze as I tasted her, and she writhed under my touch and made soft kitten noises.

"Now," she demanded simply after a couple of minutes.

"Yes, ma'am." There would be time for more leisurely explorations the next time. And the next time. And the one after that. I think it was that thought as much as the sensations I was feeling that made me so happy.

I raised myself and looked her in the eye while I entered her, only a little at first. Her eyes were wide and as dark as night. She wrapped her legs around me, bringing me down to her, deeper inside her. I heard myself groan and entered her fully in one smooth stroke. We both gasped and then began to move. She met me stroke for stroke, her body fitting to mine like we had been made for each other. I was beginning to think we had been.

She clung to me like she was afraid to let me go for fear she'd go spinning off the earth. Like I was her lifeline in a roiling sea. As for me, I was a real, living, warm-blooded man again, if only for those moments.

I felt us floating upward together toward some kind of heaven. I tried to slow my pace to make the moment last, but Connie wouldn't let me. She urged me on in her body's silent language.

We cried out as our pleasure spilled over the crest we rode together. The power of it, like nothing I'd ever felt, took us over as we surfed out every wave of sensation. We held each other tight as we floated back to the shore.

Neither of us could speak for a while. I held Connie and she stroked my chest with her fingers. "What's this scar?" she asked absently, running a forefinger along the jagged mark. "The one in the middle of your chest."

I opened my mouth to say *That's where the minié ball tore through my chest and killed me.* But I stopped, reluctant to remind both of us that I was nothing more than a reanimated corpse. Not a real, live boy after all. No, not by a long shot.

"It's nothing," I said. I took her fingers in mine, brought them to my cooling lips and kissed them. They were warm and alive like the rest of her.

"Jack, that was . . ." she trailed off.

"I know. Me too." I released her fingers and touched the tip of her nose. "Next time we'll take it slower. I promise."

"Next time," she repeated. She looked at me with such profound sadness that for a second I was scared.

"What? What is it?"

She forced a little laugh. "Nothing. It's just that we had to wait so long, and it was so wonderful, it still doesn't seem real somehow."

"It's real," I said with more conviction than I felt. "And there's plenty more where that came from." I gave her a wicked wink and she tweaked one of my nipples.

"There better be," she said playfully.

"For right now, though, I'd better get back to William's. It's almost sunup."

"One last kiss then," she said, and locked me in a tight embrace.

I kissed her like I'd never kiss her again, molding our bodies so close I hardly knew where I left off and she began. She released me slowly, and kissed the length of my arm to my fingertips as I rose from the bed. I took my clothes and dressed quickly in the living room and went back to the bedroom for one more look at her beautiful self curled in her soft cloud of a bed.

"Can I see you tonight?" I asked.

She pretended she was asleep, but I sensed that she wasn't. She was just playing 'possum to avoid my question. Or playing hard to get, more like. Some women like to be chased, and if Connie was one of them, I'd chase her all she wanted and follow wherever she led.

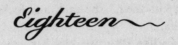

Eighteen

William

The noise was coming closer and becoming more annoying. Renee stirred, and I reached down to brush some of the dirt off of her face.

The noise was definitely coming from above. Dirt and pebbles began to rain down just feet away from where Renee and I were buried. A small opening formed, and a beam of light filled it briefly before a strange face appeared. One with a long, shiny snout. What manner of creature was this? Then I noticed that it wore a yellow hard hat.

Just at the moment I'd deciphered that the snout was really an oxygen mask, that face disappeared and was replaced with that of my son. "You all right?" he called.

"We are now," I said.

After the workmen had fitted Renee with a breathing device like theirs and a small canister of oxygen, they quickly—and wisely—disappeared.

While I began the climb out, carrying Renee, followed by Olivia and Will, I felt the earth's greed. It and whatever was just underneath us were reluctant to let us go.

Will had commandeered Hugo's house for the burned-out coven, since none of its occupants was using it anymore. On the walk there my son and Olivia explained how they had found us.

"So as soon as Olivia and I had settled everyone in, we sensed you calling for us," Will said. His wounds were already healing somewhat, and he seemed to have regained most of his strength. "We rushed here as quickly as we could, and at the site of the cave-in, we found a crew of flushers already there, all decked out in their oxygen masks and tanks. They had been sent to fix the sewer that ruptured when the cave-in started."

Olivia took up the story. "We slipped them enough cash to help us dig you out with their, uh, digging machine, and to keep their mouths shut in the bargain."

"Was it enough to keep them from asking questions about how you could breathe in the sewers and they couldn't?"

"Too right," Will confirmed. "Either that or they were too afraid for their lives."

Renee was shaken at first but was as right as rain once we got back to Hugo's. She took a bath and dressed herself in a long shirt of Olivia's while one of the vampires went out to buy Renee pizza, her favorite food. She fell asleep after one piece, so tired she collapsed onto her plate. I washed the sauce off her cheeks and chin and put her to bed.

The sun was up, and I would get my rest as well. At sunset we would fly home in my chartered jet. Under normal circumstances, I preferred to travel by sea, but these were hardly normal circumstances. I tried to call Melaphia to tell her that Renee was safe, but nobody answered, and the answering machine was not on. That struck me as quite strange. Jack's cell phone was unresponsive as well.

Will had raided the wine cellar and—not surprisingly—selected a bottle of red. "Let's have a drink to celebrate before we go to bed," he suggested.

I could tell that Olivia was torn. She was glad for having rescued Renee and me, but she still grieved that two of her vampires had been murdered the previous night. Added to that were the harsh words we'd exchanged right after the fire. For all those reasons and perhaps more, she seemed lost in her own thoughts. Still, she accepted a glass and toasted our rescue with grace.

"How fare your other vampires?" I asked.

"Already beginning to heal, thanks to Will," she said.

Will nodded and to my surprise said nothing. Humility was not his style. I could feel a new warmth developing between them. Perhaps they would be friends after all. I was glad for that, since Will had rejected my appeal for him to come to Savannah with me.

"What of Donovan?" The last I had known, he remained unconscious after Will had carried him from the fire.

"Donovan is in one of the coffins we found here," Olivia reassured me while Will stared into his wine glass. "He's almost recovered, I think."

I looked at the lovely Olivia and thought about how far she'd progressed. She had proven her bravery and resourcefulness in protecting her coven and their valuable work. She had made mistakes, but in the end she had done well.

My realization of Diana's evil helped me come to terms with what I had viewed as Olivia's betrayal. I knew now that it was time to fully forgive Olivia and move on. Her decision was the wrong one, and not one she'd soon repeat, but her motives had been pure.

"When Donovan is fully recovered," I began, "I suppose it's time to talk about relocating you and your vampires to Savannah."

Olivia swirled her wine contemplatively. "I've been thinking about that, William. I'm not so sure that would be the right course of action for my coven after all."

"Oh? Why not?"

"Now that we know more or less where the dark lords are, right here underneath us as it happens, you'll need us here to keep tabs on them."

"As well as keep our eyes and ears open for the goings-on of any powerful vampires they may lure in to do their dirty work on this level," Will added.

"It sounds as if you two have teamed up," I observed.

They looked at each other for a moment. "Olivia says I can join up with her lot if I fancy," Will said. "Since you staked Hugo and since Mummy Dearest is busy clawing herself out of the hole she dug for herself, I guess I may as well have a go with this group."

"Speaking of Diana and her predicament, do you think Ulrich was finally killed?" Olivia asked.

"It's hard to say. The last I saw of him, his head was cleaved more than half off, but that's the shape I left him in the time before, and he still managed to heal himself. My sense is that we haven't seen the last of either of them. More's the pity."

When we'd finished our wine, I said, "I'm going to retire now, and at sundown Renee and I will leave for the private air strip in the country. But before I leave you, I want to say how impressed I am with the two of you. Not only did you team up to save Renee and me, but you saved Olivia's coven, moved them and their work into safe new quarters, settled your differences and planned your future—all in one night and day. There's no telling what you can accomplish from here. And I, for one, am glad, Will, that you have found such a suitable new home where you can be safe."

"Good thing, too," Will said, looking at Olivia. "Dad here tells me that there are at least four people in the States who've sworn to see me dead."

Just then the door leading up from the cellar opened; in the doorway stood a redheaded Welsh vampire. Donovan had crawled out of his coffin again, and he was staring daggers at Will.

"You! I swore by the goddess I'd drain you as dry as dust, you son of a whore!"

In a split second, Olivia was at Donovan's side, holding off the weakened vampire. She glared at Will. "Friend of yours?"

"In another life." Will got to his feet and took a defensive stance, but he was able to relax when Donovan collapsed into Olivia's arms. "It was a long time ago."

I realized that Donovan hadn't gotten a good look at Will the first time my son came to Olivia's house, and he was unconscious when Will saved him from the fire. "I don't even want to know what you did to him," I said. Something told me that Will had a checkered history with many, many European vampires. "Perhaps when Olivia explains how you saved his life last night, he'll call things even."

"I'm sure they'll be the best of friends," Olivia said. "I'm putting you back in the coffin," she told Donovan, hoisting him over her shoulder. He hadn't seemed to hear the part about Will saving his life.

"I'm getting better," Donovan insisted weakly.

"I'm going to bed," I said, and followed Olivia to the cellar.

Jack

In my dream, Connie was on top. She was riding me, and my hips were bucking, rising to meet her every movement. Her head was thrown back, eyes closed, her black hair cascading across her shoulders and down her back. Her lovely breasts moved up and down with each stroke, her skin flushed with arousal. I saw the artery pulsing at the base of her throat.

I sat up and threw my arms around her, holding her fast to me, trapping her. She cried out. I don't know if it was from pleasure or from pain. All I could hear was the siren song of that pulse beneath her creamy, warm skin, and my fangs unsheathed themselves. As if I had X-ray vision, I saw the blue of the artery beneath her skin, running like a river.

My fangs hovered over the pulsing vessel and bit down hard. Connie screamed.

I came awake in a cold sweat, tried to sit up too fast, and hit my head on my coffin lid. I threw it open so hard the lid bounced on its hinges and almost closed again. I crawled out, rubbing my eyes blearily. A nightmare. It was only a nightmare. But the scream had sounded so real.

A clap of thunder from a lightning strike just outside the house penetrated the steel-reenforced vault and reverberated off the walls. I assured myself that the imagined scream had only been thunder.

I felt groggy, sensing it was still daytime outside, but I knew between the nightmare and the electrical storm, I wouldn't be going back to sleep. I dressed, crossed to the little wet bar in the corner, and grabbed a bag of blood from the fridge. That nightmare had shaken me to my toes. I reckoned I was just one of those guys who, when they finally had something good in their life, was so afraid of losing it that the fear had seeped into the subconscious and morphed into a nightmare.

I ripped the blood bag open with my teeth and poured it in a highball glass. Doctor Phil would be proud of my self-analysis, I'm sure. I did have to admit that a romance with Connie, as much as I had longed for it, wouldn't be easy. I was a natural-born killer and she was a cop. I was evil dead, she was divine good. Yada yada yada. It wasn't exactly a match made in heaven, so to speak.

But if I hadn't been in heaven in her bed last night, then heaven didn't exist.

I flopped down into William's easy chair, propped

my boots on the ottoman, and went over the last night in my mind. She'd driven me half crazy with every blessed touch, heat-filled glance, and whispered word. Even her playing hard to get there at the end made me hungrier for her than ever.

A guy always wanted what he couldn't have.

Another deafening clap of thunder made me jump. I thought about adding a little splash of Jack Daniel's to the blood to calm my nerves, but I didn't want to go to Connie's later with whiskey on my breath. Let's see, what else had Connie said last night? I wanted to remember every little thing.

I think I know what I have to do to be at peace with events from my past, she'd said. And then she'd added that she had some work to do on that score. I just hoped she'd finally given up the idea of going to the underworld. I'd assumed that she had dropped that plan. Had she said that, or had it been wishful thinking on my part? Suddenly her statement about knowing how to be at peace started to bother me.

I wracked my brain trying to remember more of what Connie had said to me. I was so damned horny she could have recited the Gettysburg Address and I wouldn't have noticed. Then, something else came to me like the thunder ringing in my ears.

I want you to know that whatever happens later, even if something goes wrong, you mustn't blame yourself.

I had assumed she was still afraid I might be hurt during our lovemaking. But what if she was talking about something else? Something yet to happen? A tingle of fear worked its way up my spine.

I just then realized I'd assumed a helluva lot since

the night before. And you know what they say about assuming. I was starting to feel like an ass.

For the first time, I wondered where Reyha was. It was definitely still daytime. She'd be in dog form, but she should have been sleeping, if not in my coffin, at least here in the vault. And it was entirely too quiet. Usually when I woke up too early, I could hear the muffled sounds of the active daytime household above me.

But there was no sound from upstairs, only the howls of the wind and thrashing tree branches from the raging storm outside. A storm that hadn't been forecast. I remembered glancing at the weather page of the *Savannah Morning News* yesterday to see if there would be rain for the dominance fight. The forecast had been for cold and clear weather for the rest of the week.

Something wasn't right. I reached for the cell phone on my belt clip to call Connie and make sure she was safe. The battery was dead.

Another lightning bolt made me jump. That one had to have struck in the backyard. I crossed to the windows that faced Mel's house. I separated two of the strips of steel on the metal blinds and peered out through the tinted glass.

The phone dropped out of my hand onto the floor.

I burst out the metal door of the vault and into the backyard, not caring if I caught fire and burned to a crisp. But there was no sunshine because of the impenetrable storm clouds. The sky was as black as night.

I sprinted to where Connie's body lay on the ground, dressed in a white gown, in the middle of a circle of lighted candles. Candles that were inexplicably still burning even through the fierce gale. Melaphia stood above her in a trance.

I knew in a horrified instant what this scene meant. Melaphia had helped Connie's spirit go to the underworld, leaving her comatose body behind. When William had done this, he had nearly died. I mean *final death*. If he hadn't been able to find his way back to this dimension, his body would have turned to dust and his soul would have been trapped in hell. Connie did not have the knowledge or the power of a five-hundred-year-old blood drinker. How would her spirit ever survive to return to me?

I knelt at Connie's side and cradled her in my arms. I put my ear to her chest and heard a faint, thready heartbeat. CPR would do more harm than good to Connie's body and would be no help at all in reuniting her body and spirit. I shouted at Melaphia in desperation. "Why? For God's sake, why did you let her do it?"

Mel opened her eyes and looked at me as if the answer was perfectly obvious. "I did it for you. And for William."

"What the hell are you talking about?"

Melaphia reached down and grabbed me by the collar with both hands. With a strength I didn't know she had, she hauled me to my feet, forcing me to let go of Connie. "Do you know what she is?" she shouted, bringing my face to within inches of hers.

"You told me she was a Mayan goddess."

"She is much more than that," Melaphia said. Even her voice had changed. She was speaking in the voices of her foremothers, many of whom I had helped to raise, loving them like daughters, just as I did Melaphia and Renee.

"What?" I demanded. "What is she?"

"She is the Slayer!" Melaphia released me and spat on the ground between us.

"A slayer," I repeated. Another lightning bolt struck nearby, and my mind lit up with the memory of the moment at Sullivan's funeral when Connie had grown so mad at me for not killing Will to avenge Sullivan's death. She said she guessed she'd just have to learn how to kill vampires herself, and a jolt of eerie dread had pulsed through me . . . like I'd been struck by lightning sure enough. Something inside me knew, had always known, that Connie could be the death of me. But I couldn't face that knowledge because of my feelings for her.

"Does she know?" I asked Melaphia.

"No. And with the gods' help, she never will. I have saved my baby. Now I'm going to save my fathers." Mel's own voice had returned.

I took Melaphia by the shoulders. "What do you mean by that?"

"She's not coming back, Jack. Not ever."

"You don't mean that!" I shook Mel, convinced she had lost her sanity again. "You've got to help me get her spirit back!"

"Never! If she comes back, she'll kill you. William might be strong enough to defeat her, but it's you who won't be able to escape her gifts, because you love her. Don't you understand that?"

I understood then that Melaphia would be no help to me. If I was going to bring Connie back, I would have to go and get her myself. I knelt by her body and tried to remember the prayer I prayed to the Loa Legba, the voodoo god of—what was it? The portal to the underworld or something like that. I'd screwed up my first prayer to him so bad that I'd accidentally raised Huey from the dead. I was drunk then and sober as a judge now, but I was so nervous I couldn't remember a thing. I was going to have to wing it.

I took up a candle in each hand. "Loa Legba, hear my prayer!" I shouted above the howling wind.

"Jack, what are you doing?" Melaphia demanded, tugging at my arm.

"Open the portal to the underworld!"

"Jack! No!" Melaphia's high, thin scream became one with the shrieking of the storm.

Nineteen ~

William

The jet's engine purred like the proverbial kitten. Renee was strapped into the seat beside me, and she sighed as I smoothed her hair. She was eagerly perusing the stack of books I'd bought her on our way out of London.

"I already have this one," she said, holding up a copy of *Alice in Wonderland* by Lewis Caroll.

"Yes, but that is a first edition. It's very rare and valuable."

"Oh," she said, looking it over carefully. "I think I still like my copy best."

"Why is that?"

"Because it's the one you and Jack have both read to me from since I was a little girl," nine-year-old Renee said.

"I see." That was the first time I consciously noticed her referring to Jack without the sobriquet *uncle*. I supposed my little girl was growing up. They always do.

She was remarkably calm for all she had been through. Still, I worried about lingering mental trauma and psychological scars from what she'd experienced, some of which she wouldn't even talk to me about. I decided the best thing for Renee would be to help her forget.

"Renee, look at me."

The child of my heart turned her eyes up to me, and I began to concentrate my glamour on making her forget what happened after her kidnapping. After a moment, she frowned, reached up with a slender brown hand so like her mother's, and gently put her palm and fingers across my eyes.

"Don't," she said. "But you can tell Mom you did."

"Why?" I asked. I dropped the glamour, took her hand in mine, and kissed her fingertips.

"Because I need to remember. It's Mom who needs to forget. Understand?"

I looked down into the deep, dark eyes of a mystical old soul in a child's body, and I realized she carried the wisdom of a thousand years of wise women in her blood. Every bit of knowledge, no matter how unpleasant, added to that wisdom. Ultimately, that wisdom would help her to survive.

"Yes," I said. "I understand."

I leaned my head back and closed my eyes, leaving Renee to her books. I would be glad to get back home, but it would never seem the same without Eleanor. Now that Renee was safe and sound I let the grief of my loss wash over me.

I was still unable to reach anyone on the phone at the house, and Jack's cell wasn't even going to voice mail.

In the back of my mind I considered the possibility that something was wrong, but—despite my better judgment—I refused to entertain the notion that anything bad could spoil the victorious arrival of Renee.

Under cover of darkness we made our way home from the airport in my chauffeured limo. My butler and occasional driver, Chandler, assured me that the staff at the plantation house was fine and there was nothing amiss at the house on Houghton Square that he was aware of.

When Chandler dropped us off curbside, I stood for a moment and looked at my home as Renee scampered toward the front door. So much had changed in the few scant days since I'd left. My once-beloved Eleanor, who was to have been the lady of this house, was dead by my own hand. I was about to find out if my faithful companion for years yet lived. Normally, Deylaud would have eagerly anticipated my arrival home, whether from a day at the warehouse office or a lengthy spell abroad. Where was he now?

Renee squealed as two slender faces appeared in the panes of glass on either side of the front door. One was Reyha, the other her darling brother Deylaud. I began to laugh, holding my arms out wide. The front door burst open and Melaphia ran out in her nightgown and slippers. She scooped Renee up in her arms and spun her in a circle, covering her giggling face with kisses. Melaphia seemed barely to notice the bandages on Renee's arms. For now, she was just happy to have her baby back, though I knew I would eventually have to tell Melaphia of her dear child's trials.

Reyha and Deylaud ran to me. Reyha had only a

slight limp, and Deylaud, though thin and pale, looked nearly healed. They leapt upon me and kissed my cheeks. I embraced them, bringing their heads together against my chest. "Is Renee all right?" Deylaud asked, peering around at the little girl.

"She is perfectly well," I assured him, anticipating with dread what his next question would be. He locked eyes with me and asked it silently. It's remarkable how creatures with whom we live for generations can communicate with us even without words.

I looked at Deylaud and stroked his silken hair. His love for Eleanor in his way had been as great as mine. He had been almost as devoted to her as he was to me. I shook my head solemnly. "I'm so very sorry," I said. "Eleanor isn't coming back."

He nodded, buried his face in my chest, and sobbed. Reyha let go of me and took him in her arms, comforting him as only a littermate, someone with whom she had shared the closeness of a womb, could.

"I bought you some welcome-home presents," a laughing Melaphia was telling Renee. "Go into the parlor and see what you can find." Renee gave her mother another kiss and ran up the steps and into the house. I could imagine the mound of presents Mel would have lined up for her, as a testament of her faith in my ability to bring Renee home safely. They would probably take hours to unwrap and examine.

"She'll be spoiled rotten," I said. I hugged Melaphia and kissed the top of her head.

"And I'll enjoy every minute of it," Mel said. "Thank you. I knew you'd get my baby back for me."

"Yes," I agreed. "Your faith in me was invaluable."

The twins joined us, and we walked up the steps and

shut the door against the cold. Once in the foyer, I handed my suitcase and overcoat to Deylaud. "Reyha," I said. "Why don't you call Jack at the garage and tell him to come home. We want him to join the celebration."

This time it was Reyha who broke down in tears. Her brother, looking grave, peered downward at the hardwood floor. Melaphia's demeanor changed so dramatically that I took a step backward. Her smile disappeared and her eyes took on a remoteness that I'd never seen before.

"Come with me, Captain," she said. It was the name by which her grandmother's grandmother had called me and it dated back to the Civil War, when I wore the uniform of a Confederate cavalry officer in order to ease my passage across moonlit battlefields in search of fresh blood.

She looked at Reyha and Deylaud. "Go into the parlor and stay with Renee. Don't let her come downstairs."

A frisson of fear rippled through me as the twins hurried to join Renee. I turned to demand that Melaphia tell me what was going on, but she was already halfway to the stairs, and I could do nothing but follow.

All the candles were lit in the little recessed altars on either side of the stairway. She touched the hidden electronic button that opened the way to the vault, a kind of steel-reinforced safe room.

I was totally unprepared for the sight that greeted me at the bottom of the stairs. Horror rose like bile in my throat as I fought not to scream.

The lifeless bodies of Jack and Consuela Jones lay side by side on the floor, surrounded by lighted candles and strewn with herbs. As peaceful and still as the grave, they looked for all the world like that most famous of star-crossed lovers, Romeo and Juliet, in their final repose.

"My son . . ." I heard myself whisper. "What did this to you?"

Stunned, I turned to Melaphia and saw in her eyes something I'd missed before. She was quite mad. Her mind, which I had been convinced would heal once she saw her darling daughter again, remained broken. The gods only knew what had happened here.

As if reading my mind, she sought to reassure me. She reached out, took my hand, and said, "Everything is fine, Captain. I have much to tell you."

Twenty

A Final Word from the Council

The demons sat in a circle around a cauldron of fire. "Ulrich has failed us again," said one.

"So have half measures," said another.

"We need a new champion," said a third as he drank from a goblet of fresh blood and passed it to the fiend on his right. "Especially now. The end time of five years has begun, and the Slayer is among us. So it has been prophesied."

There was a general murmur of agreement amongst the dozen or so blood drinkers, all so ancient that their leathery flesh had turned oily and baked to a reddish hue.

"I believe we have an applicant," said a serving vampire from where he cowered against one earthen wall.

"Show that vampire in, and be quick," said an old lord covered with sores as he idly scratched his scaly chin.

The minion backed toward the opening to the cavern

and grasped the sleeve of the long, hooded cape of the young vampire who was waiting outside. The young one shook him off and the servant resumed his place in the shadows.

"What have you there—an offering?" asked the first demon. "Bring it forward."

The hooded vampire tossed the unconscious body of a young woman toward the circle. A tattoo on her shoulder read SID V. FOREVER.

"Very well then," said the second old lord. "We've heard of your exploits. But in your own words, tell us why you should be the one to further our cause."

The cloaked vampire lowered the hood and began to speak.

An ocean away, a weathered vampire, driven mad by his isolation and trapped in a granite sarcophagus beneath Savannah, began to laugh.

For a sneak peek
at Raven Hart's next novel

The Vampire's Betrayal

read on.

Jack

I pressed my cheek against Connie's face and tried to will the warmth back into her. How could a dead man bring life back into her body? She was always the one who made *me* feel alive again.

I knew how Romeo must have felt when he entered the tomb and saw Juliet lying dead. If I had some poison on me I would drink it.

As if that would kill me.

William and Melaphia had told me nothing could be done to save her and surely that was so. They would have helped her if they could, but I guess the powers of good decided to hold her forever in that heavenly place. It was a place I could only see through squinted eyes, like someone staring at a total eclipse of the sun.

Why, oh, why did she have to be taken away from me now, just as we'd truly found each other? I thought about the night we'd spent together, and I cried out in pain. I held her from me and gazed into her face, searching again for some sign of life, but there was none.

I studied her lips, her eyelids, her cheekbones, chin,

memorizing her while I could. As painful as it would be, I wanted to be able to remember the lines of her perfect face if I lived to be a thousand.

But I didn't have to live to be a thousand. I didn't have to live at all.

The vault had no windows, but I sensed it was daylight outside. I didn't need poison like Romeo. All it would take to end this pain would be to step out the back door, feel the sun on my face one last time, and it would all be over.

With Connie in my arms, I stood. "We're going now," I told her. "I love you. Good-bye." One last kiss, I thought. One last kiss.

I lowered her feet to the floor and held her tightly. I put my lips on hers, for once as cool as mine, and kissed her long and hard, pressing her body ever closer. She still smelled like lilacs, and I pretended that she was there with me, alive and well again.

I brushed one thumb across the soft skin of her throat and stroked her long, ebony hair. I gathered some of the silky mass into my fist and rubbed it against my cheek, savoring the softness. Her every curve and texture was what a woman should be. She was a goddess indeed.

I thought about how we had slow danced at Werm's club, and began to sway with her, playing over and over again in my head the Elvis Presley song we had danced to. *Wise men say, only fools rush in.* I'd been a fool to think that falling in love with a mortal would lead to anything but disaster.

I'd had too many relationships with human women to count, but only this one had lead me to forget myself and to become reckless. I'd never loved any woman the way I loved Connie and never would again.

I should have left her alone, I told myself. *She'd still be alive if it hadn't been for me.* But true to my nature as a demon, I had thought only about myself and what I wanted. And, my god, had I wanted her. I saw my red-tinged tears fall onto her gown, staining it, spoiling its pure whiteness, and I cried.

I cried for myself and I cried for Connie. My body shook with sobs. The music in my head stopped, and I stood still, hugged her, and gave in to my emotions. Our dance was over now.

But Connie had other ideas.

I felt what I thought was an intake of breath against my chest. I had to be imagining things in my grief, becoming delusional. Then I saw Connie's head move. In another moment she was looking up at me.

"Jack," she whispered.

I covered her face with kisses, pausing just long enough to cup her face in my hands and stare into her eyes to reassure myself that I wasn't dreaming. Then I kissed her some more, her nose, her brows, her cheeks. "Thank god," I said. "You're really alive."

"I feel like I've been on a long journey, but I can't remember what it was all about. Wherever I was, you brought me back, though, didn't you?" she asked.

"Yes. Everything's going to be fine now."

"But I can't remember what happened. I think I had a job to do. Something important. Did I do what I . . . set out to do?"

"Yes," I told her. "Everything's all right. You can

put all your sorrow behind you." I wrapped my arms around her and gave her a squeeze. "Pinch me so I can believe we're both really back."

Laughing, she reached around me and pinched my butt, and I laughed with her. Then we looked into each other's eyes again and the laughter died on our lips. It was as if I was seeing her for the first time. I saw the same wonder and awe that I was feeling reflected on her own face. She flung her arms around my neck, and I kissed her again like I'd never kissed anyone before—or been kissed in return.

I carried her to the chaise lounge and sat her down, kneeling in front of her. She cupped my face in her hands, then lowered them to my shoulders and chest, stroking her way to my waist where she grasped my shirt and pulled it out of my jeans and over my head. I reached beneath the white dress and swept it up and off in one smooth motion. She was naked underneath, glorious and perfect. If I hadn't already known for sure that she was a goddess, I would have felt it in my bones. She lay back and I began my worship of her.